# HOW TO DUMP A VAMPIRE

## JAMIE DALTON

This is the fade to black edition of How to Dump a Vampire. If you are wanting the open door spice scenes, those are available for purchase as well.

To all who have ever felt the need to hide from parts of your past...

it may be painful, but I'm glad you're here.

NECIA

PRINCE ASHER'S HOME

LILLITH'S LAIR

# RODEL

# TRETERRA

# 1

## THORN

The icy wind nips at my cheeks as I trek through the forest, hushed outside of my boots crunching the fresh blanket of snow. A stubborn lock of raven hair covers my eye, escaping the warm confines of my crimson woolen hood. I blink away frozen tears as the wind whistles past, threatening to tear away my fur-lined cloak.

These woods have been locked in winter's grasp for endless weeks, but today, it has loosened its icy grip just enough for me to step outside and stretch my legs. I know I can't linger long. The ancient magic that thrums through the forest warns me the blizzard is soon to return. I can feel it in the brittle air. The trees creak and groan under their frosty burden.

Out here, no one can find me or judge what I am. My little cottage awaits, beckoning with its promise of tea and a crackling fire. Here, I'm far from the backstabbing leeches who tried to kill me. Twice! You would think one murder attempt would be enough.

Some "rulers" they turned out to be, the vindictive bastards. I tried reforming their corrupt world once. I thirsted for justice and revenge. I dug up their dirty secrets. But I also learned the hard way you can't force change on the unwilling.

So I freed myself instead.

Now, it's just me and the elements. This winter storm is especially nasty. I pull my hood lower as icy flakes assault my cheeks. The things I endure for some peace and quiet.

I curse under my frosty breath, quickening my pace. I can't wait to be home sipping tea by the fire, my safe little sanct—

What's this? A man is face-down in the snow up ahead.

Cautiously, I approach, ready to defend my part of this forest from any threat, but as I draw near, I see he poses no danger in this state. Rather, *he* is in danger.

I kneel down and turn him over. His skin is frozen, lips tinged blue. Clumps of white snow stick to his black hair. My eyes widen. He could almost pass for one of my kind with those sharp features, but I haven't seen another in ages. Well, I haven't seen anyone really, but who's keeping track?

I glance around warily. Where did he even come from? Is this an ambush or trap?

Everything looks clear, though, and I can't just leave him out here. With a reluctant sigh, I brush the snow from my skirts, loop my arms around his shoulders, and prepare to drag him back to my cottage.

"You better not be trouble, buddy," I mutter, hefting him up.

He's slender but tall, and I'm out of practice using my preternatural strength. Still, I manage to hoist his limp form and start dragging him toward shelter.

I don't need this complication. As soon as he's conscious, I'll give him some supplies and send him packing. Back to my peaceful, solitary life. That's the plan.

So why does part of me want to unravel the mystery of this stranger? And why, when I glance down at his angled features, do I feel an odd stirring in my long-guarded heart?

Bah! Just the cold playing tricks on my mind. Once we're inside by the warm fire, I'll tend to him, get some food in his belly, and wave goodbye without a backward glance. No twist of fate can dictate my future or who I give my heart. My life is mine alone now.

I'm in control of my destiny. The past and whatever strange magic stirred here tonight will stay buried, where they belong.

Trudging through the drifts, I half-carry, half-drag him toward the shelter of my cottage. Tendrils of smoke wisp cheerily from the stone chimney, contrasting the stranger's dire condition. The structure is small and modest, nearly hidden amongst the naked winter trees, but to me, it's perfect.

I pause at the heavy oak door, gathering the energy to move him enough to open the door. The inside of my home is calling me—the woven rugs covering worn floorboards, strings of drying herbs, a crackling fireplace casting warmth through the single-room abode all my own, away from any who would think less of me.

Shifting the man's weight, I unlatch the door one-handed. We practically fall across the threshold in my haste to get him near the fire. I settle his limp form on the thick fur in front of the hearth, my breath coming fast. His fate now depends on my skills, long disused.

Kneeling by the fire, I peel back the stranger's tattered cloak and search for injuries. There are none, only the unnatural pallor indicating his weakened state. I place my palms on his chest, seeking a heartbeat. It thrums slowly, so unlike my own rapid pulse.

Closing my eyes, I delve into long-restrained abilities. A conduit opens between us as I channel restorative energy into his body, only a trickle at first, probing cautiously at the breach between life and death, and then more forcefully, sensing his fading life force.

Suddenly, his back arches, body convulsing violently. His striking silver eyes fly open, meeting my gaze with a blaze of recognition. Inexplicably, his life essence entwines with mine, two strands knotting together. The cottage darkens around us.

No! This can't be!

I recoil, breaking our connection. The stranger collapses back, breathing labored but regulated as he falls back asleep. I stagger away, clutching my chest as unwanted heat courses through my veins. The ancient magicks of a fated mating bond flicker to life.

Hands clenched, I can't stop pacing. Sorcery has meddled here, that much is clear, but I'll be damned if some ancient mate-bond with a random starving man will ruin the solitary life I've built.

I learned the hard way that destiny and "meant to be" are fantasies. Trusting them only leads to disaster. I refuse to give up my freedom a second time.

Kneeling by sleeping handsome here, I study his face in the firelight. He has no clue that fate thinks we're a match made in heaven or that he now has power over me, and he never will.

When he wakes up, I'll play dumb about all this magical connection stuff. As far as he'll know, I simply took pity and helped a stranger in need. I'll get him back on his feet, send him on his way with some supplies, and pretend this never happened. No twist of fate can dictate my future or who I give my heart to ever again.

My safe little cottage, my rules. I control my destiny now. The past and whatever magic stirred here tonight will stay buried.

After settling the stranger's unconscious form by the fire, I rise to stoke the flames. The howling of the gusts of snow has only grown louder since I returned, so I add another log and prod the embers, sparks dancing up the chimney.

As the fire regains warmth, I glance back to check on him. Still as death he lies there, raven hair framing his angled features. A closer look makes me freeze. His lips are partially open, revealing the lengthened fangs of a vampire.

Carefully, I move closer to see if they are, in fact, fangs. In my shock, I fail to notice his hand shooting out to grab my wrist in an iron grip. Before I can react, he pulls it toward his mouth, teeth poised to pierce my skin.

I cry out, yanking my arm back desperately. The reflex seems to stir him, just enough for his fangs to retract and release me as he sinks back into unconsciousness.

I stumble away, staring wide-eyed and cradling my wrist. "Shit," I breathe aloud. This is no mere lost traveler. A weakened vampire in my cottage... This can't be happening!

Yet the puncture wounds I expected do not bloom. Some part of him, even deeply unconscious, resisted the urge to feed, but the primal instinct will only grow as starvation sets in.

Thoughts churning, I pace in front of the fire. When he awakens, his tenuous control will be all that stands between decorum and violence. I can't risk his bite. It could make the bond between us harder to break, if not impossible.

The solution comes to me in a flash—the asrbloom elixir, a tea that can sustain a vampire, abating the thirst for blood. It may be this stranger's only hope... and mine.

I rise from his side and make my way past the dried bouquets adorning my timber walls. At my carved oak cabinet, I sift through jars of dried flower petals, bundles of herbs dangling from the rafters, vials of essential oils, and hand-sewn pouches holding rare ingredients—treasures I've slowly gathered, transforming this little cottage into a sanctuary imbued with nature's magic.

I sift through the various pouches and jars filling my cabinet, glass clinking, until my fingers close around a small linen pouch tucked in the back. Pulling it out gently, I loosen the drawstring and peer inside at the precious contents—a fine powder with a shimmering crimson hue, flecks sparkling like rubies in the fire-light.

Asrbloom pollen, harvested from a rare magical flower that only blooms beneath the full moon. So potent is its magic that simply steeping a pinch in hot water can nourish a weakened vampire without the need for blood. It is a secret my mother uncovered through decades of studying botanical lore, one few in the realms know.

This stranger's only hope is the restorative tea this pollen can produce.

With care, I sprinkle a small amount into the iron kettle hanging above the fire, but as the water starts bubbling, the pot suddenly shakes violently then explodes in a spray of shards that rain down onto my worn wooden floors.

I stand stunned, gaping at the wreckage now scattered across the woven rugs. Never before has my magic acted so volatile when crafting a curative elixir. What disturbance has shaken my intuitive talents so?

When our energies connected briefly, it was as if a rock dropped into a still pond, disrupting the calm flow. That must be why my attempt to bring this stranger back from the brink of death affected my magic oddly.

Taking a deep breath, I center my focus, grab another kettle, and begin brewing a second batch, willing my magic to flow calmly. This time, the healing tea steeps perfectly. Gently cradling the man's head, I lift the mug to his colorless lips and administer the steaming crimson liquid.

As the tea restores faint color to his cheeks, relief washes over me, yet it is short-lived. When he wakes, I must ensure no sign of my true nature is revealed. My existence depends on secrecy. Better he believes I'm merely a humble herbalist who took pity on a lost soul than for him to learn the truth.

The sooner he's on his way, the less likely our crossed paths will dredge up secrets best left buried. If distance comes quickly, perhaps this mate bond between us will fade back into dormancy before he recognizes it. I can't risk the alternative, especially not with a vampire. The fated mate magic grows stronger with proximity.

Once he's healed, I will give him provisions and directions through the forest and hope I never gaze upon those piercing silver eyes again. It is for the best, no matter the whispered protests in my conflicted heart.

# 2

## DRAVEN

My head is pounding like a battalion of trolls went to town on it. I pry my eyes open and squint against the flickering firelight. Wooden rafters swim into view overhead. Where the hell am I? Where are my men? Where is Lord Anthony? We've been friends since childhood. He wouldn't just leave me.

I try sitting up to get my bearings, but my limbs feel like jelly. Seriously, it's like some sorcerer sapped all the strength from my muscles.

Lying here on a fur rug, I take stock of my surroundings.

Small, rustically furnished room. Herbs hanging to dry along the walls. The comforting crackle of logs burning in the hearth. A quaint little cottage, by the looks of it. Pretty swanky digs compared to the frozen forest floor I last remember. Still no clue how I ended up here, though.

Let's retrace my steps. I was journeying westward through the mountains on an urgent quest, making for Everdusk. Got ambushed by a freak winter storm along the desolate high pass. Snow came down so thick I couldn't see two feet in front of me.

I must have been separated from my men in the storm. As much as I hope they are safe, I'm not sure I would be of much help to them at the moment feeling as weak as I do.

The wind cut right through my cloak like shards of ice. I pushed on for gods know how long, each step heavier than the last as the drifts froze my legs. Thought I was tougher than some harmless frozen rain. Pride goeth, and all that.

Finally, my stubbornness gave out along with my weary limbs. Collapsed face first into the snow. Considered just lying there and letting the cold embrace take me. Would've been a disappointing end for a noble son of Trettera.

The last thing I recall is the world fading as icy tendrils crept through my veins instead of blood so how in blazes did I end up cozied by a fire in these snug quarters?

I catch movement from the corner of my vision. There's a woman across the room with her back to me. Slim build, black long braided hair. She's grinding some herbs with a mortar and pestle, oblivious to my awakening.

Well, whaddya know? This woman must've rescued my sorry, half-frozen ass and hauled me back here to thaw me out. Seems I'm in her debt. Doesn't sit right, owing some peasant a boon. If the boys back home heard about this, I'd never live it down.

As I shift to sit up, the wooden floor creaks under my weight. The woman's head whips around, eyes wide. Whoa...those eyes. Bright emerald, keen as a hawk's, with a gaze that bores right through your soul.

Those are not the dull, bovine eyes of a simple commoner. Intelligence glimmers in their depths, hinting at knowledge and talents far beyond what her plain garb suggests. The mysteries beheld in those eyes could swallow a man whole.

My body relaxes a smidge as I realize she can't be the woman I'm looking for. Well, the one I was looking for when I got lost in the snow. A rumor claimed that a powerful vampire who was thought to be dead was hiding in this forest and was, in fact, alive. This can't be her, though. While I never saw the woman who nearly tore down all of vampire noble society myself—I was too young to be involved at the time—her descriptions don't match the woman before me.

"I see you've awoken at last," she says, voice sweet as birdsong. "You've been asleep for almost three days. I wasn't certain you would surv—"

Her words catch as my own eyes flash silver. It's a trick vampires can do when our emotions run strong. Right now, hunger rages within me, so my gaze betrays the predator inside. My fangs itch to extend, to sample the lifeblood that flows so near...

*Whoa there, down boy. Reel it in.* Mustn't lose control and repay my rescuer's kindness by turning her into dinner, but gods above, her aroma is maddening. Like a fine vintage wine calling to me, whispering promises of succulent nourishment if I just embrace my true nature.

*Get ahold of yourself, man. You're Draven Valisar, esteemed prince of Trettera. Not some rabid fledgling who bites anything with a pulse. Have some class.*

With immense effort, I suppress my baser urges. My eyes resume their normal icy gray, and my ivory fangs relax.

The woman's guarded expression softens. She's reassured I don't mean imminent harm. Little does she know how narrowly she just avoided becoming a late-night snack.

"Pardon my distressing reaction," I rasp out. My throat burns, parched as the desert realms far south from here. "It has been some time since sustenance of any kind has passed my lips."

She nods in understanding and wordlessly brings me a steaming cup. I don't ask what's in it, just guzzle the contents down, too desperate to soothe this wretched thirst. Rich, velvety warmth slides down my throat, chasing the rawness away. Strangely, I feel my depleted reserves replenish just a bit, despite the drink not being blood.

As my more civilized bearing returns, I take a moment just to look at this woman who plucked me from death's maw. Fair of form and delicate in her features, yet she possesses an undeniable strength. She's clad in a simple woolen dress of forest green, adorned with embroidered vines and blossoms along the bodice and sleeves. A homespun apron protects her front, stained with hints of dried herbs and earth. Her feet are laced into leather boots lined with fur, little tufts peeking out the top, sensible for trudging through drifts. A knitted shawl of undyed wool, which she might have spun herself, wraps around her shoulders, its fringed edges swaying as she moves about.

At first glance, one might see a rural herbalist or cottage tender humble in appearance, but something stirs in me. She exudes confidence, and my instincts scream there is something more beyond her pastoral facade.

"What cruel twist of fate dropped me at your cottage door?" I ask, intrigued. "The gods surely steered me along an unusual path to have our lives intersect."

She tenses at my probing, avoiding my gaze as she busies herself stacking firewood. "Merely chance. I only did as conscience demanded in sheltering a fellow soul battered by winter's fury."

Her careful words spark my curiosity further, ringing both true and false, and I can't figure out why. She's being evasive about herself and her reasons for aiding me. Something about her intrigues me to no end.

"Well then, you have my deepest gratitude for heeding conscience's call, mysterious hermit lady," I say with an exaggerated bow from my seat near the hearth. That gets a flicker of a smile from her somber lips. "May I know the name of the fair soul who plucked me from icy oblivion?"

She pauses, wary again. I half expect another deflecting response, but finally, she answers, "Thorn. Just Thorn will suffice."

"Well met, Lady Thorn." I dip my head respectfully, hoping to earn more of her trust.

"Do *not* call me lady. Don't go giving me titles that I want no part of."

Interesting.

We regard each other in contemplative silence, two strangers brought together by improbable circumstances. She saved my life when she could've left me to perish. This doesn't make sense. While I'm appreciative to not be a frozen husk left in the snow, this part of Treterra isn't supposed to be inhabited. The forest is known to be wild and dangerous. Unless... surely our crossing paths is not mere happenstance.

The wind continues its relentless howling outside, rattling the shutters of the humble cottage. After hearing it deal me such merciless punishment on my journey, I find its haunted cries almost mocking as I rest safely by the fire.

"One more day of rest and nourishment will restore you well enough for the journey home. Besides, until the storm lets up, you wouldn't make it more than a few feet before becoming lost and returning to the same state I found you in," Thorn says as she brings me another cup of the revitalizing tea. Her tone brokers no argument.

I let out an exaggerated sigh. "Your concern for my constitution is duly noted, my lady."

She arches one brow skeptically. "I told you not to call me lady, and is that pride or stupidity speaking?"

I gasp in mock affront. "You wound me! I thought my constitution the very picture of health? You don't even know my name, and yet you feel comfortable enough to insult me so."

"The picture of stubbornness refusing to acknowledge his limits, more like." Her eyes glint.

I put a hand to my heart. "I know when I am beaten. Very well, divine healer. I shall submit to one more day of your restorative care or whenever the gods will ease their stormy anger outside."

She gives a solemn nod. "A wise choice." The corner of her mouth quirks in a hint of a smile. "So, what should I call you?"

A laugh escapes me. *You're curious, aren't you?* "Draven. The name's Draven."

We share a look of amusement at our huffy formalities disguising mutual understanding. Thorn's company provides a comfort and challenge I have not known before. Our banter comes easy as breathing, our true thoughts spoken in the spaces between sarcasm.

I must learn her secrets, and I'm not leaving this cottage until I do.

She putters around the cottage, sneaking glances at me when she thinks I don't notice. *Yes, I see you, Green Eyes. Who are you trying to kid with that timid deer act?*

Don't get me wrong, the skittish thing is kind of cute, but I know there's more to Thorn than her humble peasant garb suggests. Beneath those wide emerald eyes glimmers sharp intelligence. How do I get past her prickly exterior to uncover whatever secrets she's hiding? I'm not necessarily curious. I just don't like not knowing things, which is totally different, right?

I give her my most disarming grin. "So... I don't think I caught where exactly we are?"

She tenses over the herbs she's grinding, like she wants to make a run for it. "Remote areas. Doubt you would know this region."

I chuckle. "Oh, I'm a man of many talents, sweetheart. Try me."

Her eyes narrow at the casual endearment. That's right. Take the bait. Let's see some of that fiery spirit I caught a glimpse of earlier.

"The Sylvain Forest," she replies after a pause. "South of the mountains."

Well, what do you know? The little witch is right. This neck of the woods is remote, mostly uncharted except by creatures and not of the human variety. What's a woman like her doing in the big bad forest all by her lonesome?

I study Thorn as she goes back to grinding herbs. Wisps of black hair escape her braid, framing delicate features set in concentration. She's kinda cute when she's focused. You know, in an unaware, woodland creature type of way. Doesn't hold a candle to the court ladies I'm used to back home, though something about her still draws me in.

I give my head a shake. I need to focus. Time to turn on that old Valisar charm and get what I want.

"Well then, my mysterious forest nymph, might I know the name of the lovely woman who rescued this lowly traveler?" I flash a smile guaranteed to slay.

She bristles, shoulders tensing. Ooh, struck a nerve there.

That prim mouth of hers presses into a firm line. "I told you Thorn will do."

I clutch my heart dramatically. "You wound me! After all we've shared? Come now, humor a man whose life you saved."

Her eyes flash green fire. There it is, that latent spark just under the surface. My grin widens. *Looks like I'm getting somewhere with you after all, sweet cheeks. What else ya got?*

"Just. Thorn." Each word clips out sharply. "And I don't appreciate your endless questions or foolish flattery, so leave off."

She turns away, effectively shutting me down. For now, anyway. I don't deter that easily. Everything about this woman rubs me the wrong way some-

how...which makes me even more determined to unravel her.

Game on, Thorny. I'm just getting started with you.

# 3

## THORN

This man is going to be the death of me and not in the romantic, destined soulmates type of way. More in the "I'm about to strangle him with my bare hands" type of way.

I aggressively work the dough, imagining Draven's perfect smirking face in place of the innocent lump of bread. Punch, fold, flip. Punch, fold, flip. It's therapeutic usually.

Baking always soothes my nerves, but it's not working today. Not with Mr. Tall, Dark, and Infuriating lounging by the fire, critiquing everything I do as if he's the gods-gifted authority on the art of bread-making.

It's barely been a few hours since he woke up, yet he's already made himself quite at home here, strolling

around my cottage uninvited and inserting his opinions where they aren't wanted. He's been peppering
me with all manner of invasive questions in that posh
voice of his.

Where am I from? Why am I alone here? What
are the full extent of my healing talents? How does a
humble peasant woman know vampire physiology so
well?

Yeah, hard pass on sharing my life story with this
stranger, fate-bound or not. I don't care how muscly
his forearms look when he folds them behind his annoyingly perfect head of raven hair. A girl's gotta have
her boundaries.

So here I am, embracing the peaceful cottage life,
doing my adorable little homesteader thing. Just an
ordinary forest witch with a slightly aggressive bread
technique. Nothing to see here!

But can I get a moment's peace? Nope! As I knead,
Draven lounges on like a lazy housecat, criticizing
and questioning my every move. He even critiqued
the "haphazard" way I hang my dried herbs, insist-
ing on reorganizing them alphabetically "for maxi-
mum efficiency." Then, he scoffed at my "primitive"
wood-burning stove and lack of proper silverware.

Apparently, he's accustomed to five-course meals at some fancy vampire castle.

Oh, and let's not forget him raising that arrogant brow at my hairbrush with twigs for bristles. He just can't comprehend life without his diamond-encrusted, sphinx hair combs or whatever lavish grooming accessories nobles use.

He won't tell me who exactly he is, only that he's rich and everyone waits on him hand and foot. If I judged him by his clothing alone, I would find this claim hard to believe, but no one other than a noble could be this self-entitled, arrogant, and clueless and survive.

Now, he's moved on to insulting my bread technique as if he's the gods' gift to baking. I swear, just a few more smug comments about my incompetent dough kneading skills, and I'll—

*Deep breaths, Thorn. You've got this. Just keep punching and folding. Don't let Sir Fangs-a-Lot ruin your peace.*

"Is that really how you knead dough where you come from?" he muses, tapping his chin in mock scholarly observation. "Seems rather brutish. You'll choke the poor yeast's spirit mixing it so violently."

I grit my teeth and keep kneading, refusing to acknowledge him. *Just keep working the dough, Thorn old girl. This loaf is your baby, your pride and joy. Don't let Fangs McGee ruin your peace.*

"You know that dough owes you no offense, right? No need to teach it manners by punching it into submission," he drones on.

Sparkles of energy crackle across my palms where I'm aggressively massaging the dough. Dammit. My magic always gets testy when I'm worked up, and whatever this mate connection has done to my magic is just making it worse. I take a deep breath, trying to steady my emotions before Draven notices anything amiss.

*Get it together, Thorn. Your secretive solitary lifestyle depends on keeping these mystical talents under wraps. Last thing you need is giving Mr. Tall, Pale and Handsome more reasons to stick around probing into your business.*

"Might I recommend letting the dough rise near the warmth of the fire before baking?" he muses, peering at my work with vexing authority. "Could add a lovely airy texture to the crumb."

That does it. This loaf isn't the only thing getting kneaded into submission today.

I brush my hands off on my apron, walk to the nearest book off my shelf, and whip it at his aristocratic head. "Here! Make yourself useful for once and read this quietly while I finish, you yammering pine cone!"

With an infuriating grin, the wretched man snatches the book from the air without even glancing up. Blast his stupid vampire reflexes. Probably just showing off at this point.

"Such hostility over a few helpful suggestions," Draven tsks, looking far too delighted by my outburst. "And here I thought we were getting along famously like old friends."

"Old friends? About as famously as a troll and a unicorn!" I scoff. "Now read your book in silence before I shove those unsolicited opinions about proper dough-handling technique right up your—"

"As the lady commands," he interrupts with an exaggerated bow, settling into the chair by the fire.

Mercifully, he opens the book and starts reading, finally giving me some peace, but did he just call me lady again?

I blow an errant strand of hair from my forehead and get back to shaping the rounded loaf. As soothing as baking usually is, my insides are churning worse than the dough after Draven's constant needling.

Who does he think he is anyway, this stranger I pulled from the jaws of death? Waltzing in here and acting like he knows everything with his posh accent and stupidly perfect raven hair and strong arms that probably feel amazing wrapped around—

Ahem. Anyway. Where was I? Right, angrily kneading dough.

At least he's quiet now, though as I sneak glances across the cottage, I catch the insufferable smirk playing on Draven's unfairly kissable lips. No, not kissable. Oh, he's enjoying getting under my skin, the scoundrel. Thinks he's so clever.

Well, two can play at this game. I'll get him back for being the most aggravating, vexing, distractingly handsome thorn in my side and send him off to never be seen again. But first, I need my daily bread to get through whatever antics you have planned next.

As I knead the dough, an idea strikes. Perhaps I can weaken the unwanted bond between Draven and I before he recognizes it.

Moving quickly, I gather a pinch of dried asrbloom leaves from my herb cabinet. They have nullifying properties useful for suppressing magical effects. I crumble the leaves and work them into the dough, chanting an incantation under my breath.

The bread takes on a faint shimmer as the magic spreads evenly through it. There, this should help block Draven's senses when I eventually serve the loaf, keeping the mating bond clouded. He'll eat it without knowing a thing. Our paths will then part ways with no cosmic strings attaching us. I release a breath, satisfied.

*You're clever, Draven, but not as clever as me.* This vampire might think he has the upper hand, but I have tricks up my sleeve too. Let's see that over-confident grin when he tastes my spell-laced bread.

Magic zaps through me unexpectedly, and I yelp, shaking my singed hand. Blast! Gotta be careful not to overdo it while the loaf bakes. Just enough to mask the bond, not torch the whole cottage down.

I sneak another glance at Draven. Soon, fate's meddling will be muted, and we can go our separate ways. It's for the best, no matter the ache the thought strangely stirs in my heart.

*Game on, Draven Fangface. Let the battle of wills commence, but fair warning—I'm no damsel to be trifled with. If you think one lethally aimed book was the extent of my retaliation, you've got another thing coming. This sassy sorceress always gets payback.*

I finish shaping the loaf with a satisfied smile. *Round one goes to me, vampire boy. My cottage, my rules.*

\*\*\*

The bread safely tucked away to bake, I settle into the worn velvet armchair by the fireplace and take up my knitting needles and yarn. If I can just lose myself in the steady click-clack of the needles, maybe I can tune out the vexing vampire currently invading my home and ignore the urge to watch his every move. I need this mate bond to be gone. This is ridiculous. I'm no teenage girl. I'm over three hundred years old for crying out loud!

Knitting has always soothed my nerves. Something about the repetitive motion lets my mind empty of all worries as I focus only on the soft yarn gliding through my fingers. With each new row, I can feel the tension easing from my shoulders.

I glance to where Draven lounges across the cottage, hoping he takes the hint that I'm now occupied. Wishful thinking. He peers at my knitting curiously, head cocked in that infuriatingly endearing way he has.

"And what might that be you're working on so intently?" he asks.

I sigh, resigned to conversation. "A scarf. For myself, not you, so don't go getting ideas."

He puts a hand to his chest. "You wound me, Lady Thorn. I would never presume such familiarity when we've only just met."

"Uh huh. Then be a good vampire and leave me in peace while I finish this, why don't you."

"Alas, I fear reading has taxed my spirits," he laments dramatically. "Might I regale you instead?"

I resist the urge to chuck my wooden knitting needle at him. Barely. "Do as you wish. Just keep it down. I'm trying to focus."

Ignoring my tone, Draven rises and peruses my overflowing bookshelf, head tilted as he scans the cracked leather spines. I tense, wondering if he can sense the power that thrums from some of those ancient tomes, but he merely selects a book of Tretteran poems, flipping idly through the pages.

I exhale, returning my attention to the scarf as I finish another row. The fire crackles low in the hearth, spreading comforting warmth across my cheeks. My muscles finally start to loosen their tension knots. Maybe Draven will actually stay silent for once.

No such luck.

"Ah, this one," he murmurs. Clearing his throat, he begins to recite in his rich, velvety voice:

"On the dawn wind's breath, the old magicks rise,

Two souls entwined by fate's design.

The blood moon reveals that which hides inside,

Awakening the beast you caged within..."

My knitting needles freeze mid-click. Blood drains from my face. It cannot be chance that led him to read those ominous words aloud.

I force a shuddering breath, schooling my features before facing him. "You might want to be more careful what you wake here with incantations," I say as lightly as possible.

Inside, my heart hammers. Does he know? Suspect what we are? I've made sure not to touch him again, and I've kept my distance. This bread has to finish cooking soon!

Draven lifts one brow. "Come now. It's merely verse. What harm ever came from poetry?"

"Words hold power, vampire," I reply sharply. "Not all strings in this cottage are safe to pull."

His grin only widens at my warning. "You almost sound as if you have something to hide." He taps his chin in exaggerated thought. "Now whatever could that be, I wonder?"

I bristle at the glint of anticipation in his silver eyes. Everything is a game to him, a dance of veiled words. He seeks to provoke a reaction that will betray my secrets, but I will not oblige.

Holding his gaze steadily, I set my knitting aside. "Enough riddles. If you insist on keeping me from my work, then make yourself useful." I gesture to the bubbling pot hanging over the stove. "The soup needs tending while I ready the bread."

With far more enthusiasm than the task warrants, Draven snaps the book shut and saunters to the kitchen. I grind my teeth. *You're only encouraging his pestering, Thorn. Sometimes you're your own worst enemy.*

But I cannot sit idle while that poem's meaning sinks in. Better to keep busy preparing our meal.

The rich scent of baking bread now laces the cottage air, my empty stomach rumbling in response. Strange, this connection with Draven seems to have increased my appetite threefold.

Crossing to the oven, I slip on a hand towel and pull out the perfectly browned loaf. After all that nonsense working in the nullifying herbs, at least the dough baked up nicely. I inhale deeply, taking comfort in the familiar simplicity of fresh bread.

Behind me, I hear the bubbling hiss of soup spilled across the stove, followed by Draven's muffled curses. I whirl to find him frantically mopping up splatters of scalding liquid from my worn countertop while clutching his hand.

Despite myself, I have to stifle an exasperated laugh.

"Not accustomed to managing a common hearth fire?" I quip, crossing my arms.

He glowers at me, sucking his scalded fingers with a petulant look. "Pay it no mind. Merely... testing your reflexes."

I shake my head, lips twitching in a smile. "Here. Run cold water over the burn."

Draven lets me guide his hand under the pump, leaning closer than necessary so our shoulders brush. Tingles erupt across my skin at the contact. I focus on the cold water rinsing away the angry redness, trying not to notice how pleasantly cool his skin feels against mine.

*Get a grip, Thorn. We're just two people preparing dinner. Nothing out of the ordinary about this at all.*

When I glance up, however, Draven is staring at me with an intensity that makes my breath catch. His eyes seem to bore right through me, as if glimpsing all the secrets I cloak in shadow.

Heat rises in my cheeks. I step back and busy myself slicing thick pieces of the fresh bread.

*Focus on the food. Safe, mundane soup and bread. Not the magnetic pull of the man now watching your every move.*

Gods, when did this cottage shrink so small?

"You take the bowls. I'll dish up the soup and bread," I say briskly, avoiding his gaze.

Draven obediently sets the table while I ladle steaming soup and arrange the bread, studiously keeping my gaze from wandering his way. Just one more meal.

Tomorrow, this strange, vexing bond between us will wither away once he departs.

The crust crackles as I cut, and I arrange slices of the freshly baked bread on faded ceramic plates. Wisps of savory steam rise up, making my mouth water.

Draven places worn silverware and chipped bowls on the small wooden table near the fire.

I ladle the hearty vegetable stew, filled with potatoes, carrots, and greens, into each bowl. The chunks of potato soak up the rich broth eagerly.

Draven's eyes widen as I set the filled bowls down, along with a small crock of fresh butter.

"Please, enjoy," I say, gesturing for him to dig in. No need to stand on ceremony here in my cozy cottage.

Draven waits until I've seated myself across from him before lifting a spoonful of stew to his lips and blowing gently. His eyes drift closed in bliss at the first taste. I hide a smile and duck my head to my own bowl to try the stew.

The broth is fragrant, with pops of flavor from herbs I grew and dried myself. The carrots and potatoes are perfectly tender. I peel flakes of crust from the bread and swirl them through the stew to soak up more of the savory liquid.

Across the table, Draven makes quick work of the stew, pausing to liberally butter a chunk of the bread and take an appreciative bite. I notice a spot of butter cling to his upper lip and have to stifle a laugh. Table manners clearly weren't a priority in vampire training.

We eat without speaking, the only sounds the crackling fire and the scrape of our spoons on bowls. It's a simple meal, oddly comforting on this snowy evening. It's almost like we're old friends. I blink away the thought. Nope, I can't let my mind wander like that. He'll be gone in the morning, and that's for the best.

I sneak glances at as he enjoys the bread and stew with gusto. The furrow between his brows has smoothed, the set of his mouth relaxed. The nullifying herbs seem to be working, dampening the demand of our unwanted bond.

Soon, we will be strangers once more. As it should be.

I take another warm bite, savoring the brief companionship before our paths diverge. The bread tastes bittersweet on my tongue.

I clear my throat and keep my tone casual. "This storm should break soon. If we're lucky, by mid morning, you can gather supplies and be on your way again."

He stills. "You are so eager to be rid of me?"

There's no masking the note of hurt in his voice. Against my will, guilt pricks.

I set down my spoon and face him. "It's not that I don't... appreciate you as a guest," I say carefully, "but you have your own path, as I have mine. It is not wise to overstay a welcome."

His expression turns contemplative. "And if fate intended our paths to now merge?" He leans forward. "Would you still force me to leave?"

My throat tightens. Is he feeling it? I thought the bread would work.

I stand and begin clearing dishes with finality. "Fate rarely considers individual will, and it's often wrong. Get some rest. You've a long road ahead come dawn."

I don't need to glance back to feel his stare. Holding in a sigh, I make a show of preparing for sleep, moving about to extinguish candles and bank the fire. The cottage descends into shadow, only the dim orange embers casting a faint glow.

Draven stands, hands clenched at his sides. I avoid his gaze, heart heavy with regret. This long night is nearly through. With the rising sun, two strangers will finally part ways, memories of their encounter fading until they are once again nothing.

It is better this way.

# 4

## DRAVEN

I awake with a start, the echoes of some half-remembered dream still clinging to my mind. As
I blink sleep from my eyes, the cottage remains still
and quiet. The fire has died down to faintly glowing
embers in the hearth, and a shiver runs down my
spine.

What roused me? I sit up slowly on the lumpy
pile of blankets, senses straining for anything amiss.

There. A faint creak of floorboards.

I turn to find Thorn standing over me, gazing
down with eyes closed in slumber. She sways gently
in her long white night shift, raven hair spilling
loose over her shoulders. Her feet are bare, her expression serene yet troubled.

"Thorn?" I ask softly.

She does not stir or respond, locked in some somnambulant trance. Odd that she would rise from her bed and wander over here while still deep in dreams.

I eye her warily.

Thorn reaches out slowly, seeking. Before I can react, she kneels, her warm palm comes to rest along the edge of my jaw. My breath catches at the contact as she begins to gently trace the line of my face. I should stop this and guide her back to bed. Instead, paralyzed by her touch, I find myself leaning into her hand. When has anyone last touched me with such tenderness? It's almost like I can feel a hum from her touch.

Her fingertips brush my lips, sending a tremor through my entire body. Gods, what am I doing? I close my eyes, losing myself to sensations long forgotten...

My trance breaks when Thorn sways forward, her knees tangling up in the blankets on the floor. Still asleep, she tilts toward me, features serene yet imploring. The rational part of my mind screams she is senseless and unaware, but base hunger surges up, and I find myself wishing to accept what this dream tryst offers.

Clenching my fists, I slip from the blankets and stand swiftly moving away from her. Thorn frowns, fingers grasping where I'd been as if searching for lost contact. The sight spears my heart with hot guilt and longing in equal measure. I'm better than this.

As gently as possible, I grasp her shoulders and turn her about, guiding her back toward her own bed. She follows without resistance, but her head twists to keep her sightless gaze on me over one shoulder.

The shy hope inscribed on her face proves my undoing. I pause, lifting one hand to cup her cheek. She nuzzles into my palm, and I thrill at the softness of her skin and the warmth of her sigh against my wrist...

*You fool*, I chide myself. She is not awake, not aware.

With a pang of regret, I withdraw my touch and firmly steer Thorn the last few steps.

Once she is safely bundled back in her bed, I pull up her quilt and smooth the covers over her shoulder. Let her wake believing this midnight encounter merely a forgotten dream.

I leave Thorn tucked safely in her bed and make my way back across the cottage, each step weighed down by restless thoughts. Sleep will not come easily after that strange encounter.

Kneeling by the hearth, I add a few more logs to the fading embers, stoking flickering flames back to life. Orange light fills the small space as I sink down onto my blankets.

The fire now crackles steadily, warming my face, but its heat cannot thaw the ice within my conflicted heart. Thorn's touch unlocked foreign sensations I dare not examine too closely.

I've known this woman barely a day, yet in that brief span, my soul feels irrevocably changed. Her nature tempts me to cast aside my own armor in turn, to walk away from the responsibilities awaiting me and let one of my siblings take my father's place on the throne of Trettera. He hasn't chosen his heir yet, and I imagine my life here would be much more entertaining than if I returned to court.

But come daylight, I must don my princely mantle once again and return to a life of protocol and appearances. My world has no place for such vulnerability as Thorn evokes within me.

I stare into the freshly fed flames, wrestling with truths too disquieting to confront. When sleep finally claims me, my dreams are haunted by emerald eyes that see far too much and by the lingering ghost of her touch against my skin.

\*\*\*

The howling wind outside pulls me from restless dreams. Blinking up at the rafters of the rustic cottage, I need a moment to gain my bearings. Right. I'm still stranded here with Thorn.

Speaking of whom, I lift my head to see her already up and bustling about. She pauses to stoke the logs in the soot-stained hearth and then glances my way briefly before busying herself hanging a kettle over the awakening flames.

I sit up and scrub a hand over my face. My makeshift bed of hand-embroidered blankets on the hard wooden floor provided minimal comfort.

Yawning, I try to shake off the lingering unease from my fitful sleep. Something about sharing such confined quarters with Thorn all night puts my instincts on edge, even as my treacherous heart stirs at her nearness. I don't get feelings. Toward women, I should say. Do I become angry, sad, happy, or find someone attractive? Yes, but it's always fully under my control.

Thorn is getting past my walls, and I'm not entirely sure how I feel about that.

Crossing creakily to the frosty window, I peer outside at the bleak vista. An impenetrable wall of swirling white obscures the forest beyond. I can scarcely make out the woodpile a few yards from the cottage beneath the mounting drifts.

Any hopes I harbored of escaping this enforced proximity with the prickly witch are quickly dashed. We're both snowbound here, it would seem. Just marvelous.

I turn back to deliver the news, only to find Thorn already watching me resignedly. She stands clutching two steaming mugs, the firelight playing over her delicate features.

"So it seems we are fated to enjoy each other's company a while longer," I announce wryly. No point denying the obvious, given the weather's unrelenting fury.

Thorn's mouth presses into a thin line as she hands me one of the mugs. "Obviously. Drink. It will take the edge off the... discomfort."

I eye the beverage curiously before taking an experimental sip. Rich, earthy flavors coat my tongue, at once foreign yet distantly familiar. The warmth infuses my belly, seeming to spread restoring tendrils throughout my entire body.

I blink in surprise as the ever-present hunger pangs of my vampire nature ease, my empty reserves somehow replenished by the mysterious contents of this brew. Most astonishing. Not even blood itself could provide such instant satiation.

"This tea is good," I remark, swiping my lips clean. "What's in it?"

Thorn tenses almost imperceptibly. "Just a restorative tea from herbs found in these parts," she murmurs evasively.

My eyes narrow, but she avoids my gaze, busying herself with menial tasks. Clearly there is more to this than she cares to share. I filed that away for later consideration.

I drain the last of my mug, warmth spreading through me. As Thorn collects our dishes, I offer, "Allow me to tidy while you cook."

She only nods and I look around for what to do.

Tidying is new to me. As the second eldest son of a noble family, I never had to. Such tasks fall to servants.

Selecting the stoutest broom, I sweep with vigor, but where a sword handles light, this tool bucks in an unfamiliar grip. Thorn watches subtly from her work, eyes dancing though her face remains neutral. Her gaze prickles my skin.

Pausing, I declare, "Fear not. The situation is well in hand."

No sooner do the words leave my lips than the broom slips, scattering debris. Thorn's lips twitch as if to smile, but she says nothing of my fumbling. Her discretion intrigues more than mockery might have.

With her instruction, my sweeping proves more adept. As the final dust bunnies are dispatched, I glance to where Thorn works. Her focus on the task at hand seems complete, yet something in her eyes betrays more observation than she lets on.

I stride over to the rough wooden shelf holding Thorn's random assortment of spices and jars. "How about I whip us up something tasty?" I declare enthusiastically, grabbing ingredients without really looking too hard at what they are.

Behind me, Thorn makes a strangled sound. I glance back to see her watching my haphazard ingredient selecting with barely disguised horror.

"Or... perhaps you would prefer to handle the culinary matters," I concede reluctantly, carefully replacing the items in no particular order.

Thorn presses her lips together, mirth glittering in her green eyes. "A wise choice."

I fold my arms across my chest. "Yes, well, clearly one cannot be skilled at all manner of tasks."

As if to emphasize my point, Thorn turns back to the bubbling kettle hanging in the hearth and promptly knocks it askew. Steam and scorching water hiss over the burning logs.

"Seriously?" she exclaims, shaking her damp skirt.

I can't help but chuckle. "See? We all have our clumsy moments, do we not? At least I refrained from sending boiling water across your humble cottage floor."

Thorn shoots me a piercing look, spots of color blooming on her fair cheeks. "My *humble* home is all that's keeping you alive right now, and my clumsiness is your doing, vampire," she mutters.

I lift my hands in bafflement. "I fail to see how nearly upending your own kettle could possibly be my fault unless you intend to blame the confines of this cramped space?" I gesture broadly around us.

Thorn simply presses her lips tight and turns her back on me. "Just stay out of my way. I don't want to scald myself further on your account."

I stare after her, totally confused. Everything I do seems to annoy her more. Being crammed in this tiny cottage wasn't my idea. Why is she so irritated with me?

# 5

## THORN

I crack the eggs against the iron pan's rim, letting the yolks and whites spill out to sizzle. The scents of butter and porridge waft through my little cottage, temporarily masking the lingering traces of Draven's spicy, masculine scent that somehow permeates the small space.

As I stir the simple breakfast, I try to ignore his looming presence behind me. Why must he insist on hovering whenever I cook? It's a small miracle I haven't burned down this place with my magic acting up so badly.

I hear the clinking of jars being removed from my shelves. I don't have to glance back to know Draven has taken it upon himself to again "help" with the meal preparation, likely grabbing ingredients at random with no concept of how to cook.

Sighing, I turn to find him scrutinizing a handful of mismatched spices and herbs.

"I've got this covered, thanks," I say tersely, plucking the items from his grasp before he can upend them haphazardly into the porridge.

Honestly, parsley and nutmeg? What does he think I'm making? Soup dumplings? The man knows nothing about cooking.

I firmly guide Draven away from the kitchen area with an insistent hand on his back and ignore the tingle I feel on my fingertips. Touching him is a mistake.

He grumbles but allows me to sit him near the fireplace with a book taken from my shelf. Anything to keep him occupied and out of my way.

"Here. Read this, and let me focus. I will tell you when food is ready," I state, earning a dramatic sigh from him.

Still, Draven cracks open the aged tome, apparently accepting temporary literary imprisonment if it earns him breakfast. I'll take the reprieve, no matter how fleeting.

Soon enough, we eat in strained silence, and I desperately wrack my mind, trying to think of activities to occupy Draven's attention. Our forced togetherness in my tiny cottage is painful without some kind of diversion.

My gaze wanders around the room as I search for inspiration. I could teach him to knit his own scarf. It's tempting just for the look on his entitled face, but we would probably kill each other halfway through. Teach him basic chores again? Equally risky. Herbalism lessons? Not on your life, vampire.

I eye my box of polished spell stones atop the mantle. Their smooth surfaces reflect the firelight hypnotically. Crafting a checkers set could work... although that would require interacting collaboratively. I sigh, letting the notion go. Better to avoid fueling conversation.

The fire crackles, sending a cascade of sparks up the chimney. I watch their glowing dance, transfixed by their ephemeral beauty. If only distracting this restless vampire were as simple as reading tea leaves or tossing bones. Divining his future would at least pass—

Wait! Now there's an idea. Perhaps I could disguise a reading as a part of chess. I could create a board with markings of the gods on my divination stones for our pieces, and I could read how they are arranged after the game. He would never need to know, and perhaps I can discover who this vampire really is.

"Here. Take these back to the hearth," I direct, allowing no room for argument.

Draven's eyebrows lift, but he complies without verbal protest, returning to the fireplace with the new reading materials.

Satisfied he's settled again, I scour my cabinets in search of suitable supplies. In a lower cupboard, I unearth a section of sanded pine board leftover from some forgotten project, its surface smooth and intact. Perfect for crafting the grid.

Next, I rifle through baskets and jars until I find my paints—pigments painstakingly derived from plants, minerals, and other natural sources. I select two rich contrasting tones—deep emerald and burnt umber. Their vibrancy will lend life to the otherwise mundane board.

Finally, I retrieve my box of polished spell stones from the mantle. I pick through the array of translucent crystals and marbled minerals, seeking eight each of two complementing colors. The stones feel pleasantly cool and grounding against my palms as I roll them between my fingers, enjoying their soothing energy.

With my materials assembled, I settle myself at the table and lose myself in crafting our makeshift checkers set. First, I mark out the grid pattern on the board using a ruler then begin carefully applying contrasting coats of paint to the squares.

The smell of the pigments mingles with lingering wood smoke in the air. I find myself breathing deeper, the familiar scents and focus required for the delicate work loosening the persistent knot between my shoulders. Creating with my hands has always calmed me and helps me find my sense of self again when the outside world grows overwhelming and strange.

As I turn the board to complete the alternating pattern, I feel Draven's gaze on me from across the room. I don't acknowledge him openly, but I slow my brush strokes, suddenly self-conscious under his silent scrutiny. What must he think of me, whiling away the snowy hours on childish diversions? Not exactly mysterious and enchanting behavior befitting a witch.

Shaking off the self-doubt, I square my shoulders and continue painting. So what if I indulge in simple arts and crafts? It centers my spirit in this chaotic, unpredictable world. I refuse to explain or defend my private passions, especially to a vampire interloper.

At last, the board is complete, two tones traversing the grid in perfect contrast. Setting it near the fire to dry, I turn my focus to the stone playing pieces. I inspect the stones, enjoying the way the firelight dances across their glossy surfaces.

Though crafted from mundane minerals rather than enchanted, these stones impart a subtle sense of calm and balance, their natural magic seeping gently into my skin. I handle each in turn, channeling my focus into imbuing the ordinary objects with intention—to bring distraction, levity, and fellowship for two isolated souls. A simple spell yet profoundly needed.

I quickly paint on the markings of the gods to the bottom of each piece and wait for them to dry.

Occupied with my crafting, I'm caught off guard when Draven appears at my elbow. "This game possesses quite an elaborate battlefield for mere child's play," he remarks, inspecting the painted board.

I resist the urge to cover it protectively and meet his gaze challengingly. "Deceptively so. Don't assume it lacks sophistication based on familiarity."

Draven's lips quirk upward. "Point well taken," he acknowledges. "I shall reserve judgment until you educate me on this mysterious game.'"

I nod in satisfaction and turn back to drying the stones, blowing on them gently with a hint of my magic to speed up the process.

He returns to his seat by the fire and opens his book. I can feel his gaze every time it glances my way, but I can't let it get to me. Nothing is allowed to happen. *Ignore the bond, Thorn.*

With the painted checkers board dried and stones marked for my covert divination, I set the makeshift game atop the table. Though I crafted it as much for personal insight into my vampire guest as entertainment, I cannot deny a spark of eagerness to test my wits against Draven's.

"The board is prepared. Are you ready?" I call over, feigning casual disinterest.

Draven lifts one brow in silent appraisal but closes his book and approaches. He studies the painted grid and stone pieces with an analytical eye, saying nothing.

Suppressing a flicker of annoyance at his haughty scrutiny, I launch into explaining the rules before he can make any disparaging remarks. "The gameplay is simple enough even for you to grasp," I say pointedly. "We take turns moving diagonally to capture each other's pieces and block advances. Whoever removes all their opponent's stones wins. Understand?"

Draven blinks then flashes me an annoying smirk. "Straightforward, though I may need a practice round to get the hang of this treacherous battlefield."

I purse my lips. He's clearly trying to get under my skin. Well, I won't give him the satisfaction of taking the bait.

"Then pay close attention to this first match," I reply coolly, taking my seat.

After a dramatic pause, Draven settles across from me, moving smooth and graceful as a cat. I ignore how the firelight catches his sharp features.

"White stones go first," I state, nudging one of the carved crystals forward.

Draven copies me, and we're off.

We play in tense silence, the only sounds the periodic crackling fire and clacking stones. I notice Draven studies the board hard before each move, cautious and shrewd despite his casual vibe.

When he makes a surprise diagonal hop to nab two of my pieces, I mask my shock with effort.

"Not bad," I bite out.

Draven's mouth twitches. "Your generous praise overwhelms me."

I nearly fire back a scathing retort but catch myself. The infuriating vampire is intentionally trying to throw me off. He will not mess with my focus.

But as we play on, keeping composure gets tougher. Draven keeps making annoyingly smart moves, predicting my strategy and dodging capture. That knowing glint in his silver eyes fans my temper.

We both reach for pieces at the same time, hands barely brushing. I jerk back instinctively from the electric sparks that brief contact ignites. Draven's nostrils flare, but he stays silent, just scanning the board again.

After agonizing minutes, he finally slips up. I pounce and capture three of his stones fast.

He leans back with a rueful chuckle at my win. "Well played. Seems you'll take this round."

I bite my cheek to keep from grinning, still flushed with victory, but tallying the remaining pieces wipes the smile away. We're only two stones apart. Hardly a decisive victory.

Draven notes my expression and laughs. The rich sound washes over me in irritating waves. "Come now. Revel a bit longer in your oh-so-narrow win."

"It is victory nonetheless," I retort, yet the hollow words only deepen my annoyance. I should have bested this pompous vampire by a wider margin.

"Indeed, but such a close call suggests I am a quick study of your little game," Draven points out, insufferable smugness returning. "Perhaps a rematch is in order?"

I bristle at the challenge in his words. Does he think I will back down?

Squaring my shoulders, I begin gathering the scattered pieces with more force than necessary. "Oh yes, we shall play again, and this time, I will be sure to win by a more significant lead."

My pride will accept no less.

Draven's eyes gleam, seeming to relish provoking my competitiveness.

We reset the board silently. As much as his arrogance grates on me, I cannot deny a small thrill at the chance to test my wits against him once more.

This time, I make the opening move. Draven counters quickly, but I anticipate him. Within three turns, I capture one of his stones.

He lifts a brow. "You are playing more ruthlessly this round, I see."

I offer a thin smile. "I am simply demonstrating the full potential of my own strategy now that you have grasped the basics." Unable to resist taunting him in turn, I add airily, "Of course, if you require more time to familiarize yourself with the rules, we could take a break."

Draven snorts. "That won't be necessary." His eyes flash with steely determination.

Game on.

The real battle kicks off then. We play quickly, neither willing to give ground as we maneuver our armies of stones across the painted grid.

I gain a slight edge with aggressive offense, but Draven refuses to yield, always finding creative ways to dodge capture and put my pieces in vulnerable spots.

Our hands keep colliding as we move our stones, eyes locked challengingly across the table. My pulse races with exhilaration at this test of wits. For now at least, vampire and half-witch are total equals, too focused on strategic victory to care about petty divisions.

The endgame approaches, both our forces badly battered. I'm only one stone ahead of Draven now, not the advantage I'd envisioned.

Sitting back, I realize I've revealed too much of my own skill here, usually reserved for solo play. What will I tell Draven when he remarks on my talent? That it was a childhood hobby in the remote village where I grew up? There we kids scratched grids in the dirt, using rocks or seed pods as markers...

My spiraling thoughts are cut off by a clack as Draven makes his last move. I stare at the board, stunned. Somehow, between mental math and racing pulse, I missed his path to nab one final crucial piece.

We're left with a single stone each, perfectly tied.

For several tense seconds, neither of us speaks. The crackling fire seems muted beyond our locked gaze.

Draven straightens first, exhaling slowly. "A draw then. How very interesting."

My cheeks burn, half embarrassed about losing focus, half ticked he forced such a close match. I should say something scathing, resentful.

But meeting Draven's quirked brow and dancing eyes, I'm surprised to feel my mouth twitching upward. The sincere joy of a challenging game wells up, melting away defensive irritation. When was the last time I matched wits so equally with someone? It was... invigorating.

"Well played." I nod in acknowledgement. "Seems we're evenly matched in this arena."

Draven's grin widens, softening his sharp features into something more roguish and warm. "Indeed. I haven't enjoyed such stimulating sport in many years." He extends his hand across the table.

After a heartbeat's hesitation, I clasp it in mine. A tingle runs up my arm and floods my body instantly, leaving my head feeling as if it's drunk.

Draven releases my hand and rises from his seat, stretching his arms overhead. An ache immediately settles in my heart at the loss of his touch, but I shake it off. This can't happen. I don't want this. I can't get attached.

"I shall add a log or two to the fire before we commence with a third round," he declares.

I nod absently, eyes following him as he crosses to the woodpile. Once Draven's back is turned, I seize the opportunity to study the marked stones still scattered across the board and the ones he's placed on his side. Every little movement he made with these pieces leaves traces for me to read.

My fingertips skim over the arcane symbols, mentally deciphering their mystical import. Let's see. The rune for deception lies by the home row, suggesting disguise of true intentions. Temptation aligned with recklessness points to rash impulses. Oh, fate, you fickle temptress you.

I quickly commit the other auspicious and ominous patterns to memory before Draven turns back around. There is much to unpack from this covert reading, but I must ponder it later.

For now, I sweep the stones into a pile and begin setting up the board once more. Draven returns to the table, oblivious to my surreptitious divination.

"Ready for me to best you this time?" he asks lightly, though determination glints in his eyes.

I lift my chin. "Bold words. Why don't we let the stones decide?" I nod to the reassembled board between us.

Draven grins, sharp and wolfish. "By all means. Let the games continue."

He settles back into his seat as I make the opening move. My mind whirls with revelations from the runes even as I refocus on the strategic battle at hand. I must tread carefully indeed. This vampire may prove more complicated than anticipated.

# 6

## THORN

The last checker stone clicks into place as I soundly trounce Draven for the third time in a row. He leans back with a huff, raking a hand through his unruly dark hair. I would say it was nice to see him slightly disheveled, but if I'm being completely honest, it's just making it harder to ignore our mate bond. Why is he so damn attractive no matter what he does? How can I still want him when half the time he makes me so... frustrated?

"I must concede that your skill far exceeds mine at this game," he states begrudgingly.

I can't restrain a smug smile. "Perhaps with more practice, you'll provide me a true challenge someday."

Draven narrows his eyes at my gloating, though the corner of his mouth quirks. "Such confidence from someone I nearly bested last round. How do you know I'm not just letting you win?"

"Nearly being the key word," I retort with relish, enjoying this rare upper hand over the vexing vampire.

Inwardly, though, I'm troubled. He might be right. He's losing the game in an almost laughable way. A way that usually requires knowing the game well enough to intentionally lose. On top of that, the marked stones revealed little insight into Draven's true nature when reading their scattered patterns. I need him to eat more of my spelled bread to keep his senses clouded to our bond.

As if summoned by my thoughts, Draven leans back lazily in his chair. "That was quite the mental workout. What say you conjure up another of those delicious loaves to replenish us?" He pats his flat stomach for emphasis.

I hide my smile, oddly pleased he enjoyed the bread so much despite its magical ingredients. "Fresh out at the moment, but I was just about to prepare another batch."

Draven's eyes light up. "Well then, I shall eagerly await the fruits of your skillful baking, my lady."

"If you call me lady one more time, I'm going to slip something into your bread that will make your stay far less comfortable."

I shoot him a wry look as I tidy up the game. We seem to have moved into a cautious rapport, interacting almost... pleasantly. I mustn't forget Draven leaves at first chance. Whatever cAudreyderie we build here will make that parting no easier.

Clearing my throat, I gesture for him to pull up a seat near the stove's warmth. "If you insist on observing, at least make yourself useful and stoke the fire."

Draven grins and grabs the iron poker while I assemble ingredients for the dough—flour, salt, yeast. Kneading bread always steadies my thoughts, and I need that now after the checkers game rattled me with its glimpse at his layered nature.

As I work the dough, I feel Draven's gaze on me. I straighten my shoulders under his silent scrutiny and add a sprinkle of nullifying herb to the mixture, softly chanting the suppression spell. If only this snow would cease so the vampire could take his mysteries and be on his way!

Yet as I sense him studying my baking, curiosity about what goes on behind those clever eyes pricks at me.

I sneak a glance up from the loaf I'm shaping. "You seem surprised by my dough technique," I note. "Don't common folk bake where you come from?"

Draven blinks as if startled to be caught watching. "Oh yes, of course. I'm sure they do. Just admiring your skill at handling such a... temperamental lump of food."

I snort. "You almost sound disappointed it isn't fighting back."

"On the contrary. I prefer my meals passive," he retorts, yet a shadow crosses his face that gives me pause. For all his teasing, much about this vampire remains closed off.

My instincts bristle, warning me not to prod deeper.

We pass the time with lighter conversation until I need to place the dough by the warm stove to rise, covered with a tea towel. Draven lounges with his usual casual entitlement, but I notice he sticks close, eager to talk or offer unsolicited opinions. I tell myself that he's just bored and that he doesn't truly enjoy my company.

"You know, once this storm passes, I will be quite famished after our bread and porridge diet," he remarks. "How about making a pack for my return? Maybe an extra loaf to go?"

The thought of Draven leaving twists my gut strangely.

I keep my tone light. "Eager to escape me, are you?"

He tilts his head. "I have things and people who are relying on me. I need to return as soon as I can, but I admit it's tempting to stay." His voice drops lower, warming me more than the fire.

I still my hands, heartbeat quickening. Drat this bond tightening between us!

"Well then, you will be glad to hear that you won't be walking anywhere. I can use my magic to send you home. We just need to wait the storm out first."

"You can do that? Why didn't you send me home right away?"

"First, you weren't exactly coherent when I found you. Second, the storms in this part of the forest are filled with wild magic. It could affect the spell and send you somewhere completely random… if you reappear at all."

A smirk spreads on his face, "You're concerned for my safety so much you couldn't bear the thought of me coming to harm?"

I turn away, flustered. "Let's check your fire. I'll need much more wood for baking."

Draven frowns at the deflection but obediently grabs the iron poker. I exhale in relief as he crouches before the hearth, stoking the logs back to crackling life, then swiftly crosses the creaking floorboards to peer outside.

My heart sinks. Snow still falls in relentless sheets, coating the landscape in undulating dunes. The weather remains firmly against us. Against me, specifically, it sometimes seems, preventing Draven's departure and this troublesome attraction brewing between us.

I bite my lip, scanning the wooded horizon until my gaze snags on the snow-capped shed. The firewood stores! Between distracting games and conversation, I've let them dwindle far too low for Draven's voracious appetite these past few days.

I turn back to suggest he take an inventory, only to find him watching me expectantly from his casual sprawl in my armchair.

"We're nearly out of firewood," I announce. "I'll head to the woodshed while the dough rises. There's a rope to help me find it in the snow."

Draven is on his feet in an instant. "Nonsense. You've already done plenty of cooking and cleaning. You're exhausted. Allow me."

He grabs his cloak off its hook before I can respond. I watch, bemused and conflicted as he wraps the woolen garment tightly around his shoulders. Odd to see someone else volunteering to do the household chores that normally fall solely to me, though likely Draven aims more to escape boredom than assist.

I nod. "Very well. There's a rope from door to shed. Don't let go of it, or you will get lost in the storm."

Draven scoffs but indulges me with a slight nod.

I bundle him up further in my thickest cloak, muffler and mittens, trying to ignore his distracting nearness. Last, I put a bracelet on his wrist with a small charm and whisper a spell of connection. Gods, his hands brushing mine almost kindle sparks through my body again. I quickly step back once finished.

"Be quick, and call if you need me. The storm is loud, but I will be able to hear you with this," I say brusquely to cover my fluster as I point to the bracelet.

Draven's eyes gleam at my poorly masked concern, but he simply hefts the snow shovel and strides out into the swirling whiteness. I watch his silhouette fade, an odd anxiety twisting my gut. Draven is clever, I tell myself. He won't take unnecessary risks.

I occupy myself preparing the oven, but as the minutes creep by, unease mounts. Draven should have returned by now. I glance outside but can barely make out the shed's shape through the deepening snow banks.

A strange tingling feeling pricks at the back of my neck, like invisible strings tugging me out into the storm. I frown, rubbing the odd sensation away. Is it some mystical prompt from our unwelcome mate-bond spurring me to action? Or simply my own conscience worried for the safety of a guest under my care?

I hesitate, uncertain if going after Draven would make the pull of fate between us even stronger.

The premonition intensifies, my heart growing anxious as I imagine him lost and disoriented in the blizzard's fury.

Worry wins out. Securing my second warmest hooded cloak around me, I whisper a warming incantation into the fibers before braving the blizzard, staying tied to the rope. Snow whips around me, but my cloak's magic keeps the worst chill at bay.

I find Draven midway, laden with an armful of split logs, or, rather, I crash right into that armful as he sways disoriented in the maelstrom. The impact knocks us both down into the snow.

"What are you doing out here?" Draven exclaims through chattering teeth, dropping the spilled logs.

"Rescuing you, it would seem!"

I help Draven to his feet, pulling his arm over my shoulder and clasping his waist. Together, we battle back up the now wholly obscured path, my cloak fortunately large enough to shelter us both in its enchanted space with a few logs still in his arms..

I halt us just outside the glowing cottage window, its light blurred behind ice crystals. "What happened?" I pant. "You were taking too long."

Draven shakes his snow-crusted head ruefully. "Got turned around in the whiteout. I'd still be lost if you hadn't come to find me. Seems I owe you my life again."

He looks down at me, our faces flushed from cold and close proximity. I read the question in his eyes, the same nameless draw I feel.

I clench my gloved fists, shaken. We cannot keep tempting fate this way.

"You shouldn't have let go of the rope. It was right next to you, but you couldn't see it because of the storm. *Never* let go of the rope if you can't see it." I huff and try to calm my frustration, reminding myself that he isn't someone who usually does this himself. "Let's get inside."

I hurry us in before he can speak further. Once we're sheltered in the cottages warmth, I force myself to step back, busying myself stoking the stove's fires.

When I finally turn back, Draven stands shivering, his numb fingers fumbling unsuccessfully to remove his snow-encrusted outer layers.

"Here. Allow me," I say gently, approaching to help peel off the sodden cloak and muffler.

Draven exhales, shoulders slumping. "Appreciated. My hands have gone quite useless."

He surrenders to my ministrations, silver eyes intent on my face as I carefully unwrap the frozen garments. I feel suddenly shy under his gaze but continue steadily freeing him from the clinging wet fabric.

With his tall frame bent toward me, an intimate hush falls over us, broken only by the crackling fire. I peel the last soaked glove from his hand, pathetically numb and white. Clasping it between my own, I begin gently massaging warmth back into his icy fingers.

Draven's breath catches. His skin thrills under my touch as blood flow returns. I diligently focus on restoring sensation to each digit, acutely aware of his nearness.

When at last his hands are rosy and flexible again, neither of us moves to break contact. Our eyes lock, heat rising between us. I know I should step back, but some magnetism keeps me transfixed.

Slowly, Draven lifts his free hand to brush a raven lock from my cheek. His cool fingertips trail sparks across my skin. Entranced, I lean into his touch, my breaths coming fast.

"Thorn..." Draven murmurs, low and thick with longing. He begins to dip his face toward mine.

At the last moment, panic grips me. I turn my head sharply, his lips just grazing my hair instead. The half-forged moment shatters.

I pull back, the loss of his touch a palpable ache, and I force a teasing tone to cover my turmoil. "Let's get you warmed up with some tea."

I don't meet Draven's eyes again as I busily retrieve the kettle. The cottage air now hangs heavy with dangerous possibility.

With effort, I ignore my racing heart. I must keep my wits about me. Much more is at stake than mere attraction.

Yet as we sip tea in brooding silence, I cannot deny part of me wishes I surrendered to the fire blazing between us.

# 7

## DRAVEN

The tea's rich, earthy flavor coats my tongue, the warmth seeping deep into my chilled bones, yet something about the restorative brew continues to nag at me. Ever since waking in Thorn's cozy domain, this beverage has mysteriously sated my hunger, keeping the gnawing thirst for blood at bay.

I study Thorn over the rim of my mug, watching steam wreathe her delicate features. She avoids my gaze, posture tense, as we sip tea in brooding silence. The near-kiss haunts the scant space between us.

Setting down my empty cup, I clear my throat. "Forgive my curiosity, but this tea of yours intrigues me. Where did you find such a unique blend?"

Thorn's shoulders hunch almost imperceptibly. She busies her hands preparing a fresh pot, not meeting my eyes. "It's merely an herbal tisane I discovered through my studies."

I lean forward intently. "We both know that is not the full truth. No simple tea could so thoroughly satiate a vampire's thirst." I keep my tone gentle, hoping to earn her trust. "Please, Thorn. I only wish to understand."

With a weary sigh, Thorn's composure wilts. She gazes into the flickering hearth as if seeking answers in its glowing embers.

"It's called Asrbloom tea," she says at last. "Made from the pollen of a rare crimson flower that only blooms under the full moon. Steeping a pinch invigorates a weakened vampire as potently as blood."

I sit back, stunned. In all my centuries I've never heard of such a botanical marvel. "Asrbloom, you say? Remarkable. You discovered it yourself?"

Thorn shakes her head, raven braid swaying gently. "My mother was the gifted herbalist, not I. She unearthed the flower's properties and passed the knowledge to me."

"A family secret then. Intriguing." My curiosity burns to know more about this mysterious flower.

However, the subject clearly pains Thorn, so I hesitate to pry deeper.

We sip the fresh tea in silence until Thorn sets her cup down with decision. "Come. I will show you."

Mystified, I follow her to a carved cabinet, watching as she retrieves a small linen pouch from its shadowed depths. Cradling it gently, she loosens the drawstring and tilts the contents into her palm. Crimson dust spills out, fine as ground jewels, catching the firelight in subtle shimmers.

"Asrbloom pollen," Thorn murmurs. "Collected under last month's full moon."

I bend to examine it, awestruck. The translucent grains possess a pearlescent quality unlike any pollen I've seen, even in my long years.

Thorn lets me take a pinch between my fingers, watching closely as I study it. The particles feel cool and finely textured, seeming to hum with latent power. I half expect them to disintegrate from my touch.

"Incredible," I breathe. "And such a tiny amount can satisfy a vampire's thirst?"

"Yes, though I use sparingly. It's quite precious. As far as I know, it only grows in this part of the world."

Thorn gently sweeps the glittering dust back into its pouch.

I nod thoughtfully as she returns the Asrbloom to its cabinet nook, my earlier doubts creeping back. "Something still puzzles me. You live alone here. Why keep such a supply on hand?"

Thorn goes very still, her back turned to me.

I press on gently. "Did you... hope to encounter my kind? To put this botanical discovery of your mother's to use? Perhaps use it against a vampire?"

Thorn whirls to face me, cheeks flaming crimson. "Don't be absurd. Do you think I wanted to harbor a starving vampire in my home?"

I lift my palms placatingly. "I only wondered—"

"I prepared it for myself!" Thorn interrupts. Eyes widening, she turns her back again.

Herself? What could she mean by that? Why would she need it?

"Thorn, please," I implore gently. "Help me understand."

After a long tense silence, she continues softly, "My mother created it long ago to help newly turned vampires control their rabid hunger when they had no other recourse. She hoped it could teach restraint and prevent senseless violence. When I was young, we lived in an area where noble vampires had a habit of hunting and allowing their thirst to overwhelm them so they turned vampires instead of using self-control and stopping before that point."

I watch the rapid rise and fall of her shoulders, shame and defiance warring in her tense posture.

Stepping closer, I lay a tentative hand on her shoulder. "Thorn," I ask quietly. "What are you not telling me? Were you turned?"

She shudders under my touch but does not pull away. At long last, she whispers, "The tea does not just revive vampires."

I wait, breath suspended, as the fire crackles steadily behind us.

Thorn closes her eyes. "It helps... restrain cravings. For blood. It's able to somehow supply everything that a vampire needs to survive without drinking blood directly. The results can be amplified with blood added to it, but it's not needed."

Stunned understanding sweeps over me. Thorn has had to protect herself from vampires alone. In a kingdom full of vampires. A safe haven for them while a death sentence for her. Asrbloom is as much her refuge as mine.

My voice catches thickly in my throat. "You hide this truth to protect yourself from being turned or worse."

From people like my brother and father, a fact I do not say aloud. I wouldn't put it past them to be among those Thorn mentioned turning humans into vampires and leaving it to be someone else's problem. They truly believe they are at the top of the food chain. The worst part is that they would still look down on and persecute any being that isn't a natural-born vampire no matter how restrained they are or if they themselves created the being. From what I've read and heard, this was what Vivian, the vampire I'm looking for, was so against and why she was hellbent on taking down my family.

Revulsion twists my gut at this ingrained prejudice. Treterra is unique because it's a kingdom ruled by vampires and one of the few fairly safe places for our species.

"There is no shame in what you have," I vow fiercely. "The shame lies with those who are unwilling to control themselves."

Her eyes glisten with surprise at my words. After a shocked moment, her lips curve into a tremulous but warm smile. "You are unlike any vampire I have met, Draven. My past isn't what you expect, and it's not something I'm willing to share with others. Don't pity me. I've chosen this life, and I quite enjoy the little world I've built. I quite like the tea anyways. Why not sit and have a sip with me?"

Her words ring with quiet conviction, a subtle warning not to tread where I am unwelcome, yet curiosity leaves me unsatisfied.

As she takes another sip, I shift closer in the wooden chair, an elbow on the table, and lean toward her until I am near enough to feel the heat of her body. Thorn tenses but does not pull away or halt her clicking needles.

"You know so much of me," I murmur low near her ear, "yet you remain an enigma."

I reach out slowly, brushing back a raven lock that has escaped her braid. My fingertips graze her neck, feeling her quickened pulse. Still, she sips, refusing to meet my gaze.

"Does the tea truly satisfy?" I ask, trailing my fingers along her jaw. "Does a vampire never crave more?"

Thorn inhales sharply at my intimate touch, fingers faltering, and a small amount of tea splashes over the lip of her mug. The flickering firelight deepens the roses blooming on her cheeks.

"As with any creature, restraint is a choice." Her voice remains steady, and her words ghost warm against my wrist.

I lean in closer, emboldened. "What of carnal yearnings? Does it help those too?"

My thumb caresses her chin. With my heightened senses, I can hear her heart thundering and smell the heady spice of arousal kindling beneath her skin. Still, Thorn does not pull away.

"Some hungers run too deep to be suppressed," she whispers, slowly placing her drink on the table with a small thunk.

"And if such dangerous cravings arose?" I brush my lips against her temple, gritting back my own pounding need. "Would you surrender or resist?"

Thorn turns at last to face me. Her pupils are blown wide, lips parted, breaths coming fast, yet resolve glimmers in her fierce emerald gaze.

"I surrender only by choice." Her fingers twist in my hair, pulling me closer. "Never by force."

With that, she closes the distance between us. Her mouth claims mine in a searing kiss that steals my breath and scorches my very bones. I am lost, consumed by smoldering desire as she bares the truth of her passion. Here is the wild side she keeps locked away, unleashed at last by my reckless taunting.

Her touch ignites my body, and I find myself yielding completely. Consumed by Thorn's fire, what remains but to burn?

Thorn's kiss sears through me, volcanic and urgent. Her fingers twist almost painfully in my hair, pulling me against her petite but surprisingly strong form.

For a moment, I am lost, drowned by relentless waves of passion crashing through my senses, but slowly, an alarm bell cuts through the haze of desire. Something is off. Thorn trembles now, her gasping breaths tinged with fear, not craving.

With monumental effort, I pull back, breaking our frantic embrace.

Thorn stares at me wide-eyed, lips swollen from our kisses, before she turns away in shame. "Forgive me," she rasps, wrapping her arms around herself. "I don't know what came over me. I never surrender control like that."

Confused, I reach for her shoulder but stop myself short, unsure if my touch is wanted. "There is nothing to forgive, Thorn. I'm the one who pushed too far."

Thorn shakes her head sharply. "It was weakness. I swore I would never... We can't..." She trails off, refusing to meet my gaze.

The softly spoken words pierce my soul. My chest aches, seeing her torment. I want to pull her into my arms and soothe away whatever ghosts haunt her, but forcing intimacy now might only drive her further behind her walls.

So instead, I simply sit in quiet support, letting the crackling fire fill the tense silence. Thorn's tremors slowly subside, tension draining from her slender frame, but she keeps her body angled away, the maintained distance heartbreaking.

Neither of us speaks further. An invisible wall between us has fallen. We move about the cottage with a newfound ease, chatting lightly as Thorn empties the cold tea kettle and prepares dinner. I notice she stands a bit closer now, angles her body more openly toward me as we talk. Each subtle shift thrills me.

Later, as we eat thick stew ladled over slices of fresh bread, I can't resist voicing part of my earlier curiosity.

"This Asrbloom tea," I remark between bites, "you say you carry it with you when traveling alone?"

Thorn pauses, spoon halfway to her mouth. Her eyes take on that mesmerizing ferocity, like an emerald blaze. "In case of crossing your kind, yes," she says pointedly. "I walk unseen usually, but you never know what will happen."

I nod, hoping my prodding will not break this delicate accord between us. "A reasonable precaution, though I promise you don't need to fear me." I infuse the vow with utmost sincerity.

Thorn studies me for a long moment before inclining her head in acknowledgement. There are still ghosts of distrust between us, but I pray continued understanding will help lay them to rest.

We pass the rest of the meal in thoughtful quiet. I sense Thorn observing me when she believes I'm not looking, as if trying to solve a complex riddle. I pretend not to notice, hiding my smile.

After we finish eating, I help Thorn clear the table then stoke the glowing embers in the hearth. Neither of us is eager to sleep just yet, so we settle together before the fire as the wind continues its lonesome howling outside.

Thorn takes up her knitting, needles clacking rhythmically, while I page idly through a leather-bound book of local myths and legends. We don't speak, but the silence wraps around us with tender comfort. Each time I glance up, I find Thorn already watching me over her clicking needles, an affectionate half-smile teasing her lips.

I know I should bank the fire soon and try to sleep, putting emotional thoughts to rest, but solitude is not what my restless spirit craves tonight. Not when this extraordinary woman sits close enough to touch, each shared moment knitting our hearts closer than her yarn.

# 8

## THORN

My hands tremble as I hastily gather up the abandoned mugs and kettle, clattering them loudly in my distress. The tea items rattle on the tray, evidence of my inner turmoil I cannot seem to still.

What came over me? Kissing Draven without a second thought. I have so many secrets that would get me killed, and I just gave a vampire that I don't really know anything about a massive clue to learn who I am.

I chance a glance over at him where he sits watching me. Heat rises in my cheeks. I avert my gaze quickly, afraid he'll read the truth spelled out in my eyes—that, for a blissful moment, I forgot myself entirely and gave in to desire.

Such foolishness cannot happen again.

Breathing deeply, I brace myself on the edge of the wash basin. The past has taught me that passion only brings pain. In this case, Draven's involvement threatens the safe solitary life I've built, away from prying eyes and powers intent on using me.

I must regain control. Apply logic. Establish boundaries. Suppress dangerous feelings that would only lead to heartbreak again. I am the only one who can shape my destiny, and I will not have it derailed by an ill-fated mate bond and my own pathetic longing.

Gods above, what did I just unleash by kissing Draven like that?

Draven's still watching me with those penetrating silver eyes, no doubt wondering what in fiery blazes has come over the forest hermit who was snogging him senseless moments ago. I quickly avert my gaze.

*Get it together, Thorn!* This cannot happen again. That smoldering passion only brings pain. I need to be logical and set some boundaries between us before I do something reckless like smile or make eye contact.

I ignore Draven's confused staring and hunker down at my table to scratch out a list of rules for keeping myself in check.

*No touching the hot vampire whose kiss still smolders through your veins.*

*Seriously, stop fantasizing about his hands on you!*

*And no more gazing dreamily into his eyes either or you'll spill all your secrets.*

The quill scratches loudly on the parchment as I outline precautions against getting closer to Draven. I see him stand cautiously, looking like he wants to say something, to ask what's wrong, but I keep scribbling, willing him to leave me be with my frantic list-making.

He hesitates then sinks back down by the fire, his expression going from confused to hurt in a flash. Great, now I've wounded his pride. Honestly, it's for our own good. I cannot let myself fall any deeper under this man's spell, or I'll end up burned again.

I continue filling the parchment with strict rules to keep my dangerous heart in check.

*Light topics only.*

*No discussion whatsoever of unbreakable bonds or my mixed bloodline. Way too risky, like dancing with fire.*

There, guidelines established!

I survey my list critically, checking for any loopholes. Satisfied I've got enough here to avoid further entanglements, I set aside the parchment. No need to

---

explain all this to Draven. He'd argue fate has it out for us or some nonsense. I have to start following these rules pronto before we do anything else we'll regret at sunrise.

Having decided on this logical course, I rise to fix us a bedtime snack, avoiding his eyes. I focus wholly on slicing bread and cheese, willing my hands to be steady. Nice and simple food prep. No more intimate dinners that end with us gazing longingly across the table.

I hear Draven approach behind me, his footsteps cautious. My shoulders tense instinctively. *Don't turn around. Don't you dare make small talk or let him get close again!* I brace myself on the worn countertop as he hovers over my shoulder.

"Thorn." His voice is gentle, full of questions I can't answer. "Have I done something to upset you? Please, talk to me."

My treacherous heartbeat picks up at the sound of my name on his lips. *Shut up, stupid fickle heart. We are sticking to the plan.*

I shake my head, keeping focused on fixing these sandwiches. From the corner of my eye, I see Draven start to reach for me then think better of it. Even his near touch raises goose bumps on my arm. Dangit! I quickly step away to put more space between us. *Take that, pesky mate bond.*

Looking uncertain, Draven stands there in the middle of my cottage, seeming so lost it tugs at my blasted soft heartstrings. *Get it together, Thorn.* This temporary cold shoulder routine is necessary if we're ever to break free of each other.

As I arrange the food on two plates, I hear Draven approach behind me, cautious as one might creep up on a cornered wolf. I brace myself, gripping the table edge. *Do not turn. Do not invite conversation or the temptation of his nearness.*

"Thorn." His voice comes gently over my shoulder. "Why won't you tell me what I've done? We don't know how long we will be stuck together in here. Does it have to be so painful?"

My eyes flutter half-closed. Just the melodious sound of my name on his lips sparks a warm blossoming in my chest that spreads and aches. I harden my heart against it. *You will not sway me from logic, vampire.*

I shake my head mutely, keeping my focus on preparing the snack. Out of the corner of my eye, I see

Draven's hand raise as though to touch my shoulder then fall away once more. The ghostly impression of his touch lingers on my skin. I shiver and step out of his reach, crossing the room to set his plate on the far end of the table. Distance. Yes, that's best.

Draven stands uncertain in the center of the cottage, eyes clouded, looking utterly lost. I feel a pang at being the cause of such sadness in his striking features, but this standoff cannot be helped if we're to have any hope of breaking this accursed bond.

I gesture woodenly at the seat opposite me, not meeting his gaze. "Come. Eat before it gets cold." I know it makes no sense. The sandwiches are already cold, but I can't think clearly anymore. I need him to leave before I slip up and go too far.

He doesn't argue, though a muscle in his jaw twitches as if he's biting back questions.

We eat mostly in silence, my rules a chaperone forcing space between us at the small table. When Draven's hand accidentally brushes mine as he reaches for his mug, I jerk my own back swiftly, ignoring the tingling remnant on my skin.

We make stilted small talk about the weather, the food, and the firewood, inane topics like two strangers forced into close quarters, not whatever it is this mating bond seeks to make us.

I endure Draven's brooding silences and sad-eyed glances with stoic resolve. It is better this way, I remind myself, even as my chest twists at the absence of our easy banter. Never should we have allowed such familiarity between us. Once the storm clears, things can go back to how they were before fate meddled—Draven free to his wanderings and I, once more, blissfully alone. Two lives woven only by the barest filament now painstakingly severed.

It doesn't matter if my cottage will feel several degrees colder, missing the lively fire Draven sparked within me. This numbing emptiness is far safer than the terrifying precipice of hope and intimacy I briefly peered over before fear yanked me back. His kind are why I am here, why I have to stay hidden. I can't let myself soften for any reason.

No, it's decided. My rules will steer us clear of that chasm's edge until Draven can safely get on his way and I can get back to my solitary existence. We only need to endure the discomfort of this new awkward tension between us a little while longer. Once the snow melts, hopefully this fated mate connection will melt away too, like footprints in the drifts outside.

At least that's what I keep telling myself.

By the time we've cleaned up the quiet, stilted meal, I'm exhausted from constantly battling my feelings, which keep getting in the way of logic. I need a break from those soulful silver eyes, which seem to peer right through my fortified walls.

Murmuring some excuse about being tired after nursing an ill Draven—which isn't a total lie—I retreat to my bed in the nook by the fireplace and pull the curtain closed for privacy. Only then, in the sanctuary of shadow, do I finally unclench my jaw and allow my shoulders to slump, drained from keeping up that rigid, impersonal facade all day. Denying my desires is proving more difficult than anticipated, but I can't let myself weaken, or Draven might rekindle flickers of hope in my heart. I can't do that. I've already learned what happens when I let hope blossom. It never turns out well. I've lost everything before because of it.

I sit, listening to the muffled sounds of Draven moving quietly about the cottage. Thanks to our supernatural connection, I'm annoyingly attuned to his presence even through the divider curtain. He probably thinks I'm being fickle and moody, getting all passionate with him one minute only to give him the cold shoulder the next. If only he knew the ghosts of my past that make it too perilous to act on our feelings.

I rub my arms against the pervasive chill despite the fire crackling steadily in the hearth. Keeping my distance from the man I'm meant to take comfort in leaves me feeling hollow and lonely. I chose this guarded separation between us for our own safety. So why does it have to sting so bitterly?

*** 

Ugh, these old pages are making my nose itch something fierce, but I've gotta keep searching through this spellbook if I'm gonna find a way to break the mate bond that is still somehow forming between me and Mr. Tall, Pale, and Mysterious over there.

I tip the heavy leather tome titled Cryptic Spells at an angle so Draven can't peek at the contents from where he's sitting and poking at the fire. As far as he knows, I'm just casually perusing some light reading to pass the time in our snowy imprisonment together.

If only he knew the truth—that I'm desperately trying to find some untraceable magic to undo whatever supernatural connection is sparking to life between us before it's too late. Before he realizes we're being tied together by the red strings of fate and uses that power to get all controlling and suffocate my freedom.

Been there, done that. To them, I wasn't a person, just a powerful monster to be controlled and exploited. Then, it all turned on me, literally, and I was hunted by the very people I helped.

I force several deep breaths to calm myself down. This tricky mating bond could destroy the safe little world I've built if I don't find a way to snip those tangled ties pronto.

I must stay focused if I'm gonna uncover some solution here, even as my inconvenient crush on Draven wars with my logic. Isn't there a spell for dissolving connections without a trace? I skim past confusing incantations for summoning spirits, forgetting memories, and manipulating feelings. Ugh, nothing helpful!

I risk a peek over at Draven, who's rising from his chair all sinuous and cat-like. A sliver of pale skin shows as he stretches, making my pulse skip embarrassingly. *Get it together, Thorn! Focus on research, not the hot vampire whose kiss you can't stop thinking about!*

"Gonna grab some more firewood before it gets dark," he says casually.

I make a vague sound of reply, pretending to be lost in my reading. Honestly, I'm hyperaware of his every movement, our bond pulling me toward him like a magnet.

I have to shake myself out of staring at the door long after he's gone. *Pull yourself together!* This weird attraction is exactly what I need to break. With Draven out fetching wood, I can use this time to work uninterrupted. I'm sure he will make it back in safely this time. The storm is starting to edge a bit. It should be safe to send him home soon.

Okay, there's got to be some hidden jewel in this book that can save me from getting all doe-eyed over Mr. Can't Keep His Smug Smirk To Himself. Come on, come on... Aha! A spell called Rite of Sundering. That sounds promising!

Skimming the description, it seems like it can sever metaphysical connections. Perfect! This mystical witch's brew of herbs shouldn't be too tricky to whip up either. The ritual's incantation is elaborate but doable if I focus. Tonight when the crescent moon rises, we'll be free!

I'm carefully brewing up the magical draught when Draven shoulders his way back inside, arms loaded with logs. Snowflakes twinkle in his windswept hair, and he flashes that infuriating grin. "Couldn't go another minute without me, huh?"

"Hardly," I retort with an exaggerated eye roll. "Just looking forward to not freezing to death overnight once you actually haul in enough firewood." I pointedly bury my nose back in the spellbook.

He chuckles, clearly trying to get a rise out of me, and starts rebuilding the fire.

I sneak glances at him over the top of my book, admiring how the flames bring out reddish hints in those raven locks. Part of me hates how appealing he looks bathed in firelight. *Cast the spell first. Moon over the hot vampire later!*

Once the cottage is again filled with crackling warmth, I retrieve the brewed draught. In the flickering firelight, I pour all my magic and intention into it, reciting the spell's shaping incantations. The liquid starts to glow and hum with power.

I look up to find Draven watching me curiously. Before he can ask, I quickly close my eyes. Just gotta focus on the mystical connection between us and sever it with this rite.

I start chanting the Sundering spell under my breath. The temperature instantly plummets, and an ominous creaking shakes the entire cottage. My eyes fly open, but it's too late to back out now.

Draven jumps up, looking spooked as stuff starts rattling violently on the shelves. "Uh, Thorn? Wanna tell me what you're up to right now?"

I don't answer, pouring all my will into completing the volatile ritual, but my control is slipping, and the spell takes on an explosive life of its own. I have to see this through! I can't let the havoc that the mate bond is wreaking on my magic take control.

Shouting the final verse, I direct the breaking point of the ritual squarely at the link between me and Draven. A deafening crack splits the air. At the same moment, a psychic rope snaps tight in my mind.

"Argh!" I double over from the rush of foreign emotions flooding my senses—confusion, concern, anger at my betrayal...

Crap. Felt that loud and clear. The spell backfired and connected our minds instead of cutting us off.

I glance up to see Draven looking just as shell-shocked, gripping his head.

"What the hell did you do?" he demands. "I can sense your feelings... hear your thoughts!"

Oh no. Please tell me he didn't just pick up on my raging thirst to jump his bones. Awkward.

I turn away so he can't see my flaming cheeks. "Um, slight magical mishap? Meant to restore our peace and privacy." My voice comes out shaky and unconvincing. So much for stealth.

Warm fingers catch my chin, gently turning my face back toward him.

I brace for anger but see only earnest concern in his searching eyes. "You wanted space from me. I understand." His thumb strokes my cheek. "But my presence does not have to be an intrusion."

My treacherous heart flutters at his nearness. Words bubble up before I can stop them. "I wish I wasn't so afraid..." Mortified at the unchecked confession,

I pull away. No more risks while he's leashed to my unfiltered mind!

Pulse pounding, I rush to the window. Thank the gods, the weather's eased up quite a bit more than I had realized.

I start gathering up Draven's things, movements jerky. "Storm's passed. Time to be on your way!"

He frowns in confusion as I shove bread and his cloak at him, but I'm hyper-focused on preparing the transportation spell before our mental link gives me away completely.

Channeling crackling magic between my palms, I bark out, "Where am I sending you?"

"The royal castle in Everdusk," Draven answers slowly. "But couldn't we discuss—"

Everdusk? Ice floods my veins. He is really nobility? Every primal instinct in me shrieks trap.

I cut off his unspoken plea, forcing stiff composure. "And your position there?"

"I'm one of the princes." His empty smile and guarded eyes spell reluctance.

Time's up. The spell is fraying!

Clawing back tattered magic, I cast the transportation orb with my last shred of control and unceremoniously dump a baffled Draven into its vortex.

The absence hits me like a sledgehammer, and I collapse, gasping.

Well, I got my wish. No more entanglements or heartache. Just me and solitude once more.

Why does victory feel so cold and hollow?

I curl around the gaping wound in my chest, sobs wracking my frame. I've never experienced agony like the severing of our short-lived bond. It smothers me until I'm numb, and I long for just one more moment by the fire with him, secrets be damned.

# 9

## DRAVEN

The wind gets knocked outta me as I'm spat out right in front of the royal castle gates. One second I'm standing in Thorn's cozy cottage, the next—bam—back in civilization faster than you can shout "goodbye."

Still catching my breath, I gape up at the imposing fortress of stone looming above. Everdusk Castle's spiked towers pierce the cloud-streaked winter sky, banners emblazoned with House Valisar's crest flapping from the parapets. The last dregs of daylight wash the pale stone edifice in rosy hues. Looks like I made it back to the vampiric nest right on target.

As I get my bearings, memories of Thorn's panic-stricken face flood my mind. Her voice echoes in my mind. "Storm's passed. Time to be on your way!"

Then, poof! Teleportation spell to the face and here I am.

What the hells went down back there? One minute, we're all snuggled up sipping tea. The next, she can't blast me outta her life fast enough and right after that spell mishap too, the one that somehow psychically tethered us before she got spooked.

I press my palm to my chest where an odd ache throbs. It feels like she clawed into my ribcage and ripped something vital out. Is this some lingering effect of our mental connection snapping so suddenly? Yet, this hollow pain feels deeper than physical, like a piece of my soul got left behind in her little cottage. So damn bizarre.

The creak of iron gates shake me from my daze. Right, oughta actually enter my ancestral abode now that I've spent who knows how long awkwardly loitering outside the place. The guards stare at me like they've seen a ghost as I stroll past into the bustling courtyard, which is carpeted in a fresh dusting of snow. Can't blame 'em. Last they heard, I got buried in a freak avalanche on my travels. Yet here I am, without a scratch somehow. Well, besides the gaping emotional wound anyway.

The guards' shock mirrors my own. I was warm and content in Thorn's cottage. Now, I'm back in the imposing coldness of the castle courtyard.

"Prince Draven, you're alive!" another guard exclaims, rushing forward.

I nod vaguely, still dazed. "Yes, I... managed to take shelter in a cottage before the worst hit."

My words come out distant, my thoughts still consumed by Thorn's panicked face as she shoved me into that transportation spell. Why had she been so frantic to make me leave?

The guards chatter excitedly, but their voices blur together into meaningless noise. Pain continues to pulse through my head and heart—hers, not mine. Our severed bond must have left some faint echo of connection.

I sway on my feet from a fresh wave of crushing heartache. Again, hers. Thorn must be in pure anguish for it to bleed over into me like this. I press a palm to my chest, willing my own emotions to remain separate.

"Prince Draven?" The guard's voice filters through again, tinged with concern now. "Are you well? We should inform the king right away of your return."

I blink hard, trying to focus on his words. "No need to trouble my father yet. I'm simply... weary from travels." I attempt to smile reassuringly. "Let me rest before presenting myself."

The guards exchange a look but don't argue. I take advantage of their lingering awe to extricate myself and make my way swiftly across the courtyard before more servants descend, pelting me with questions I cannot answer.

Not when my every thought bends toward Thorn.

Foreign emotions—pain, regret, and sorrow—batter my mind like a hurricane. Thorn's anguish bleeds through our fading bond, assaulting my senses.

I press my palm harder against my chest, struggling to stay upright under the onslaught. Her weeping echoes faintly, as if carried on the wind. My fingers dig into the stone walls for support as we pass through the grand archway.

Thorn's presence surrounds me, though she's nowhere to be seen. It's like I carry the ghost of her within me. I blink back hot tears that are not my own. I must retain control and keep my fractured composure...

"Draven!"

My mother's voice cuts through the haze as she sweeps into the courtyard, flanked by her ladies-in-waiting. Queen Vespera's emerald gown billows around her, the skirt's golden embroidery glinting in the torchlight. An ornate silver circlet crowns her flowing raven hair streaked with white. Her ageless pale face is lined with concern, cheeks flushed from hurrying outside to greet me.

I straighten instinctively before her assessing gaze. It's her eyes, the same piercing silver as my own, that truly give me pause. They see through veils and shadows to cut right to the heart of matters. I resist the urge to shrink back from their knowing stare.

"We had feared you lost to the winter's fury," she says, cupping my cheek with cool hands weighed down by heavy rings. Her gaze searches mine intently, likely finding the secrets etched there before I can utter them aloud. "Yet it seems fate spared you once again."

I open my mouth, but words fail me. How can I explain my mysterious survival? That a strange witch risked all to save me, only to cast me abruptly out again? Another wave of sorrow crashes through my mind, stealing speech.

Mother's brow creases, fine lines furrowing. "You are unwell. Come, we shall tend to your needs." She deftly takes my arm, steering me away from the guards' prying ears. Her voice drops to a murmur meant only for me, soft yet steely at once. "There are shadows in your eyes, my son... You have brought something back with you."

It is not a question. Her ancient instincts never miss anything.

I shudder out a breath, the first step to unburdening my chaotic heart. "Yes, but I don't yet understand it myself."

Mother nods. "Then we shall unravel this mystery together. For now, you need rest."

"My men, Lord Anthony, are they safe? Have they returned?"

"Yes, they were how we knew you were missing. They returned in hopes of gathering more men and supplies to find you, but they are all safe."

Relief floods me. I need to find my childhood friend later.

Too spent to resist, I let her guide me through the twisting corridors to my chambers. Thorn's spectral presence clings to me like mist, a living ghost I cannot exorcise. Not until I understand why she haunts me so.

Inside the sanctuary of my rooms, blessed stillness settles over my mind. Thorn's sorrow retreats to a dull ache as my mother tends the fire. I sink into a chair, rubbing my throbbing temples.

"Now tell me everything, Draven." Mother's voice anchors me as she takes the seat opposite me. "Omit no detail. The truth shall set you free of these shadows."

I meet her eyes, finding patience and wisdom etched there by centuries of wear. Taking a deep, steadying breath, I grasp for where to even begin explaining the tangled events that brought me here.

"I... was saved by a witch after I got lost in the storm and separated from everyone," I start hesitantly. "She healed me in her forest cottage."

Mother's gaze remains studiously neutral. "Go on."

"She tended me for several days there, until the storm passed. Then, she sent me back here." I spread my hands. "That is all."

"Somehow, I doubt the full truth is quite so simple." Mother's piercing eyes seem to peel back my evasions. "Son, if she harmed you..."

"No!" I cut in hastily. "She asked nothing in return, only for me to leave once recovered."

I fall silent as echoes of Thorn's weeping reach me. I press my palm harder against my chest, willing the sound away. Not now!

Mother scrutinizes me closely, missing nothing. "You did not wish to leave her."

I open my mouth to deny it then slump back in my chair. What point is there in concealing the truth from one so perceptive?

"No," I admit wearily. "I found myself... drawn to her... but I'm needed here."

Mother nods thoughtfully. "You care for this witch, though you hardly know her. Curious."

I stare at my hands, blistered now from the few days of honest labor. How much have I changed from the prince who left these gilded halls?

"She is an enigma, and now..." I trail off as sorrow stabs through me once more.

Mother reaches over, clasping my hand firmly until the fit passes. Her brow furrows. "My son, what magic has this witch worked upon you?"

I shake my head helplessly. "I wish I knew."

My fingers brush against the bundle of bread and cloak in my grasp. How strange that Thorn pressed such humble gifts on me.

I take a thoughtful bite of the bread, savoring the rich flavors that hint at the complexity of its maker.

Mother watches me closely. "May I?"

I pass her a piece. She chews slowly, tasting, assessing, and her eyes widen fractionally.

"There is old magic woven through this bread. Subtle but unmistakable." She fixes me with a piercing look. "What has this woman been doing to you?"

I stare at the half-eaten loaf, remembering the herbs Thorn mixed in. What had she been trying to accomplish with such spells? Had it all been a lie?

Before I can dwell on that distressing idea, sorrow knifes through me again. Thorn's muffled sobs echo relentlessly, clawing at my composure. Not deception, surely, but desperation.

I meet my mother's eyes beseechingly. "Please, I need rest now. My mind is... tired."

Mercifully, she rises without argument. At the door, she pauses, gazing back with ancient wisdom. "There is much left unsaid between us. When you are ready, we shall unravel this mystery of your witch together."

The door closes behind her with an ominous finality, leaving blessed silence. Still, Thorn's sorrow haunts me, her muffled sobs echoing relentlessly in my mind.

I stare down at the remnants of spelled bread in my hands. What desperate magic had she worked into this innocent loaf? And why had it caused her such anguish to make me leave?

Had it all been a deception on her part? The thought pierces my heart like a dagger of ice. Surely one who saved my life at risk of her own cannot be wholly false?

No. Her tears are real. Thorn regrets my absence as much as she fears my presence. Of that much, I am now certain.

I rise on shaky legs, hands clenching into fists. I cannot find answers here behind sheltered walls. The only path is back to that hidden cottage, wherever it may lie, back to the mysterious Thorn who even now calls to my soul from afar. First, I rest. Then, I will find her and get my answers.

\*\*\*

Bolting upright with a gasp, I clutch the silk sheets now damp with sweat. Panting raggedly, I rub my throbbing chest as the lingering agony from the dream fades. Gods, it felt so real, like razor-edged icicles shredding my heart. Probably just stress after recent chaotic events.

Blinking against the daylight filtering through stained glass windows, I take in the lavish suite of rooms. Gilded furniture, velvet drapes, a ridiculous excess of plush pillows on this massive canopy bed. Definitely not the rustic cottage I've spent the last week in. Home. My home.

As I awake, things become more clear. Thorn's magical transportation orb zapped me back here to the royal castle. Back to the vampire nest.

A hollow pang hits my gut at the thought of her. No doubt Thorn is relieved to have her humble abode back to herself without this high-maintenance prince crashing on her floor.

I grimace, kneading the persistent ache behind my breastbone. It almost feels like... longing. Absurd. I only knew the witch for a few days before she sent me packing. Too bad the silken tassels on these obnoxious pillows can't fill the void left behind.

Clearly, Mother was right about me needing rest. Nothing else explains such self-pitying thoughts over a near stranger.

With a groan, I peel back the velvet coverlet to rise. Time to face the inevitable royal duties awaiting my return.

Except the second my feet hit the ornate rug, all strength flees my body. I crash to my knees with an inglorious thud. It's like the floor dropped out from under me. This fresh wave of agony rips through my chest even worse than the haunting dream. I gasp raggedly, clawing at my sternum which now feels eviscerated. What's happening to me?

*Get it together. You're a deadly vampire prince, not some mewling human infant.*

Gritting my teeth, I crawl my pathetic self back onto the massive bed, focusing on breathing through the pain. Maybe more rest will sort out this strange sickness.

Except the torture doesn't ease. It only intensifies. This crushing pressure keeps building until I want to claw my way out of my own skin for relief. A faint sound pierces through the sheer anguish—the soft hitch of a stifled sob. What the...

Forcing myself motionless, I strain to listen past the roaring in my skull. There, beneath the frantic pounding of my heart, comes the whisper soft sound again—a woman weeping quietly.

Thorn.

Her name cuts through the mental haze with crystal clarity. It's her sorrow I'm somehow feeling. The spell, right? That was what she was doing before she sent me back. Is this from that?

My fangs punch down reflexively with an animal snarl. Who dares reduce my fierce witch to such helpless tears? I'll shred them to tattered meat! No, calm down. I'm a rational vampire. She was crying after I left too, right? Besides, Thorn doesn't belong to me. More importantly, if I'm sensing her desolation over here, does it flow both ways? Is my own anguish compounding hers? The last thing I want is to deepen her distress.

I force my fangs to retract and try measured breathing instead, focusing on sending calming vibes through our peculiar bond. Can't have both of us coming unglued. I'm stronger than this.

After several minutes, it seems to help marginally. The crushing pressure in my chest eases a fraction as rational thought trickles back in. Thorn's muted weeping continues, but it's more distant now. At least one of us is keeping it together.

Now that I've regained some measure of sense, I know what I must do. Get the blazes back to that cottage by any means necessary.

Throwing aside silk sheets worth more gold than Thorn's entire homestead likely costs, I lurch stiffly from the massive bed to dress. No time to bother with the two dozen fancy clasps and buckles of formal court attire. I just yank on a simple tunic, trousers, boots and a thick cloak for the journey ahead.

I've just finished tying my bootlaces when the chamber doors burst open and a troop of guards march in, weapons glinting.

"Prince Draven, stand down this instant," the captain barks out. "Queen's orders that you remain confined to your quarters."

Like hell!

They advance with chained silver manacles, prepared to shackle me by force.

I flash extended fangs in warning, crouching defensively. "I'd like to see you try containing me. Stand aside!"

The captain pauses uncertainly.

Just then, a commanding voice rings out behind the guards. "Stand down. Now."

They instantly part as my mother, Queen Vespera, sweeps imperiously into the chamber, emerald skirts billowing. Her piercing silver gaze sizes up the situation in an instant.

"Leave us," she commands sharply.

The guards file out without protest.

Her ageless yet careworn face creases in maternal concern. "Draven, what are you doing? You still seem unwell. Where do you think you are going?"

Despite her gentle tone, I force myself to relax my aggressive posture, not wishing to seem deranged. She's always been able to see right through me, so I opt for honesty.

"Apologies, Mother, but I need to leave now."

"In such a state?" Her searching eyes bore into mine. "You are clearly... unwell, my son."

I rake an unsteady hand through disheveled hair. She's not wrong. From the bloodshot eyes to the inside-out tunic, I likely resemble a rabid animal more than a prince. Hardly reassuring.

Picking my words with care, I explain waking up connected to Thorn's sorrow and this compulsory, all-consuming need to return to her side. Mother listens silently as I describe the frayed psychic tether causing me such physical and mental torture.

When I finish, she nods slowly, sunlight glinting off her silver circlet. "What you describe aligns closely with effects of the fated mate bond that sometimes manifests between vampires or other magical beings."

I gape at her words. "You believe Thorn and I could be... fated mates? But how is that possible?"

Mother's gaze turns thoughtful. "While rare, fate occasionally intercedes to bind two souls. The call between mates becomes impossible to resist."

I grip my throbbing chest, my own impossible longing echoing her words, yet it seems fantastical that destiny could have matched us so peculiarly.

"However..." Mother taps her chin. "Bonds take time to fully root. Yours seems to have flared unusually swiftly."

I blink. "What are you suggesting?"

"Perhaps some catalyst accelerated your connection," she muses. "A ritual... or shared blood."

My thoughts race, reviewing my time with Thorn. I don't remember any sort of moment that would have triggered such a thing, but if she was using spells on me... the tea, the bread... Could such exchanges have hastened our bonding, amplifying simple attraction into something more profound?

Seeing the dawning comprehension on my face, Mother nods. "Yes, an intimate joining of blood or magic could certainly ignite a mate bond. But why so rapidly... unless... " She meets my gaze. "This witch, she is no ordinary woman, is she?"

I stare down at my hands, calloused now from days of honest labor beside Thorn. "She is an enigma," I admit. "She is gifted in the mystical arts and hides her true self."

"So fate and magic combined have woven this web between you." Mother sighs knowingly.

"I still struggle to grasp that destiny could chain me eternally to a near stranger," I admit.

Mother gives an understanding smile. "Such is the paradox of predestined love, but remember, fate may draw you together, yet the choice to nurture any bond remains your own."

Her wisdom resonates deeply, kindling fragile hope within my tumultuous heart. If Thorn is my destined mate, I cannot force that fate upon her. Perhaps together, we can unravel this mystery and then choose our own path.

Mother clasps my hand firmly. "Be patient, my son. The answers you seek cannot be rushed, only revealed in their proper time."

I nod slowly, the urgency to find Thorn tempered by Mother's calming counsel. I know my place is here for the moment, not running off blindly after a phantom bond only half understood.

"You're right, as always," I acknowledge, squeezing her hand. "I will restrain my impatient heart and bide here awhile."

Mother exhales in palpable relief. "Wise words. We have the best mages in the kingdom here. We can find a single witch no matter where she is hiding."

I manage a small, grateful smile. "With your help, I know the answers will come in time and, with understanding, control over whatever enchantment has entwined our fates."

Mother presses a swift kiss to my forehead. "Have faith. No spell endures forever unchanged. The sun sets but always rises anew in the morning."

Despite my mother's calming wisdom, the phantom agony refuses to abate. Even with distance between us, the shredded bond tortures my heart.

Now alone, I pace my chambers, yearning for relief. The lavish gilding and velvet provide no comfort, only jar my senses.

I spot the bundle of provisions Thorn packed. An idea flickers through the haze of anguish. Perhaps her bread can grant some small relief? My mother said it was spelled. Perhaps that's what it was for?

I hastily unwrap the linen-swaddled loaf and root around for a knife with fumbling fingers. After sawing off a hunk, I bring it to my nose and inhale the yeasty aroma deeply before devouring it in famished bites. Chewing slowly, I close my eyes, focusing every sense on the memories Thorn's magic evokes... her shy smile when I praised her baking... the comfort of a meal shared in easy rapport. The vice around my chest loosens just slightly. I exhale in fragile relief, forcing myself to savor another small mouthful rather than glutting more greedily.

I dig my fingers into the bread, and fresh agony knifes through me as I imagine Thorn suffering alone. What darkness drove her to push me away so forcefully? Was she so afraid of me that she couldn't stand my presence for a moment more?

There must be something I can do other than sit here futilely gnawing away anguish bite by bite! For now, though, this bread is my only lifeline to Thorn, so I wrap myself in the knitted vestige of our bond and endure this half-life purgatory swallow by swallow. Clutching the remaining loaf to my chest, I sink onto the plush bed, its comforts now alien and cloying. Somehow, I vow silently, I will find my way back to her hearth and her open heart. Back to the only place that feels like home.

Until then, I cling desperately to the lingering echoes of Thorn left in these gifted provisions, my sole solace until fate leads me to her light once more.

# 10

## THORN

I awake in agony, my chest feeling gutted as if a vital organ had been carved out. Even smothered under a mountain of quilts, a bone-deep cold seeps through me. This isn't just physical pain. It's the remains of the bond I shared with Draven slowly shredding to bits. I knew the distance would help this dissipate, but I hoped it wouldn't hurt this much.

Pressing both palms over my whining heart, I chant every healing spell I know until the magic fizzles. Too wrecked to mend this intimate damage. Fate's cruel, letting me sample true belonging only to yank it away before I could grab hold. Sure, I don't really want it, or didn't I? I don't know. I can't think straight. What's done is done.

I'm tempted to make a loaf of the bread I had been feeding my vampire guest, but I don't have the energy.

Dragging myself out of bed, I poke at the banked embers, coaxing the fire back to life, but its heat can't thaw the ice around my soul. I wrap up in my thickest wool shawl and shuffle outside into the pale dawn, hoping the frosty air will numb this endless ache, but nothing mutes the gaping absence inside me now.

My leaden legs carry me to the woodshed on autopilot. Keeping my little place stocked with firewood provides some semblance of routine amidst the chaos.

As I trudge through drifts, flashes keep assaulting me—Draven's rare unguarded laughter, his secret smiles meant only for me, our heated embrace by the hearth. I squeeze my eyes against fresh hot tears. *Fool. How could you let yourself fall for a handsome stranger? You knew how this had to end. You set your will against fate itself yet still got shattered.*

I should've turned the half-dead vampire away that first night and kept my hapless heart cased in ice against his melting charm. Now, only shards remain, broken beyond repair.

The weight of the axe nearly topples me as I weakly try to swing it. Spent and despairing, I sink down amongst the silent pines.

As I sit there, lost in melancholy, unbidden memories keep invading my mind—Draven's tender gaze, the soft brush of his fingers over my cheek, his strong arms cradling me close, shielding me from the darkness.

No. I force the recollections away ruthlessly. The past is done. He has surely returned to his family in Everdusk by now, back to that gilded cage where my former life had been so terrible a living nightmare I'd rather let the world believe me dead than remain trapped there.

Maybe I should just lay here and allow the cold to claim me. Give up this endless fight. Find some peace in oblivion.

A flash of white catches my blurry eyes—a snow fox darting gracefully between the trees.

I watch numbly as it playfully chases a mouse across the icy crust before bounding over to me. The fox pauses a few steps away, cocking its head curiously. After a moment, it approaches and nudges my limp hand with its velvety muzzle. Warmth seeps from its touch, kindling faint sparks within my hollowed spirit.

*Come now, child. On your feet.*

I startle at the gentle yet commanding feminine voice echoing in my mind.

The fox meets my shocked gaze steadily, eyes swirling with ancient wisdom.

Gobsmacked, I struggle to rise on violently shaking limbs. What magic is this?

The fox trots at my heels as I stumble back home, its presence keeping me tethered to this world. Once inside, spent physically and mentally, I collapse on the hearth rug. My strange companion hops right into my lap, curling up against me as if sensing my need for living warmth.

"Um, hello? Just what do you think you're doing?"

The fox stills, blinking up at me slowly. *I'm here to help. The healing powers of a familiar are strongest with contact.*

I frown suspiciously. "A familiar? Nope. No thank you. Never again will I be leashed to another being."

The fox huffs, setting its head back down on my knee. *Leashed? I'm not some pet pup! I chose you to guide you out of darkness, but suit yourself. Wallow alone then!* Its bushy tail thumps my leg in emphasis.

I hesitate, sensing truth in its words as wisps of warmth radiate from its touch, dulling my agony fractionally. Still, accepting a familiar means relinquishing control I've fought hard to regain. At least this creature seeks to comfort and not consume me, and if it can grant some small relief from this torment...

I stroke the fox's lustrous fur, my walls crumbling. Its rumbling contentment vibrates through my weary bones.

*This mate bond is stirring quite the chaos inside of you, hmm?* Its sly mental tone reminds me of Granny Rona's playful spirit.

My vision blurs with hot tears. Gods, I wish she were here to guide me. She could always outwit fate's tricks, but no, I'm alone. My family was hunted, and I'm the last one left.

The fox nuzzles me delicately. *There now. Dry those eyes. We will outmaneuver this curse yet. You'll see! But first, breakfast is in order. What are you making? I do love pancakes and eggs. Oh! And bacon! But only if it's crispy and not burnt.*

Its single-minded enthusiasm startles a watery chuckle from me. "We just met literally moments ago, and you expect me to cook for you?"

The fox peers up at me beseechingly, golden eyes wide. *But you're in pain, and home cooking always helps! Don't you feel a little better with me here?*

I pause, realizing my crushing anguish has eased, if only marginally, in the creature's presence. Even so, I'm wary of entangling my life with another so soon.

"I admit your warmth offers some small comfort," I reply judiciously, "but a true partnership must be built on more than that."

The fox seems to consider this, head cocked. *You make a fair point. Perhaps we might find an arrangement that suits us both? I only wish to aid you through this trying time, as any friend would. What we become after that we can let time tell. Besides, I'm not a pet to keep. I have my own life. Fate has just woven ours together as well. Not something I asked for or expected either. You two-legged beings tend to complicate matters beyond what's necessary, and that's not a mess I want to be involved with.*

Friend. Not servant, not master. The simple offer resonates within my weary soul, yet uncertainty gnaws at me. This fox appeared in my darkest hour unbidden, fate's timing no doubt. Its aid need not become a leash if boundaries are set.

"Very well." I meet the fox's gaze evenly. "You may stay, for now, as an equal companion, but only if you swear not to control or coerce me, as others have tried." My voice hardens. "I walk my own path."

I sense the fox's earnestness through our tentative bond. *You have my vow. I seek only to guide, not command. Now then, let's get something tasty brewing!*

Despite myself, I huff a laugh as we both rise. "You are as single-minded as a gale. Very well. Let's eat. What should I call you?"

*Luna.*

"It's nice to meet you, Luna."

While I fix a simple breakfast of oatmeal, berries, and tea, my new friend's playful quips lift my spirits. The white fox observes my cooking eagerly, nose twitching at the aroma of cinnamon-sweetened oats.

When I sprinkle a pinch of dried Asrbloom pollen into my steaming tea, the fox's interest piques. *Ooh, intriguing scent! I believe that rare flower is said to have potent restorative properties, if the old legends hold true.* The fox's golden eyes gleam knowingly.

I lift the cup, breathing in the delicate fragrance. "Yes, this should help clear my head and diminish lingering shadows. I didn't expect a fox to know plants and magic so well." I sip slowly, letting the fortifying warmth and floral notes soothe me.

*There's much you don't know about me, witch. Fate wouldn't choose just any fox to be a familiar.*

I only nod, taking a sip of my tea. No, of course fate wouldn't just choose anyone. Why did that make me only feel worse?

We share the meal in thoughtful quiet. For the first time since I cast Draven away, my chaotic thoughts find some steadiness. The tea is muting our severed bond's torturous effects. I can focus and think beyond reactive anguish. There may yet be hope if I proceed wisely.

The fox finishes her meal and delicately licks her muzzle. *That was delicious!*

It's a small comfort but sincere. This curious creature appeared just when I needed a loyal friend most, and though much remains uncertain, a fragile trust now bridges the space between us.

After tidying up the breakfast dishes, I retrieve an ancient leather-bound tome from my bookcase and settle into the armchair by the fireplace. Luna curls up around my feet, rumbling contentedly as I scratch her ears and flip open the dusty cover.

My eyes hurt from squinting at the faded lettering on these ancient parchment pages, but I'm determined to push through. There has to be some arcane ritual or alchemical formula in these books that can dissolve the unwanted bond linking me to that infuriating vampire prince. I refuse to give up!

As I struggle to focus on the obscure text, echoes of Draven's presence stubbornly intrude—anger, frustration, and a vague sense of his location though worlds apart. I grit my teeth, pushing the unwanted sensations down.

"I've been at this all day, and I've found nothing," I grumble, snapping the heavy tome shut and blowing errant dust motes from its musky pages. "This so-called 'ultimate grimoire of mystical liberation' is useless!"

I sink back into the velvet armchair, kneading my throbbing temples. The gilded candles on my reading table have burned down to nubs, their flickering light straining my vision further. How long have I been hunched over these ancient pages anyway?

At my feet, the white fox Luna lifts her head, golden eyes glinting with sympathy from where she's curled atop a plush pillow. *You should rest. Your spirit grows weary.*

I wave off her concern, unable to keep still when answers feel just out of reach. "I'm fine. One more cup of tea and then back to work."

My fox companion snorts delicately as I push myself up and totter stiffly to the kitchen cabinet. A wave of dizziness hits when I reach for the tin of aromatic tea leaves. Luna's right. I need nourishment after all this mental exertion. With no appetite for a proper meal, the earthy floral notes of my Asrbloom tea will have to suffice. It's not often that I let my vampire side be what sustains me—I truly love good food anyway—but right now, I don't have time or energy for more.

I sink into a chair, sweeping a hand across my disordered work table to clear space for the tea tray I then carry over. Beyond fatigue, disheartened frustration gnaws at my patience. What if there is no magic powerful enough to overcome fate's decree and dissolve this bond forever?

No. I refuse to surrender and remain magically tied to Prince Draven for eternity. There has to be an enchantment capable of severing even the most stubborn supernatural ties. I just need to find it. I'll feel much more hopeful once this tea revives me.

The kettle whistles as Luna uses her snout to nudge it off the stove's flame. I hide a smile at her resourcefulness as she trots over carrying the pot by the handle. After passing me a steaming cup, she hops up into the chair opposite.

"Isn't that hot? I could have carried that."

*I'm a familiar, not your everyday fox. I can do things you couldn't imagine, and carrying a teapot is the least of them. Drink up now. Can't have you keeling over before you're done!*

Despite my anxious mood, I huff a laugh at the fox's matter-of-fact tone, and I breathe in the tea's soothing aroma. The vapor's warmth against my face relaxes my furrowed brow somewhat. First, sustenance. Then, back to the books with fresh eyes.

I gulp the tea faster than advisable for the scalding temperature. The rich floral flavors and subtle spice invigorate me as promised. Within minutes, the fog of fatigue lifts, and I feel curiously energized. Draven's thoughts and feelings are dampened enough that I can also forget he's there. I hadn't realized how much I needed this.

Across from me, Luna laps delicately at her own tea, neatly aligned white paws peeking out beneath her furry chest. She pauses, studying me with those uncannily sentient golden orbs.

*Goodness, look at you! Practically bristling with renewed fervor. Just keep that energy in check. I can practically feel your magic rolling off of you. Are you sure your magic isn't wild?* The fox's voice in my mind emanates wry amusement.

I roll my eyes fondly at her teasing as I eagerly tidy the empty mugs back onto the tray. She's right. I feel so much better, and now that my mind is clear, I know just the empowering elixir to brew, found in an ancient text I forgot earlier. It's at the back of my cabinet.

"You know me, always the picture of magical control," I joke as I shift stacks of scrolls and tomes to unearth the handwritten grimoire I seek. Finding mystical solutions fills me with blazing purpose once more. "Actually, you don't know me, but I promise no crockery is at risk here."

The fox hops down, pacing alongside me. *Well, if you insist on more volatile spellwork tonight, I shall observe safely from the doorway.* Her mental tone turns serious. *Remember to anchor yourself, or the forces you channel may grow unruly.*

Energized confidence overriding caution, I pause my rifling to wink at her. "The only unruly magic here is whatever nonsense fate used to bind me to Mister Royal Undeadness and to you."

This time, I vow silently, my power will overcome destiny itself.

Luna snorts as I pass the rest of the night in fervent mystical preparation, my earlier fatigue completely banished. Clearing space in my small cottage proves cathartic—out with the remnants of the evidence of my unwanted guest and in with new ingredients brimming with potential.

As the last pale light of evening filters through the cottage windows, I stand back to survey my handiwork. The aged oak table now holds an intricate layout of engraved crystals, vials of enchanted oils, and dried herb bundles tied with different colored ribbons to produce specific effects. I inhale deeply, the mingling scents focused yet strangely soothing.

Candles—tall tapers of pure beeswax etched with sigils for clarity—form a circle around the most frayed and arcane grimoire from my collection. I reverently open the dragonhide leather binding, its pages so ancient they feel more like worn parchment than paper. My pulse leaps when I find the ritual I seek nestled within, a shiver of destiny raising hairs on my nape.

After meticulous purification, the space hums with simmering potential. The time has come.

Centering my will, I take my place before the makeshift altar and begin meticulously combining ingredients as the ritual instructs, whispered words of power flowing from my lips to direct the brew's purpose.

As my incantation builds, the very walls of the cottage seem to resonate and amplify the words. Added droplets of viscous oil swirl opalescent through the mixture, kindling tiny sparks. The circle of candles flares higher, their reflection dancing across the glittering crystals and glass vials.

Power arcs to my outstretched palms as I seize it, funneling the volatile energy into the brew. "Give me the power to defy even you, oh fates," I grit out through clenched teeth. Sweat beads my brow from the forces amassing around me. "Let no bond withstand this unveiled might!"

With a final thunderous shout, I unleash the spell in a concussive blast. The windows rattle violently as objects around the cottage shake and lift into the air. Out of the corner of my eye, I see the fox familiar Luna leap atop a floating chair, furiously keeping her balance.

The magic continues building, slipping beyond my efforts to rein it back. Cold realization washes over me. Fate has played me for a fool. This spell has taken on a life and will of its own. What have I done?

I reach desperately for control, but wayward tools and jars continue swirling around the room in the grip of chaotic power I can no longer contain.

"No, stop this!" I yell to no effect. The unleashed ritual will run its explosive course now.

Gritting my teeth, I focus every fiber of my will on guiding the wild magic away from anything irreplaceable or sentimental. The swirling vortex of energy slowly shifts course, sucked into the standing cabinet where my most hallowed artifacts are secured by enchantments.

With an immense blast, the tornado of magic and debris funnels into the cabinet. I wrench the double doors shut with a resounding slam, the carved oak frame shuddering violently. As the dust swirls down, I sink to the floor, lungs heaving and head spinning. Silence gradually settles around me.

*Thorn? Are you hurt?* The fox's concerned voice filters through the ringing in my ears.

I lift my head to see Luna padding cautiously toward me, picking her way through the disordered wreckage now littering the cottage floor.

"I'm all right," I rasp out, accepting her shoulder to lean on as I shakily rise.

Truthfully, I'm drained in every way, but nothing a good long rest won't mend. Physically at least. My bruised ego may take longer after this magical fiasco.

Luna makes a sympathetic noise as we survey the cottage interior. The space looks like a localized hurricane blew through, scattering everything that wasn't secured down. I grimace at a conspicuous scorch mark now marring the center of my favorite rug. So much for no damage to valuables.

"Some mystical liberation spell that turned out to be," I mutter, righting an overturned chair with an irritable swipe of telekinesis. "I'll be fortunate if I haven't cursed myself somehow."

Luna nudges me gently. *You need sleep to recover strength. The cleaning can wait.*

My fox companion is right. Magical exhaustion pulls at my limbs, the adrenaline of the ritual wearing off.

# 11

## DRAVEN

The sound of my chamber doors banging open jolts me from a daze. Before I can react, a whirlwind of glittering skirts and unbound ginger curls barrels across the room and launches onto my bed.

"Draven, you're back!" my little sister Kira exclaims, sprawling atop the silk coverlet. "We all thought you'd been eaten by wolves or something, but nope! You just took the longest winter nap ever!"

I suppress a groan as she playfully smacks my leg. Barely one hundred and sixteen, Kira assumes anything and everything is proper teasing fodder.

"Yes, yes, I've finally awakened from my eternal slumber, oh wise one," I reply drily.

Leave it to Kira not to stand on decorum, even with a prince of the realm. With her, everything is laughter and games. Normally, I indulge her antics, but today, my spirit remains too burdened for such lightness.

Oblivious to my mood, Kira props her chin on both palms, gazing up at me eagerly. "Spill! What happened out there after you got lost? Did some grizzled old trapper save you? Ooh, or was it a wandering wizard with a magic sled?"

I shift against the headboard, avoiding her shining emerald eyes so like our mother's. "Nothing quite so dramatic, I'm afraid. Just a minor mishap during my travels. Nothing more."

"Nothing more?" Kira flops onto her back incredulously. "The whole castle thought you'd died! You gotta give me more than that. Pretty please?"

She bats her lashes, somehow making her freckled face look doleful. I snort. As if such transparent manipulation ever worked on me.

"A lady does not wheedle and pout," I chide.

She responds by sticking out her tongue. Yes, the picture of courtly manners, this one.

"Fine, keep your secrets for now, you crusty old bat." Kira hops nimbly off the bed, skirts swirling. "But this isn't over. I'll get the gossip from you someday!"

With an impish wink, she darts back out the doors, leaving blessed silence in her wake. I sink against the velvet cushions, eyelids already drooping again. Peace never lasts long around here, though.

Sure enough, another sharp rap at the door stirs me moments later. I sit up with a resigned sigh as my eldest brother Theron strides in. Even with no crown yet weighing down his brow, power and obligation shroud him like an invisible cloak.

His keen silver gaze sweeps over my disheveled state. "Still in bed at this hour? I hope you are not getting lazy."

Though his words hold a note of humor, I bristle at the implicit criticism. Theron assumes the role of heir apparent comes with the right to scrutinize our every deed.

"Merely resting as the healers instructed," I reply evenly.

In truth, I've been awake since dawn, restless dreams denying any real sleep, but Theron needn't know that.

He settles into a high-backed chair opposite my bed, regarding me with familiar solemnity. "Jests aside, there are matters of court awaiting your return, Brother. Your seat at the war table has sat empty too long while you wandered the wilds, and Father's health wanes..."

I tune out his well-meaning lecture, having heard variants all my life. Blah, blah, responsibilities, expectations, destinies, and so on. The same motivational platitudes royalty recites generation after generation. Instead, I study the portrait on the far wall, rendered in lifelike detail centuries ago, anything to avoid nodding at appropriate intervals until he finishes.

"Draven?"

I blink, focusing back on Theron's expectant expression. "Yes, of course. I shall... resume my duties once I have fully recovered." I inject confidence I do not feel into the assurances.

Mercifully, Theron seems satisfied for the moment. He clasps my shoulder with one large hand as he rises to take his leave. "It heartens me to have you returned safely, Brother. We feared the worst when the blizzard struck, but the gods watched over you, it seems."

I force a smile as Theron departs, though his visit has left me drained.

No sooner does the door close than it bursts open again, this time admitting a gust of crisp air and familiar laughter.

"Ah, just the solemn company I hoped for on such a fine day!"

Despite my weariness, I can't help but grin as my dearest friend saunters in. "Anthony, your talent for timing remains uncanny."

Anthony executes an elaborate bow, wheat-gold hair glinting in the firelight. His ice-blue eyes dance with humor and affection. "I live to serve, your highness." His playful manner smooths the lingering edge from my encounter with Theron.

I sink gratefully into a chair as Anthony helps himself to a goblet of wine with easy familiarity. He was not born a vampire. Rather, Anthony was turned later in life, inheriting immortality instead of by bloodline. For this reason, Anthony faces constant disdain and exclusion from vampire high society. Turned vampires are viewed as inferior and impure by elite natural-born vampires like myself.

Despite the prejudice he endures, Anthony excels in battle and strategy. His exceptional service earned him a position of lordship in the court, though many still reject him for being a turned vampire rather than a pureblood. Never once has Anthony faltered in his steadfast loyalty or quest for honor, even when faced with cruelty because of how he became a vampire.

In many ways his status mirrors my own—respected by some for our skills and contributions yet looked down upon by traditionalists clinging to obsolete notions of vampire purity and class. Over the years of rivalry and adventures together, Anthony has become closer than a brother to me. I would trust no one more at my side.

"That was your brother I passed, looking even more dour than usual," Anthony remarks lightly, though his eyes are serious. "I take it our quest into the northern woods bore unexpected results?"

I nod slowly. "You could say that. The blizzard separated us before we could track down any real leads on Lady Vivian's whereabouts." I shudder involuntarily, remembering the bone-numbing cold and disorientation of the driving snow. "For a time, I feared I wouldn't make it out alive."

Anthony grips my shoulder, relief flashing across his face. "When we got separated, I didn't dare hope you'd survived. The thought of returning without you..."

He trails off then manages a faint grin. "At least you emerged unscathed. How did you survive?"

I chuckle weakly. "Stumbled on a witch, or rather she stumbled on me. Not the vampire we are looking for but possibly a powerful ally someday if I can ever find her again. It's too bad we didn't find any signs of Vivian, though. She could have helped with our problem with my brother."

Anthony's expression darkens at the mention of Theron. "Your brother is far too hungry for power. If he takes the crown…" Anthony shakes his head, unwilling to voice the dire possibilities.

"Exactly," I reply. "The kingdom would suffer under his rule, but if we can expose Vivian and show she deceived everyone and still lives, it will undermine Theron's power. Or, possibly, she could become his queen. She had so many supporters, many that would rather see her on the throne than him. We have to keep searching."

"And we will," Anthony vows, ice-blue eyes blazing with determination. "I swear to you, Draven, we will unravel Vivian's secrets and her present location. She claimed something in her pocket that could take down your family. If only we knew what that was."

Our impassioned conversation falters at the sound of approaching footsteps. I exchange a quick glance with Anthony, who assumes a casually relaxed posture just as Audrey appears in the doorway. She sweeps in amidst a cloud of perfume and rustling silks.

"Time for me to make a discreet exit," Anthony murmurs with a wink as my sister descends in a flurry of excited questions.

He slips away when I try to deflect Audrey's curiosity about my quest. My heart is lighter knowing whatever comes next, Anthony will be there to stand stalwart and true.

"There you are, you dreadful creature!" she proclaims by way of greeting. "We had nearly given up ever finding your frozen corpse. You had Anthony in quite the uproar. He was threatening to return into the storm and find you himself! You two are always getting into trouble."

Despite the grim words, laughter glitters in her eyes. Audrey does nothing by halves, even grief, apparently.

She arranges herself artfully at the foot of my bed, voluminous amber skirts arranged just so. At two-hundred-fifty-years-old, appearances and gossip are her chief concerns, even more so now that she's of marrying age. I brace myself for the inevitable grilling.

"So?" she prompts, flawlessly arched brow lifting. "What happened out there? Who was this mysterious rescuer everyone is speaking about?"

I resist the urge to rub my now throbbing temples. Not this again. "No one of consequence. Just a simple woods dweller."

Audrey peers at me incredulously. "A simple woods dweller who somehow hauled your frozen royal backside through leagues of blizzard and saved your butt? Unlikely. Oh, do tell me she was some witchy herbalist with a secret cottage!"

I school my expression to careful neutrality lest it reveal anything.

Audrey claps her hands together delightedly, misreading my silence. "I knew it! How utterly romantic. You must invite her to the Winter Festival so I can meet this fascinating new arrival. It's the least we could do to thank her for returning my favorite brother."

I choke on a sharp laugh at the thought of Thorn socializing in Everdusk's gilded halls. "She did not strike me as one for balls and court intrigues."

"Pity. I shall have to get you thoroughly intoxicated on wine someday and pry all the juicy details from you." Audrey sighs theatrically. "For now, I suppose your secrets are safe." With an elegant rustle of silk, she rises and sweeps toward the door. She pauses on the threshold to add archly, "Do clean yourself up though, darling. You are simply ghastly."

The resounding click of her departure seems to drain the room of color and vibrancy. I eye my disheveled reflection. Perhaps a bath and fresh clothes might lift my mood.

I've just finished dressing when the door creaks open again. My shoulders tense, but it's only Theron, my elder of five years, who enters. His shuttered expression offers little clue to whatever brings him here.

Of all my siblings, Theron remains the one I understand least. Though alike in looks with our jet hair and silver eyes, our natures stand opposite as the sun and moon. While I crave freedom and feeling, Theron cloaks himself in dutiful solemnity.

"Greetings, Brother," he offers neutrally. "I had hoped to see you up and about."

I nod warily, waiting for whatever criticism he surely has prepared. Theron loathes idleness or any perceived weakness.

"Rumors are swirling regarding your safe return. Quite the dramatic tale, though details remain scarce." His tone holds a note of challenge.

I shrug, feigning a casual air. "Little to tell. I got turned about in a blizzard and took shelter in the first cottage I found."

Theron strokes his bearded chin thoughtfully. "And such a humble abode happened to be equipped to revive a half-frozen vampire foundling?"

I bristle at the pointed disbelief in his words. Theron ever thinks he knows more than anyone.

"As you say, mere rumors and exaggerations."

"This change in you since your return... it's unexpected."

I face him, anger simmering now. "And what business is that of yours?"

Theron's eyes harden like storm clouds. "Only doing my duty. I find it odd, and odd isn't always good."

I bare my fangs on reflex, warning him to watch himself, but Theron merely studies me with that searching gaze so like Mother's, yet his lacks her warmth.

A strained moment later, he turns sharply on his heel and departs without another word.

The heavy silence left in his wake presses down on me. I rake a hand through my hair, exhaling shakily. Gods, what is wrong with me? Why am I so on edge around my own family?

I know the answer, much as I avoid examining it too closely. Ever since Thorn sent me from that warm haven we shared, I have felt uneasy. Not like myself.

After that tense encounter with Theron, I find myself listless again, drifting around my quarters without purpose. The lavish suite, once so familiar, now seems almost alien, its opulence jarring. I was only gone a few days. This is ridiculous!

Growing weary of pacing restlessly on the plush rugs, I sink onto the massive canopied bed. Just a short nap to clear my muddied thoughts, I tell myself, but true sleep has eluded me for days.

I sink back against the plush pillows, spent after the parade of questions from my family. All I crave is to sink into oblivion's embrace, if only for a few hours respite. As I drift off, my thoughts swirl with memories of emerald eyes and a flame-warmed cottage.

When I open my eyes, it takes several blinking moments to realize my surroundings. I find myself not in my lavish royal bedchamber but rather a quaint rustic cottage, its timber walls bedecked with hanging bundles of herbs and dried flowers.

Thorn's cottage.

I'm seeing it clear as day, impossibly here in this vision. There is the rough-hewn table where we shared many a meal, laughing together as we ate the fragrant stews and breads she would prepare. Over there is the worn velvet armchair she would sit by the crackling fire, needles clicking as she knitted while I read aloud to her in the evening from one of her leather-bound books of poetry or folk tales.

And there, in the little kitchen nook, stands Thorn herself, serenely grinding something with mortar and pestle. Her sleeves are rolled up, exposing slender but strong forearms that flex gently as she works. Her hair is gathered back in a loose braid, little tendrils escaping to frame her face. A face of delicate beauty is marked by a faint crease in her brow as she concentrates.

Gods, even focused on some mundane chore, she is radiant.

My fingers twitch with the phantom urge to reach across the void separating us, to come up behind her and wrap my arms around that petite but sturdy frame, nuzzling into the tender warmth of her neck.

But I remain an invisible observer to the scene, unable to interact. Still, seeing her again, being enveloped in the beloved surroundings of the cottage, is its own form of nourishment. I drink in every minute detail greedily—the motes of dust dancing in a sunbeam falling across the worn floorboards and the rich mingling aromas of crackling woodsmoke and dried herbs.

After an age of drinking in Thorn's presence, the vision begins to lose definition, fraying at the edges as I'm drawn back from the depths of slumber. I cling desperately to the last glimpses of her raven locks escaping their plait, the firelight playing across her porcelain cheek. I sear every fraction of detail into my mind before the darkness takes me, and her beloved face is lost to me once more.

I awake slowly, momentarily confused by the lavish bedchamber rather than rough-hewn rafters. Of course, I am back home in the castle, yet somehow, I am also joined to Thorn from afar. My heart aches, missing the simplicity and warmth of our time together.

"You're awake."

Mother sits near the bed, studying me with her piercing gaze that missed nothing. Without a word, she hands me a linen-wrapped package, the yeasty aroma hinting at its contents even before I unfold the cloth. A small loaf of hearty bread.

"Freshly baked, just as you mentioned," Mother says. Her eyes glint with unspoken understanding.

Somehow, she deduced the bread's secret properties from my fevered ramblings after returning, yet she does not pry or judge now, only seeks to soothe her child's unseen hurts, as she always has. The kindness brings stinging tears I blink back.

"Thank you," I rasp, overcome with gratitude.

Mother pats my hand. "I cannot claim to fully grasp this... bond you seem to share. It's rare and one that I know of only a few finding, but I know your heart will ever follow its own course, for good or ill."

I give a wry half-smile. She knows me too well, this restless spirit of mine that chafes at rules and tradition.

Thorn recognized a kindred wildness in me, and she sought not to tame but to set free.

Before I can reply, Father's gruff voice intrudes as he enters. "You've improved, I see. The illness passed?"

"I wasn't exactly ill, but yes, I'm much improved, thanks to Mother's efforts," I reply, revealing only half the truth. While the bread grants clarity, yearning still consumes me.

I take a bite as Father watches pensively.

"You can't know how relieved I was to have you returned safe, my son," he rasps at length. "Losing a child… grief from which one never recovers."

I lower the half-eaten loaf, humbled by his candid words. "I am grateful to be home," I offer sincerely.

Yet, there is far more to tell of how I survived the deadly blizzard.

Haltingly, I try conveying the essence without betraying the full truth of Thorn's identity and our bond. Father listens silently until I finished the tale.

"Seems you owe this witch a considerable debt," he remarks at last.

I start, not expecting such pragmatism. "She desired no repayment, only to see me well," I explain carefully.

Father nods gruffly. "Still, the decree of honor..." He trails off, gaze turning reflective. "For now, remain close while we determine if this strangeness between you persists. Time may yet calm such unrest. If that doesn't work, distance only makes the heart grow fonder."

I tense, wanting to argue I must find answers, but Mother's restraining hand on my arm keeps me silent. Father is not forbidding me from seeing Thorn again, only counseling patience.

I nod in agreement. I will listen... for now.

After Father takes his leave, I stand gazing sightlessly out the window while shadows claim the snowy grounds below. My emotions war within—hope and fear, logic and longing. Thorn, too, surely wrestles with what passed between us. Of that, I am now certain.

"Draven." Mother's soft voice at my shoulder draws me back. "You seem... diminished since your ordeal. When's the last time you had any blood to drink?"

I frown. Has it really been so long since I fed? I try to recall, but my time with Thorn now seems hazy, half-remembered. Surely her healing tea sustained... I freeze. The tea. With dawning shock, I realize I had not craved blood at all in the cottage after drinking it, and I haven't craved it since I returned. No wonder I am so weakened now.

Mother nods knowingly and moves to the door, quietly giving orders to someone beyond. Before long, a servant enters bearing a silver goblet that he offers with a bow.

The moment the rich iron scent hits my nostrils, my fangs punch down reflexively. Gods, it has been too long. My hands tremble faintly as I accept the vessel, hating that Mother witnessed this loss of control.

Yet, as I raise the goblet to my lips, I hesitate. Somehow, it feels like a betrayal of sorts, indulging in this side again after discovering a different way to sustain myself at Thorn's side, but denying my nature will help no one.

I drink deeply, fresh vitality suffusing my limbs with every swallow. As I lower the emptied cup, strength and clarity finally return fully to my muddled mind. My mind feels much clearer, and already, I can feel energy and health returning.

"I cannot simply pretend Thorn was merely a stranger briefly passing through my life," I say to my mother fervently. "There are powers at work here I don't understand. I feel as if a part of me is missing."

Mother listens silently to my impassioned entreaty, eyes glistening with empathy. At long last, she speaks. "The fates weave many threads to bind lives together, rarely so swiftly or strangely as was done here, but destiny can't be ignored. Give yourself time to heal. I will send out people to inquire about your witch."

I start at her words. Does she mean...

Mother smiles gently, a bit sadly. "If it's meant to be, we will find her."

She pulls me into a fierce embrace then, and I know I have her blessing to follow the mysterious call that beckons me back to Thorn's side, no matter where it leads. My course is clear at last. I will seek out my witch and finally learn if we are meant to walk this path together. Hope and fear, longing and logic, heart and mind—all seem tangled as yarn unraveled by restless kittens. I do not dare reveal the depth of this bond for fear my family will keep us apart, yet staying away feels wrong.

The vision made it clear our two fates are intertwined, however reluctantly on her part.

I splay one hand on the cold glass pane before me, imagining I'm reaching straight through and across the leagues separating us in defiance of any barriers. *Heart, show me the way. For once, let cold reason follow where you lead.*

I come back to myself with a start and find the room dim and empty save for flickering firelight. Mother slipped away unnoticed, leaving me to wrestle alone with my demons and desires. I glance down to see only crumbs left of the spelled bread gifted to me. Already, its effects are fading.

Turning from the starlit window, I sit slowly on the silken bed. Somewhere beyond the confines of this castle, Thorn, too, gazes upward at the night's luminous canvas. Or at least that's what my heart wants. The answers I crave wait out there as well.

# 12

## DRAVEN

The halls of Everdusk Castle glitter around me, decked out for the Winter Festival in crimson ribbons and emerald garlands, but even these lavish decorations can't lift my mood.

It's like I'm seeing it all through fog. Everything is familiar yet distant. It's hard to believe I only left this gilded cage a few days ago. Feels like a lifetime since the old me strode out so casually into winter's jaws.

As I wander aimlessly, servants smile warm welcomes, glad for my return. I try matching their holiday cheer, but my thoughts keep wandering back to a far humbler cottage nestled in snowy woods.

Before long, my restless feet steer me down empty corridors to a heavy oak door nearly hidden in a quiet corner. Inside lie centuries of records and oddities, steeped in magic and somehow dust free even with the limited usage. Usually, I avoid this archive, but something pulls me to sift through relics of the past. Seeking what exactly?

Clues, my heart whispers as I descend creaky steps, trailing one hand along icy stones. Insights into the mystery that is Thorn. Here in these timeworn pages lie tales of the past. If her fate is really linked to mine as I suspect, tied together by the red string of fate, there must be some hint here. At the very least, there should be a birth record since all citizens' births are recorded and saved in the archives for our kingdom. Turned vampires' records are kept in the lower levels and purebloods in the upper along with their accomplishments. Our historians are a busy group of dedicated vampires.

Even the archive has been decked out for the upcoming festival. Evergreen branches adorn the shelves and sconces, scenting the air with pine that mingles with the must of ancient parchment and candles.

"All right, let's see what I can find," I mutter, rubbing my hands briskly.

Overwhelmed by decades of texts, I grab a massive tome off the nearest shelf. Flipping through reveals ancient spells, meticulously penned by some long-dead scholar. Could it contain the recipe or secrets behind Thorn's Asrbloom tea?

Feeling motivated by this new quest, I start gathering any book or scroll related to herbalism and stack them on the table. I search through the pile, totally absorbed in hunting for some hint about Thorn's magic tea that controls a vampire's hunger. After all that dusty research, I come up empty. Just more frustrated than ever. There has to be some hint somewhere about this woman who rattled my world.

Annoyed, I shove the stack aside. A heavy tome tumbles down, falling open to reveal not spells but ornate dates and decrees. It seems to be a royal record. I'm about to close it when a symbol catches my eye—the black rose crest used only for formal matters. Odd to see it here on an entry from two centuries ago. Why does it give me such a sense of foreboding?

With an icy prickle down my spine, I read the chilling details. Soldiers had been dispatched to slaughter a powerful witch child and eradicate her "accursed" village. Led by the vicious Royal Enforcer, they left only smoldering ruins, killing all... except the half vampire half witchling who somehow escaped.

I sink onto a chair, gutted by the horrific tale. This ravaged village, could it have been Thorn's home when she was an innocent child? No, she's only a witch, not a half vampire.

But she did have the tea for vampires. It would be odd to have such an item if you didn't intend to use it. Did she give me an excuse?

If so, no wonder she hides from the rulers of this land. To her kind, my royal crest must represent terror and death itself. Revulsion twists my insides at the cruelty enacted by my forefathers. No, my father. No wonder she sent me away so quickly after discovering who I was.

Bolstered by fragile hope, I delve deeper into the archives, seeking anything about this painful history. Near the back, I find a wall of scrolls, their faded contents sealed by cords. Scanning the dates, I look for records from that bloody era. If I can find documents of the Royal Enforcer's deeds... aha!

I carefully work out one yellowed scroll. Unfurling it on the table, I pin down the curled ends and squint to decipher details of Captain Reign's supposed victories. The horrific acts described just sicken me. How could such cruelty be considered valor? Why were they hunted?

A loud thump makes me jump, but the archives remain still and dusty. Probably some book settling on the weary shelves. Still, an uneasy tingle creeps up my neck. I'm certain I'm not as alone as I thought.

The candle nearest me flares brighter, throwing twisting shadows against the walls. I swallow hard and turn cautiously, seeking the source of a sudden, unexplained chill.

"Hello?" My voice echoes eerily in the gloomy vastness, and I scold myself for indulging fancy. Just some draft from the upper passages most likely.

But I can't shake the uncanny feeling of prying eyes tracking me. When muffled scraping sounds from the aisle's end, it's too much.

"Show yourself!" My shout sounds feeble against the shadows.

Only silence greets my bravado. The archives remain unchanged, gently swirling dust. Just jumpy nerves from reliving grim tales best left buried.

Shaking off my skittishness, I return to the records. There's still more history to unravel about Thorn's past. When I lean toward the scroll again, icy tingling dances across my scalp. I freeze, listening beyond my hammering heart. Was that faint... laughter?

Before I can react, a resounding crack shatters the hush. Around the archive, creaks sound as if invisible hands push open leather spines in unison, unleashing a chorus of ghostly cackles and whispers. Panicked, I stumble back into the shelves as the table begins to violently shake.

"Enough, I beg you!" I manage to cry out through chattering teeth, but my pleas go unheeded in the gathering spectral cacophony. This foreboding place clearly keeps its secrets well-guarded.

The whispered laughter and violent rattling start up again as I hastily gather the scrolls strewn across the table. I abandon the rest of the useless tomes and make a break for the stairs, taking them two at a time in my rush to escape.

The ghostly whispers and scraping sounds intensify again. Clearly my presence here is unwanted.

After bursting through the heavy oak door, I stop to catch my breath, leaning one hand against the weathered wood. Well, that scholarly quest was a total bust. Unfortunately, those chilling details I uncovered refuse to leave my mind.

If Thorn really lived through that vicious purge as an innocent child, it makes sense why she seemed wary of me. As a prince, I represent the royal line responsible for slaughtering her people and razing her village. I need more of the full story if I'm ever going to make things right somehow. There must be more answers out there.

I push off the rough door, determination sparking within me. There has to be someone else still living who remembers this scarred history firsthand, someone nearly as ancient as the kingdom itself... Of course, the castle mage! He's old enough to possess a deeper understanding of this painful past.

I stride swiftly through the torch-lit halls, leaving the archive's oppressive air behind. The insights I seek now lie up in the mage's isolated tower stronghold and, hopefully, also a chance at redemption for my father's bloody sins.

My determined steps echo on the stones as I climb the winding staircase leading up past empty floors to the very top of the mage's lonely tower. Strange scents waft down—odd herbs and acrid potion ingredients. I've only braved visiting up here a handful of times over the centuries. The mage is friendly in his own eccentric way, but he prefers solitude for his mystical studies. I can only hope he will oblige my probing questions.

Once I reach the heavy iron-bound door etched with arcane symbols, I rap sharply. "Master Eodan? I come seeking your counsel."

Silence within.

I frown and consider simply entering, but I'm wary of interrupting volatile spellcraft. As I raise my hand to knock again, scraping sounds from behind the barrier followed by shuffling steps reach my enhanced senses.

The door creaks open, revealing the stooped, shrouded form of the ancient magus, leaning heavily on a gnarled oak staff. Though he's clearly weary from the exertion of answering my call, keen intelligence yet glimmers in Eodan's rheumy gray eyes beneath tufts of wiry white brows. Those eyes pierce me with a look far too shrewd and assessing for one supposedly half out of his wits with age.

"Prince Draven," he rasps in his reedy, papery voice. "You seem... changed, since last you stood at my threshold." The mage studies me cryptically. "Well?

Speak. What questions trouble you so to scale my tower this eve?"

I meet his gaze steadily, unfazed by the intensity of his stare. "I seek your knowledge of the past, Master, of events from some two centuries ago."

Eodan's bushy brows rise higher. "The past, you say? Come then."

He shuffles back inside, beckoning with one knotted, claw-like hand.

Ducking beneath the low beam, I step cautiously into his cluttered sanctum. Every surface overflows with ancient tomes, curious instruments of glass and bronze, and jars of pungent preserved specimens. I pick my way carefully over to a rickety wooden chair opposite his work table as Eodan eases himself down with creaking joints.

"Now then." He steeples his fingers, eyes gleaming. "What matter pulls your thoughts so far back through the mists of time?"

I hesitate, uncertain how much detail to reveal. Something in the old man's piercing yet not unkind gaze decides me. Taking a breath, I confess everything—finding the damning royal account describing the massacre of the witch child's village and my suspi-

cions that Thorn herself may be this last survivor. Eodan listens silently to my fervent tale, craggy features
unreadable in the room's gloomy candlelight.

At last, I finish with a desperate appeal, "So you see,
I have to learn more. Can you shed any light on this
part of our history and those affected?"

The ancient mage leans back, stroking his long
white beard contemplatively as he gazes at me sidelong. "Perhaps. Much has faded, but some few details linger." He taps his gnarled fingers on the scarred
table. "There was talk even then amongst the com-
moners of an unusually gifted child born in the outer
provinces. Fear drove the king's command, fear that
the child was powerful enough to take the throne by
force if they desired."

Cold truth settles like a stone in my gut. To think
petty insecurities led to such tragedy and bloodshed.
That my own father had given that order...

Eodan gives me a knowing, commiserating look.
"The past can be painful to exhume, but the future
yet remains unshaped."

I sit silently absorbing his wisdom as Eodan creakily rises, moving about the cluttered space to prepare
hot tea over a small brazier. Perhaps he is right, and

I should focus on forging a new path forward, not dwelling on the unchangeable past, but to do so, I must find Thorn again and try to make things right somehow. Our fates feel linked, whatever her true origins.

I rise to take my leave with a respectful bow. "You have been more helpful than I dared hope, Master. I thank you for your time and trust."

Eodan smiles wanly, walking over to and holding open the warped wooden door. "My tower lies open should you require an ear again for your musings." His eyes glint as I duck through.

I emerge back out into the drafty torch-lit corridor feeling somehow lighter despite the grim insights learned. With understanding comes power to choose change. I intend to help guide my kingdom toward a more just future, if Thorn will walk that road with me, but first, I have to find her and try to atone for old wounds.

Lost in thought, I descend the winding steps and emerge back into the main castle. My conversation with the mage must have taken longer than I realized. The castle corridors are empty now, most folk having retired for the evening except on nights when...

I halt mid-stride. The war council. They regularly hold strategy meetings late into the night. Of course I haven't actually been cleared to resume my duties yet after my extended absence, but perhaps I can observe from the fringes for now.

Changing course, I stealthily make my way toward the council chambers. The guards at the heavy double doors straighten in surprise as I approach.

"Prince Draven. We did not realize you were here." The captain eyes me uncertainly. "Are you certain you should be up and about so soon after your... ordeal?"

I give him my most reassuring smile. "I am quite recovered, thank you, and eager to resume my responsibilities." Before they can object further, I slip between the imposing doors left slightly ajar.

Inside, the large round table is packed with advisors and military leaders. My best friend Anthony, my eldest brother Theron, and my father occupy the central seats. Their grave voices trail off as all eyes turn to me in shock at my unannounced entrance.

"Draven." Father is the first to find his voice, bushy brows lowering. "What are you doing here?"

I lift my chin, injecting confidence into my words. "Presiding over the war council, of course. Rumors of my invalid state seem premature."

Theron shoots Father a questioning look, but the king simply gestures for me to take my seat. "If you believe yourself fit for duty, we welcome your input." His tone makes it clear this probationary return will be closely scrutinized.

I avoid meeting Theron's skeptic gaze from across the table as I take my appointed chair.

The stern-faced council members eventually resume their reports, though many pause to glance at me curiously throughout. I try to focus but find my thoughts wandering after the discoveries in the archive.

How many around this table sanctioned that horrific purge under my father's rule? Did they view it as a just and necessary strategy to protect the kingdom against a supernatural threat, or was it more about their pride and fear of losing their power and wealth? And now here I sit among them, bound by blood and duty to these men I no longer know if I can trust.

I'm relieved when the meeting concludes without me needing to contribute much.

The other council members file out, and I catch Theron's arm, steeling myself to question him. As heir to the throne, he may know more details of that shameful history.

"A word, brother?" I ask evenly, despite the unease churning within me.

Theron pauses, eyeing me curiously. "Of course." He waits as everyone else leaves until it's just us two alone in the huge council room. He folds his arms, face impossible to read. "All right, what do you need?" he asks in that impatient way he has.

I bite my tongue to keep from firing something equally snippy back. I need to verify a few things from him, so I play nice.

"Just a few questions about some military history." I force a smile. "Was hoping you could clear up some stuff I dug up in the records about when I was too young to notice."

Theron lifts one thick black brow, looking anything but eager to indulge me. "So now I'm your own personal royal scholar?"

He goes to brush by, but I step to block his exit and catch his sleeve.

"Come on. Hear me out. I think leaving the past buried could spell trouble later." I give him my most convincing pleading look. "There was this massacre of an entire family. Of a village hiding a seriously gifted kid."

Theron instantly tenses up, face closing off. After a painful pause, he yanks his arm back roughly. "Raking up old garbage is pointless," he snaps. "Find better things to occupy that nosiness of yours."

His tone makes it crystal clear he knows more than he's admitting. Now I'm really steaming.

"There's no expiration date on making amends," I shoot back. "Why all the secrecy if it was for a good reason?"

Theron's eyes flash with anger, and his jaw gets all tight. "Drop it, Draven. Get back to your rest and recovery. Stay out of my way, and you'll see why some things stay buried."

He spins on his heel, cloak swirling behind him as he storms out, leaving me alone with a hollow pit in my gut. I should've known Mr. Practical would stonewall about this bloody history.

I rake both hands through my hair, exhaling heavily. Trying to take shortcuts just made a huge mess, but I can't pretend I never learned any of this. There's got to be a way to make it right someday. I need to prove to Thorn I aim to be worthy, no matter how horrible my royal ancestors were.

Steeling myself, I head back to my room. The past can't stay buried forever, and when I finally expose the full ugly truth, I vow to help right these wrongs.

Even if it means defying tradition or my own family.

# 13

## THORN

The frigid winter wind nips at my cheeks as I make my way across the snowy forest path to the frozen lake, my fishing pole over one shoulder and a woven basket with bait and supplies hanging from the other. My boots crunch satisfyingly on the fresh powder with each step. Despite the chill, it's a crisp, clear morning—perfect weather for sitting out on the ice and hopefully catching some dinner.

Luna darts ahead of me, her white coat blends in perfectly with the white landscape as she bounds through the drifting snow. That playful fox seems thrilled just to be out of the cottage for a change of scenery. Can't say I blame her. We've both been cooped up inside for days now, thanks to that nasty bout of blizzard weather.

I breathe deep, savoring the fresh, piney air. The quiet serenity out here is exactly what my restless spirit needs. Between obsessively waiting for the fated mate bond with a certain infuriating vampire prince to fade and futilely researching ways to quicken that process, I've hardly left the cottage. Being surrounded by nothing but snow and trees gives my overworked mind a much-needed break.

As the trail levels out, the frozen expanse of the forest lake comes into view through the barren trees. Luna is already waiting eagerly on the rocky shore, practically bouncing with excitement. That fox never runs out of restless energy. Her bushy tail swishes wildly, scattering fine powder that glitters in the slanting morning sunlight.

I pick my way carefully down the snowy bank to join Luna on the lakeside. "Someone's raring to go this morning," I remark wryly, setting down my gear.

Luna yips, darting in playful circles around my legs. Then, she stops to inhale deeply. *Ah, the crisp air whets my appetite already. I can practically taste the mouth-watering trout we'll soon catch, drizzled in lemon and thyme. My friend Sasha centuries ago knew how to prepare fish to perfection. I think you would have liked her.* A touch of wistfulness enters her voice.

I glance at her curiously as we make our way to the lakeside. "Sasha? You've never mentioned her before. Was she a past companion of yours?"

Luna's green eyes grow distant with memory. *Yes, a dear friend. We met when I was just a young fox learning to use my magic, and she took me under her wing.* " A small smile plays on her lips. "Sasha was clever and vivacious, with a spirit akin to your own. She taught me so much before her time came to depart this world. She was the first mortal I became a familiar for.*

I settle onto the icy lakeside, intrigued by this glimpse into Luna's long past and erstwhile friend. She has clearly lived a rich life, full of adventure, joy, and sorrow. I'm honored she now calls me companion. There is still so much more to learn about my mysterious familiar.

"All right, all right, give me a minute to get set up first." I laugh, nudging her away gently with my boot. That fox is lucky she's so adorable.

Kneeling, I clear off a wide patch of ice near the shore until the solid surface is revealed. The ice feels satisfyingly solid and thick beneath my gloves—perfect conditions for fishing. Once I chip open a hole with my small axe, I unpack my supplies and drop the fishing line in, giving Luna a grudging pat on the head when she peers down the hole with boundless curiosity.

"There. Now we can just sit back and wait for some unlucky fish to come investigating this tantalizing worm I've provided." I cock my head toward the rocky outcrop nearby. "Why don't you play in the snow over there while I focus on catching us dinner?"

Luna gives what I can only assume is meant to be a fox grin before scampering off gleefully. Chuckling under my breath, I settle myself comfortably on the rough wooden stool I brought and turn my gaze to the open ice hole at my feet. A tinge of cold seeps into my boots from the ice, but it's tolerable for now. And peaceful. It's been too long since I allowed myself such stillness, listening to the gentle lap of water against the frozen shore and the occasional crackle as ice shifts and settles across the lake. I've been keeping myself busy, doing anything I can think of to prevent my mate—no I can't give him even that—to prevent Draven from entering my thoughts. My home has never been so clean or organized.

Out of the corner of my eye, I watch Luna roll exuberantly in the fresh powder before popping up and shaking herself, sending snowflakes scattering in a sparkling cloud. The sight brings a small smile to my lips. I don't doubt there's some deeper purpose that drew her into my life right when I needed companionship most, but moments like this are reminders that she's still a fox at heart.

As I keep one eye on the motionless line in the water before me, my thoughts begin to wander . My attempts to clear my mind fail. It keeps returning to the fateful events a few weeks ago that upended everything—stumbling upon a certain injured vampire out in this very forest and taking him in, only to end up magically bound to the infuriating yet captivating man despite my best efforts to resist.

My heart squeezes with that now familiar ache of something precious found and lost in quick succession. I shouldn't have let him get so close. Shouldn't have allowed myself to feel anything for Draven besides wariness.

Then again, fate apparently had other plans. It threw us together and linked our souls without consent. At least I think it was fate's meddling. The alternative is too unnerving to consider. It can't be that this intensity sparked to life between us naturally.

A sharp tug on the line jerks me from my turbulent thoughts. I quickly start reeling, eager for the welcome distraction. Soon, a fat trout breaks the water, shimmering and plump. Perfect.

As I busy myself unhooking the fish and rebaiting the line, I hear Luna trot over, nails clicking against the ice. She peers down at my catch and licks her chops eagerly.

I shake my head in amusement. "Patience. I'll have this cleaned and cooked up back at home soon."

Luna huffs dramatically but seems to accept my logic, settling down on her stomach near my stool. I sneak a glance at her as I cast the line out again. Her golden eyes gaze back steadily, seeing far more than just the quiet, snowy landscape around us. Sometimes, it feels like she sees straight through to my conflicted core.

"What?" I ask defensively. "Don't go prodding at my sore spots right now. I'm barely holding myself together as it is."

Luna's expression and gentle mental tone hold only compassion. *Thorn, it's all right to open up about what's troubling you so. Keeping it all bottled away can't be healthy.*

I bristle, clutching the fishing pole tighter. "I don't bottle anything away. You just caught me lost in thought. That's all."

Luna levels an eerily human-like look of skepticism at me. *Come now. I may be only a fox, but I sense the sadness in you clear as day. Please, let me carry some of the weight you bear.*

I stare down at the hole in the ice, watching my faint reflection waver on the inky water. Luna's right, of course. The burden of concealing my true self and history from everyone has worn on me, even if going it alone was my choice. Still, opening that floodgate feels risky, like I might drown in all the old ghosts that could come pouring out.

I settle back on the wooden stool, turning my attention to the fishing line in the icy water. This quiet moment of solitude is exactly what I need right now.

Luna pads back over, head tilted inquisitively.

I smile but gesture her away. "Go on. Let me focus on catching us some dinner."

Luna huffs in resignation but scampers off again.

As I wait patiently for a bite, I find my thoughts wandering to Draven once more, despite myself. I've been trying so hard to sever our bond, to get him out of my head, but it seems impossible. I shouldn't have let him—

Suddenly, I'm seized by a vivid burst of fury. Draven is locked in a bitter argument with his father. I wince at the anger boiling between them, thick as blood. Pressing a hand to my temple, I try to block out the sensations flooding through our persistent bond.

But the effort leaves me distracted. As I shift my seat, the ice below groans alarmingly. Before I can react, it fractures completely. I plunge into the dark water, the piercing cold an explosion of pain. I thrash weakly as the icy water engulfs me. I never was a strong swimmer, and the cold makes it hard to move. My robes tangle around my legs. This is how it ends?

A dark shape appears above. Luna! She plunges her head into the hole, teeth gripping my cloak. Bracing her paws on the solid ice, she pulls with all her might. I feel myself rising, the light above growing closer. With a final mighty heave, Luna hauls me out of the hole and back atop the frozen lake surface. I lay gasping and sputtering, overwhelmed with gratitude for her selfless loyalty.

The chill winter breeze bites at our soaked fur and clothes, making us shiver uncontrollably. We're far from warm, but being out of the frigid water is some relief. With chattering teeth, I slowly push myself to my feet. My waterlogged clothes cling icily, weighing me down. Luna presses close, trying to share what little body heat she has.

I spot the fish I caught earlier, frozen on the ice. "Grab that, will you?"

Luna carefully picks it up in her jaws. At least our fishing trip won't be a total waste.

We begin the arduous trek back, each step heavy and clumsy. I try summoning magic to warm us, but my powers fizzle weakly. Luna nudges my leg, and I feel a small surge of magic flow from her into me. It helps steady me as we trudge on.

The walk seems to take ages before the cozy cottage finally appears between the snow-laden trees. Never have I been so happy to see my secluded home.

After stumbling inside, I make straight for the hearth. My frozen fingers can barely grasp the tinderbox, but finally, a flame catches, and I quickly pile on logs.

As warmth slowly spreads, Luna collapses gratefully in front of the growing fire, fish still clamped in her jaw. I settle into my chair nearby, aching but alive thanks to her.

Perhaps it is the dancing firelight or the lingering chill, but I find myself softly opening up to Luna. "Thank you for saving me." I pause, trying to decide just how much to share. "You deserve to know... why I hide here alone." I stare into the flames, voice hollow. "My family was hunted. Entirely wiped out by the reigning family. Something about my mixed blood made me a threat to them, and they were killed while protecting me." I blink back tears. "I only survived because my mother, the last to survive, left me with another family and lead them away."

The familiar pain rises in my chest. Luna's eyes radiate compassion.

"They were human. After they were gone, I was angry and wanted revenge." I pause, not ready to discuss that part of my past yet. "I had to disappear or risk being hunted again." My hands clench into fists. "I won't let anyone else suffer for harboring me, so I stay hidden, alone."

I fall silent, the old grief still raw, even centuries later.

Luna rises and lays her head in my lap, grounding me in this moment. I stroke her fur, taking comfort in true companionship after so long.

*I, too, know the ache of profound loss.* Her voice echoes gently in my mind. *Centuries ago, I was but a young fox, my parents and littermates all killed by vicious hunters. I managed to escape into the forest, lonely and afraid. In time, I discovered I possessed a gift. I could connect mentally and magically with beings. I honed this power over the long years of solitude. Never forgetting but learning to open my heart again despite past griefs.* Luna looks at me with her wise golden eyes. *Finding you, kindred spirit, has brought light to my spirit once more. Our paths were meant to cross. I am certain.*

I stroke her fur, taking comfort in this companionship after so long alone. "Perhaps one day, I will have the courage to step from the shadows again, but for now, having even you know the real me feels like enough."

*\*\**

I stare into the crackling fire, lost in thought as Luna dozes by my feet. Despite our peaceful evening, my mind is in turmoil. Ever since opening up to Luna about my tragic past, memories I've long suppressed keep bubbling to the surface. I see flashes of my childhood—playing in the village square, helping my mother in the garden, listening eagerly as my father told stories. That happy life was shattered in one horrific night when the king's men came and destroyed everything.

My heart aches with emptiness. I never properly mourned my lost family and friends after I fled for my life. Perhaps if I returned to the ruins, I could find some measure of closure...

Luna stirs, lifting her head to study me with those too-wise eyes. I force a smile, but she senses my inner conflict.

Nudging my hand gently, she asks, *Why do you close yourself off from your pain, Thorn? Confronting the past might be the only way to heal.*

I flinch, unwilling to revisit that trauma. "I've avoided it for so long. What if going back only reopens old wounds?"

Luna blinks slowly. *Sometimes wounds must be reopened to clean out infection. This burden has weighed on your spirit too long. Let me help carry it.*

Her compassion brings tears I've held back for centuries. She's right. If I don't find healthy closure, I'll stay trapped in the past forever.

I kneel down and pull Luna close, taking comfort from her warmth. "All right, my friend. We'll go together... Go home." The word feels foreign yet right.

Resolution settles over me. The journey will be difficult, but with Luna by my side, I'm finally ready to confront the ghosts of my childhood and begin to heal.

# 14

## DRAVEN

The pale winter sun crests over the snow-dusted foothills, casting the encampment in a soft golden glow. Breath frosting the air, nobles emerge from their tents to begin preparations for the day's hunt.

I spot Princess Audrey by the royal tent, outfitted in finely tooled leather hunting gear. Her raven hair is swept back in an elegant braid, though several unruly strands have already worked loose, as usual.

"Brother!" she calls out in greeting, smiling brightly. "Are you ready to join the hunt today?"

I return her smile, though mine lacks her unrestrained enthusiasm. "As ready as I'll ever be. You know tracking was never my strong suit."

Audrey's eyes spark with mischief. "Perhaps you should have paid more attention to your lessons instead of sneaking off for adventures."

Before I can respond, a hearty voice rings out. "Adventures build character, Princess. Isn't that right, Draven?"

I turn to see Anthony striding over, clad in practical hunting garb that can't quite diminish his noble bearing. Early morning light glints off his golden hair, cut shorter than current court fashion dictates. His strong jaw holds a hint of stubble, another sign of his disregard for aristocratic manners. Only his ice-blue eyes give away his true age and experience, their depths belying his youthful appearance.

Audrey shakes her head, a grudging smile tugs at her lips. "You two are incorrigible. Try not to cause too much trouble out there today."

With a swirl of her fur-trimmed cloak, she heads off to ready her own mount. Anthony watches her go, eyebrows raised in amusement.

"Think we can actually avoid trouble?" he muses.

I clasp his shoulder warmly. "With you by my side? Not likely."

His grin falters slightly as he catches sight of figures approaching behind me—I turn around to find my elder brother Theron and his retinue of highborn companions. Their fine raiment contrasts sharply with the sensible garb of most other hunters.

"Best get ready," Anthony murmurs before slipping off toward his tent.

An unpleasant knot forms in my gut watching him retreat. I know it's to avoid confrontation rather than cowardice. Even now, harsh stares and hissed insults follow Anthony's turned status, despite his lineage tracing back for generations.

I turn to offer Theron a cordial greeting through gritted teeth, hoping to avoid early conflict, but he sweeps right past as though I don't exist, his posse trailing behind him.

The clear notes of horns ring out over the camp as the hunting parties gather near the edge of the forest. I take my place alongside Anthony, ignoring the sidelong glares and muttered remarks from some of the other nobles.

At the front, King Nicolai raises his hands for silence. Even in simple huntsman's garb, his commanding presence draws all eyes.

"Friends, we gather today to commence the annual Winter Hunt." My father's voice booms out over the eager crowd. "This hunt marks the kickoff of our cherished Winter Festival, a tradition spanning countless generations."

He outlines the rules of the hunt—points will be awarded for different captures, with rarer and more challenging prey worth more points. A common red fox pelt is worth five points. A stag antler rack earns ten points, but the most coveted prize is the pelt of a white fox, worth fifty points.

"The hunter who gains the most points by nightfall will win this year's ceremonial fur cloak." My father gestures to the dazzling white fox fur draped nearby. "May the gods grant you skill and good fortune this day!"

I tune out most of the familiar speech, eyes drawn to that dazzling cloak on display nearby. A ripple of longing runs through me. As a child, I'd dreamed of one day winning such a prize at the hunt, but it's been centuries since I cared about such frivolities.

My father concludes his remarks, signaling the enthusiastic hunters gathered. "Now, let the hunt commence!"

A rousing cheer goes up as the parties surge into the shadowy forest. I follow at a more sedate pace, sensing Anthony matching my stride. Together, we plunge into the reaching shadows beneath the snow-laden evergreens.

We move through the hushed forest with the easy familiarity of decades-long comrades. Our footsteps glide silently over the blanketed ground as we track through the dappled morning light. No words pass between us, but none are needed. After so many hunts, battles, and adventures shared, we can communicate through glances and subtle gestures.

Anthony tilts his head, catching a scent on the crisp air. He inclines left, and I follow wordlessly, trusting him. We pick our way between massive pines, their branches laden with snow. The cold air fills my lungs, invigorating my immortal spirit.

My friend pauses, kneeling to examine indentations in the white drifts. He runs a hand over the markings then taps two fingers to his temple and points ahead. Deer tracks. I nod, and we alter course to avoid disturbing the prey.

We continue on in easy quiet, the muted forest a refuge from the chaos of court and the tensions simmering there. Out here, it is just Anthony and I, free to be ourselves beyond the confines of status and politics.

Abruptly, Anthony stops, nose lifted to the wind once more. I watch his focused expression morph to one of eagerness. Fox. He grins and is off, a blur of muted browns and gold. With a wry huff, I hurry after him, though I know with his skills, he'll find the creature first.

Sure enough, he stands leaning casually against a fir up ahead, holding a fine red pelt. "Too slow, my friend," he teases, eyes glinting.

I simply shake my head and motion that he should keep the trophy.

As we resume trekking through the wilderness, a new scent teases at my awareness. I slow, trying to pinpoint its source, but the elusive fragrance dissipates on the breeze. Frustrated, I'm about to dismiss it when a flash of white darts between snow-heavy fir trees up ahead, too quick to clearly make out the source. The possibilities immediately ignite my hunter's instincts. Could it be the rare white fox, most prized quarry of the hunt?

I glance at Anthony, but his keen senses are focused elsewhere, tracking more mundane prey. This sighting will be mine alone to pursue.

My muscles coil in anticipation. In a burst of preternatural speed, I bound after the elusive flash of white, weaving between the trees. My feet fly swift and silent over the forest floor, stirring not a single snowflake as I race onward.

The brief glimpse of white reappears closer now, bounding through a copse of birch trees. Definitely vulpine in shape and size. I push myself faster, thrilled by the prospect of such a valuable capture. The white fox pelt alone would guarantee me the winner's cloak.

More than glory spurs my pursuit. This feels personal somehow. A connection I can't name pulls me toward the unusual fox, as if we're tied by some unfathomable thread. I shake off the strange fancy and refocus on the chase.

Hurtling over a frozen stream, I landing in a spray of glittering ice crystals. The white fox is just ahead, tantalizingly close. I can make out its snowy pelt flashing between the trees, always remaining barely out of reach. Almost like it's... leading me somewhere.

Caught up in the exhilaration of the hunt, I pay little heed to my surroundings. The terrain grows increasingly rugged, but I'm too focused on my elusive quarry to notice. All my senses narrow to that beckoning flash of white always on the periphery.

The trees thin out, and I emerge into a clearing ringed by ravaged stone walls and tumbled beams. The ruins of some long abandoned village. I slow, taking in the decrepit structures worn by centuries of harsh winters.

A prickling sense of unease now tempers my earlier excitement. This place carries a somber, haunted air, like a graveyard etched by loss and tragedy. What ancient calamity befell this forgotten hamlet?

I step cautiously over the debris-strewn ground, alert for any sign of the white fox or other forest dwellers. The ruined husk of a cottage stands ahead, its roof long since collapsed. Could my unusual quarry have hidden within?

As I approach the vine-choked doorway, that nagging sense of familiarity returns, stronger now. It's as if this place calls to some hidden part of my spirit that I can't consciously grasp. I hesitate on the threshold, torn between apprehension and longing. What awaits me within these aged stones?

Before I can step inside, a voice rings out behind me, clear and strong. "You should not have come here, Prince."

# 15

## THORN

The crumbling walls of the cottage loom before me as I approach, their weathered stones seeming to lean inward as if protecting long-held secrets. How many years has it been since I last walked this overgrown path? I've lost count of the decades that have passed in my self-imposed exile.

I pause at the edge of the clearing, my boots sinking into the snow. The cold bites at my cheeks, but that physical discomfort is nothing compared to the ache in my chest. This place holds so many ghosts.

With slow, hesitant steps, I make my way to the front door or what remains of it—a few rotting planks cling stubbornly to rusted hinges. I trace my fingers over the carved oak frame, remembering the day my father hung this door with such pride.

"There!" he declared, wiping his brow. "Now our Thorn will be safe and snug in her own room."

I beamed up at him, filled with the contentment only a child can know. My world was small and perfect then. How swiftly that innocence was shattered.

Steeling myself, I duck inside the gloomy interior. The main room is just as I remember it. Modest wooden furniture sits covered in layers of dust and leaves that have blown in over the long years of abandonment. The stone hearth that once glowed warm with crackling fire now gapes cold and empty. Cobwebs shroud the corners like gossamer veils.

At the back of the room, a rickety staircase winds up to the second floor. I avoid looking at it just yet, not ready to confront those memories. Instead, I drift over to the simple wooden table, running my hand across its scarred surface.

This is where my mother would stand mixing her potions and tinctures, the shelves behind her lined with glass bottles and jars containing roots, herbs, and other mystical ingredients. I can almost see her silvery hair glinting in the firelight as she hums one of her old folk songs passed down through generations of cunning women.

Next to the table sits a rocking chair sized for a child. I picture my younger self there, curled up with a book of spells while my mother worked. I begged and begged her to teach me even the most basic magic.

"All in good time, little thorn," she would laugh. "Once you've mastered your runes and charms."

I never got the chance to learn more before my world shattered. Now, the only magic left in this place gathers as dust.

At last, I turn reluctantly toward the stairs. Each creaking step protests my weight as I climb upward. The smell of smoke still lingers faintly in the charred walls after all this time.

I pass the room that had once been my parents', unable to look within. My small bedroom awaits at the end of the hall. The door hangs crookedly off one hinge, and I duck underneath it into the shadows. A crude wooden bedframe and stool sit untouched, the mattress nothing but rags. My feet stir up swirls of dust on the floorboards.

Kneeling down, I run my hand over the whorls and knots in the aged oak floor, seeking the loose board. There. I pry it up gently, as I've done so many times before, to reveal the small hollow space underneath, the one secret place the king's men did not discover that horrific night.

Nestled inside lies a cloth doll with a smiling painted face and yarn hair—the last remnant of my lost childhood. I lift it carefully, a bittersweet smile touching my lips.

"Hello again, Nettle," I murmur. "I'm home."

Clutching the doll close, I move to sit on the edge of the bed. The ancient ropes creak in protest beneath my weight. Looking around at these ruined walls, I can almost see the shy village girl I once was, playing contently with her homemade toy.

Nettle was my confidante, the keeper of all my young secrets and dreams. I told her of my desire to become a great witch like my mother one day. I described the tall, handsome stranger I imagined would come sweep me off my feet when I was older.

The innocence of those fantasies now pains my heart. I know too well the cruelty the real world holds.

I was eight years old when the soldiers came. Like monsters from a nightmare, they stormed our remote cottage as we slept, acting on the king's paranoid fears of witches. My mother's magic could not save her or my father in the end. Her wounds were too much.

In my terror, I hid here in this secret hollow, clutching Nettle to muffle my whimpering. The horrors I heard that night haunt me still. I lost everything—my family, my home... My entire world burned down around me.

Somehow, I survived. The fact that I couldn't save her, or any of them, still haunts me. I would never place that kind of pressure on a child, yet it's hard not to place it on myself.

Over the years, I scraped by on the fringes of society, raised by a family that wasn't my own, teaching myself what magic I could, and all the while my hate for the royals festered.

When I came of age, I returned to the capital city under a disguise to infiltrate the castle. I sought to end the king's bloodline and gain vengeance for all that was taken from me. My intricate plans ultimately failed. The king still lives still, rotting in his tower.

And so, I retreated back into exile, choosing isolation over risking more loss. This cottage, both a refuge and a reminder of my past.

Looking around its ruined shell now, I see clearly how I've allowed the traumas of my past to consume too much of my present. I've kept my true self locked away as securely as I once hid from the king's men in this secret hollow.

Perhaps after all these years, it is time to let in some light, push open that crooked door, and sweep aside the cobwebs in my heart. I cannot change the tragedy that befell my loved ones, but I can still shape what future remains for me.

I tuck Nettle back into her hiding place, replace the floorboard, and stand with new resolve. The ghosts of this cottage will always haunt me, but they need not rule me. I will find a way to honor my family's memory through more than bitterness.

Stepping back out into the winter air, I feel as though a weight has lifted from my shoulders. The cold breeze no longer bites but refreshes.

I call softly for Luna, knowing my faithful friend is likely off frolicking in the woods.

As I wait, movement catches my eye. A dark figure strides toward the cottage, the morning sun glinting off silvery hair. My breath catches. Prince Draven.

I brace myself as the past collides with the present. After what we shared, things will never be the same. For either of us.

Luna suddenly darts between my legs, a blur of white fur. Before I can react, she hides behind me, peering out anxiously. I brace myself as I see Prince Draven emerging from the tree line.

He strides toward us with purpose, his pace unfaltering even as his silver eyes meet my stern gaze. I curse myself for being so distracted by the memories of this place that I failed to notice his approach through our persistent bond. I should have been more alert.

Drawing myself up, I fix the prince with a fierce look as he nears me. "You should not have come here, Prince," I state firmly, hoping the tremor in my heart does not reach my voice.

Draven halts before me, tall and imposing in his dark tunic and riding boots, but I stand my ground. I cannot allow him to further entangle our fates against my will. He has no right to invade this private haven, no matter the pull between us.

"Yet here I am," he replies, undeterred as always. His striking eyes trail over the ruined cottage behind me.

I tense, cursing the vulnerability of this moment. I do not wish to lay my painful past bare, especially to one who represents all I have lost.

Luna whimpers softly, and I reach a comforting hand down to rest on her back, bolstering my resolve. Draven may be my fated mate, but I will determine the course of my future, even if it means shutting him out, as much as the thought secretly pains me.

"Leave."

"No, we need to talk."

Draven's persistence tries my fraying patience. "I ask again. Leave this place. We have nothing to discuss."

His jaw sets stubbornly. "I cannot, not until you hear me out." He takes a step closer, and I fight the urge to retreat. "Thorn, I know we are fated mates."

I inhale sharply, stunned by his bold declaration. Fate be damned, I cannot let him sway me with his pretty words.

"Lies. I forge my own path, Prince. The fickle whims of destiny hold no power over me."

Hurt flashes in Draven's eyes, but he forges on. "Why don't you want this? Am I truly so bad?"

Anger simmers in my blood. How dare he presume to know my heart or my secrets? "You understand nothing," I bite out. "Now leave, before..."

Luna presses against my leg, either seeking comfort or trying to calm me. I take a deep breath, regaining some composure.

Draven watches me intently. "Thorn... do you know of our bond? Did you feel it too that night we met?"

I falter. The truth presses at my lips, but I force it back down. I cannot give him that power over me.

Perhaps sensing my hesitation, he steps closer, hand raised as if to touch my face. I shy back out of reach. "Please," he implores softly. "No more lies between us."

The sincerity in his eyes wars with the fear in my heart. I waver, wanting to unburden myself yet terrified of the vulnerability.

Finally, I drop my gaze. "Yes," I whisper. "I knew then of our... connection, but it changes nothing." Lifting my eyes, I pin him with a defiant look. "I choose my own fate. I don't want a mate."

"How can you deny what is between us? Do you not realize how rare it is to find your fated mate?" He reaches for me, but I step back sharply.

I harden my heart against the ache in his voice. "Please, just go. We will only bring each other pain."

Draven shakes his head. "I don't accept that." He moves closer, and my pulse quickens treacherously. "We could be happy, if you gave us a chance."

His hand catches my wrist when I try to pull away. Our skin touching ignites something deep within me, primal and undeniable. I gasp softly as our bond flares, my senses hyper-focusing on Draven with preternatural intensity—the velvet timbre of his voice, the heat of his body so near mine, his woodsy scent mingled now with mouthwatering traces of blood...

Alarm shoots through me as I realize too late it's been days since I brewed my tea to subdue my vampiric urges. Draven's nearness is proving too great a temptation. When hungry, even another vampire can be tempting as a meal.

I tear my wrist from his grasp, stumbling back. "Please, I need you to go," I choke out through the haze of thirst, "before the monster in me takes over completely. Before we cross a line there is no returning from."

Draven hesitates, confusion in his silver eyes as they search my face.

I wrap my arms around myself, willing him to leave before my fragile control shatters completely.

"Thorn, talk to me," he implores. "What is this about?"

I shake my head helplessly. How can I explain the dark cravings rising within me, threatening to overwhelm all reason?

"Go, quickly," I plead through gritted teeth.

Draven does not flee. Instead, he steps closer, radiating concern. "Let me help you. I can see you're struggling. Are you ill?"

A growl escapes my throat before I can stop it, a feral warning. Draven freezes. We stare at each other, tension crackling.

"Please..." My voice breaks as I meet his gaze beseechingly. I am losing this battle.

Slowly, Draven lifts his wrist to his mouth. My eyes widen as I realize his intent. With a flash of fang, he bites down. Crimson blooms, rich and intoxicating.

He extends his arm in offering, droplets falling to stain the snow at our feet. "Take what you need," he says gently. "A vampires blood can cure almost anything. I can help."

As my self-control crumbles, I cannot resist the primal urge that consumes me. With a desperate gasp, I grasp his wrist and bring it to my lips, eager to taste his essence. Draven's blood floods my mouth, hot and metallic and infused with his alluring flavor. Every sip replenishes my strength, fueling the intense desire that courses through my body. I'm careful not to let my fangs descend so as not to reveal myself but lap up every drop.

At last, I tear myself away, breaths ragged. Draven cups my face in his hands, his eyes locked with mine, both a plea and a promise of everything to come. In the air, there's a tension that seems to hum with energy, a current that crackles with the anticipation of our desires.

The snow crunches beneath our feet, a reminder of the cold that surrounds us, a backdrop of white and shadows, yet it's the world that seems to fade away as Draven and I become the center, the focus of the universe.

His lips hover over mine, the pure definition of all that I've been waiting for. I can't help but lean in, lost in the intoxicating pull, the undeniable force that has connected us from the start. The kiss begins tenderly, a whisper of a touch that speaks volumes about the depth of our connection and the intensity of our passion.

As Draven's lips part, a soft moan escapes me, and I surrender completely to the seductive dance we have embarked on. His tongue traces the seam of my lips, coaxing them apart in a tantalizing invitation. I grant him access willingly, our tongues meeting in a fiery clash that sets my senses ablaze.

The cold winter air becomes an afterthought as our bodies press together, seeking warmth and solace in each other's embrace. With every touch, every stroke of his skilled hands against my fevered skin, I feel the flames of desire intensify within me. The hunger that once consumed me now transforms into a fierce craving for Draven, for the ecstasy only he can provide.

He breaks away from the kiss momentarily, his stormy eyes filled with a primal hunger that mirrors my own. Without a word, he lifts me effortlessly into his arms, carrying me with a grace that defies logic. The world spins around us as he moves us into the most solid part of the ruins around us, leaving Luna behind.

# 16

## Draven

All my senses are focused on the raven-haired beauty in my arms, her lithe body pressed intimately to mine against the crumbling stone wall. Thorn meets my passionate kisses with equal fervor, our tongues tangling in a primal dance. I can still taste the metallic tang of my blood on her lips from when she fed moments before, taking just enough to regain her strength. The memory sends a spike of longing through me.

I smooth back her windswept obsidian locks, marveling that this extraordinary woman is in my arms right now and that she trusts me enough to show me her vulnerabilities, to take what she needs from me. The connection growing between us feels profound in a way I've never experienced before.

My fingers trail down her elegant neck to glide teasingly along her collarbone. Thorn exhales a quiet moan. How is it possible to want someone this much? To feel your souls resonate in perfect harmony?

"Look at me," I plead hoarsely.

Her luminous eyes meet mine, sparkling with vulnerability and trust. The openness there resonates through my soul.

I smooth her windswept hair back from her face, my touch reverent. "You are so beautiful," I breathe.

Color stains her porcelain cheeks. I hope she can read the depth of my feelings in my gaze. Though we've only known each other a short time, my heart recognizes her as my other half. She is meant for me, just as I am meant for her.

Slowly, I become aware of the cold once more seeping into my back from the unyielding stone. With utmost care, I withdraw from Thorn, shifting us into a more sheltered alcove among the ruins.

She nuzzles into me with a contented sigh, clearly not yet ready to break our connection. I wrap my arms around her securely as the snow swirls down around us. Pressing a kiss to her temple, I marvel that only hours ago she was still a stranger. Now I know with absolute certainty that I will do anything to protect this woman who has so quickly become my entire world.

We stay huddled together as our breathing gradually returns to normal. I smooth her mussed raven locks, filled with awe, but as the fierce hunger of passion ebbs, her composure seems to shift, shoulders tensing. She won't meet my gaze, biting her kiss-swollen lip anxiously.

Concern blooms within me. "What's wrong?" I ask, ducking my head to catch her downcast eyes.

Thorn shakes her head vaguely, clearly troubled. "I can't do this," she whispers.

I freeze at her words, pulse skyrocketing. "Can't do what?"

She pulls away abruptly, leaving me bereft. Her arms wrap around herself as if to shield from a sudden chill.

"Talk to me. Let me help you."

Thorn seems lost in her own spiraling thoughts, heedless of my words. "Are you staying at the royal hunting camp nearby?" she asks urgently.

"I am, but..." I trail off, baffled by her non sequitur.

Thorn begins mumbling disjointedly about knowing where the camp is from her childhood. I strain to make sense of her rambling, to understand what has sparked this panic. My heart aches to see her so distraught.

Reaching out slowly, I graze her cheek with trembling fingers. "Please, I'm here for—"

Before I can finish, the world lurches sickeningly around me. Bright light sears my vision for a split second. Then, the scenery shifts, Thorn's distressed face is replaced by... my mother's?

I stagger in shock, abruptly finding myself in the middle of the royal hunting camp, still unclothed from my encounter with Thorn.

Chaos erupts as I frantically grab for anything to cover myself, but it's too late. I am surrounded by dozens of wide-eyed retainers, servants, and royals who have looked up from their tasks to see the queen's son standing naked before them all. Mortification washes over me. Fortunately, most of the nobles and royals are currently hunting, but that doesn't mean there isn't a crowd surrounding me at this point.

My mother's surprised expression morphs into one of resigned exasperation. "Honestly, Draven. Again?"

I am deaf to her chastisement, my bewildered gaze darting around desperately for any sign of Thorn. She brought me here somehow with her magic, though I know not how or why. My heart clenches with loss and confusion. Once again, she disappeared as quickly as she came into my life, leaving me stripped bare in more ways than one.

My youngest sister, Talia, stifles a laugh as she approaches, her eyes dancing avoiding looking directly at me. "My, my, looks like someone got a bit confused on what he was supposed to be doing today. How did you go from hunting to standing here naked as the day you were born?"

I ignore her teasing, my focus bent solely on escaping the crowds as quickly as possible. Spotting my private tent just ahead, I make a beeline toward sanctuary, doing my best to ignore the whispers and stares that follow my retreat.

Once safely inside, I sink down on my cot, head in hands. The image of Thorn's panicked face still haunts me. Why did she send me away so abruptly?

My chest aches fiercely, as if she tore something vital from me in our parting. I press my palm against it, but the pain persists, a constant throbbing reminder of her rejection.

Our fated bond, so new and vibrant, now strains against the distance she put between us. I can still feel the phantom traces of her touch, the heat of her skin against mine, and the way our very essences entwined, two strands knotting together as if we were always meant to be. That sense of wholeness, of home, still lingers, but now, it's tainted by her refusal to accept it.

The high of our amplified connection has been replaced by this lingering anguish. I curse under my frosty breath. How could she have pushed me away so thoroughly? Why does she refuse to trust in that bond, that "meant to be" we share? The ache in my chest is a harsh reminder that destiny and magic are fickle, cruel things, especially when the other half of your soul denies what fate has decreed.

She has made it clear I am nothing more than a passing complication in her safe, solitary life, but I cannot give up on what we could be. Not when I can still feel the ghostly pull of our connection begging to be restored. I will find a way to break down those defenses, to make her see that we belong together.

This void she has left cannot be allowed to remain. I need her, as surely as I need air to breathe. I will do whatever it takes to make her mine.

With renewed conviction, I dress quickly and race from my tent. My feet fly over the snow-blanketed ground as I retrace my path back to the crumbling ruins where we last stood entwined, but by the time I arrive only silence greets me. The structure sits cold and abandoned, all traces of Thorn gone.

I search every corner, desperate for some sign of where she went, but the falling snow has already obscured any trail. It is as if she simply vanished.

As I stand there, devastated, one thought rings clear in my mind. I will find her again. I must. She is my destiny, and I am hers.

*** 

I trudge slowly back through the snow toward the royal encampment. The cold is nothing compared to the icy void in my chest where warmth and passion dwelled just hours before.

Each step takes me farther from the crumbling stone cottage where I held Thorn, felt our souls intertwine. Her absence hits me like a physical blow, a vital piece of myself ripped away.

By the time I reach my private tent, tears blur my vision. I sink to the cot, sobs wracking my frame as I finally allow the anguish to wash over me. I press both palms hard over my aching heart, but the pain persists, throbbing in time with my ragged breaths.

I should have held on tighter and been more attentive to Thorn's fears instead of getting lost in passion's haze. I should have had her explain. Told her what I knew about her past and that I understood. That she wasn't alone. Now, only regret and sorrow remain, foreign emotions battering my mind like a hurricane. Her distress bleeds through our fading bond, assaulting my senses even as the connection frays.

Thorn's presence surrounds me, though she is nowhere to be seen. It's as if I carry the ghost of her within me, an intangible part left behind. I blink back hot tears that feel not wholly my own.

"Forgive me," I rasp to the empty tent, imagining I can still reach her. "I'll find you again. I swear it. Just wait for me..."

My pleading words disappear into silence, unheard by their intended recipient. She is gone, slipped through my grasp like mist, and with her went the missing piece that made me whole.

Eventually, the tears slow, leaving me hollowed out and spent. Even as bone-deep exhaustion threatens to pull me under, a flicker of conviction persists deep within. I cannot give up on finding Thorn again, earning back her trust, and making her understand we belong together. I must be patient and unrelenting. She is my destiny. I know this with absolute certainty.

As I sit brooding in my tent, a familiar voice startles me from my melancholy reverie. "There you are! I've been looking all over camp for you."

I glance up to see Anthony ducking through the tent flap, his usual cheerful grin fading as he takes in my disheveled and dejected state. Without a word, he moves to grasp my shoulder in a comforting, ground-ing grip.

"I've heard the wildest tales about you today, my friend. Rumor has it you magically appeared in the nude right in the midst of the royal assembly!"

I sigh heavily, the lingering sting of humiliation flar-ing anew. "Unfortunately, the gossip is true this time. I found myself... unexpectedly transported back to camp rather indelicately."

Anthony lets out a low whistle. "That must have been quite the amorous encounter to leave the ever unflappable Prince Draven in such a state. Come, let's walk awhile," he adds, his tone gentler now. "Share your troubles with me."

As we pass the campfire pits, the smell of woodsmoke and roasting meat filling the brisk air, I haltingly tell Anthony about meeting Thorn—her intriguing combination of shy sweetness and simmering passion, the unparalleled desire that flared between us, the certainty that she was my fated mate, and then the shock of her panic afterwards, the raw ache of our severed bond when she disappeared without explanation.

My voice breaks recounting it, the loss still an open wound.

Anthony listens intently, his usual mirth replaced by solemn empathy. He knows me better than any, like the brother I never had because, let's be honest, mine is a piece of work.

"By the gods, she sounds like quite the woman to shake your composure so," he muses, "but fret not. We'll find her again. You have my oath on that. No magical teleportation can keep destined souls apart for long."

My throat tightens at his steadfast loyalty. With Anthony by my side, the bleak despair and heartache I'd been drowning in feels a little lighter.

"Thank you, my friend," I say quietly. "I don't know what I'd do without you through all my misadventures over the years."

Anthony clasps my shoulder, gray eyes warm with affection. "Oh, you'd find plenty of trouble regardless, I'm sure, but we'll weather this storm together, as always."

# 17

## THORN

The memory of his touch still burns on my skin as I step outside the cottage, bundled against the cold. Our joining should have completed the fated mate bond, yet I tore us apart in a fit of stubborn defiance before his bite could seal it. Even now, my traitorous body craves his fingers trailing fire across my flesh, our hearts beating as one. I ache at the severed connection, feeling his absence like a missing limb.

No, I cannot relinquish control, not even for my destined mate.

In the distance, a chorus of shouts shatters the perfect stillness. My breath catches in my throat as the raucous hunting party comes into view, moving swiftly through the trees. At their lead is he, his cruel visage unmistakable even at this distance.

The vampire king.

Fear lances through me, muscles locking in panic. No. It cannot be. Not here, not now.

I grab Luna close with trembling hands, stumbling back toward the cottage, but there is no time. Wildly, I look around, spying a dense copse of evergreens nearby, and I dive into their concealing branches, huddling down and willing my pounding heart to stillness.

I look back to my old home I just emerged from and groan as I realize I was already near a good hiding spot.

The baying grows louder as they draw near, the king's melodious laughter drifting above it all. Bile rises in my throat. I squeeze my eyes shut against the memories that vision triggers, of fire and anguish and loss.

After an eternity, the sounds fade into the distance once more. Still, I remain frozen, struggling to rein in my careening emotions. *You are safe,* I tell myself. *He did not see you.* But the familiar cold dread in my veins belies those words. I cannot linger here.

Shakily, I take Luna's paw. "Come," I whisper. "We must go." With Luna at my side, I focus my energy, and we vanish from the woods in a swirl of magic, reappearing in a remote snow-blanketed glen far from the vampire king's hunting party. My heart is still racing, my mind flooded with traumatic memories I've tried so hard to suppress.

I kneel in the deep snow, struggling to slow my panicked breaths. Luna whines softly and presses her body against mine. Her warmth and unconditional love help anchor me, keeping my darkest memories at bay. I bury my face in her soft fur, clinging to this innocent creature who depends on me for protection.

*Thorn, be still. Breathe the crisp, cold air in deeply. Center yourself in this moment. The past cannot harm you here*, she says, her gentle voice soothing in my mind.

Once I've regained some control, I stand on shaky legs and take in our new surroundings. The glen is utterly still and quiet, the ancient pines muffled under heavy layers of snow. Icicles hang frozen in time on their bowed branches. It's hauntingly beautiful.

In the distance, the icy surface of a half-frozen waterfall catches the pale sunlight. I make my way toward it, my boots breaking the perfect smoothness of the untouched snow. Kneeling at the waterfall's edge, I wipe away the thin crust of ice and glimpse my reflection in the water beneath.

The scared young girl who once hid from the vampire king stares back at me, but now, her eyes blaze with an inner fire. I am not that helpless child anymore. The king did take my loved ones from me, but he did not manage to steal my spirit.

I splash the frigid water on my face, letting it wash away the last shaky remnants of fear. When I rise, droplets glitter like diamonds on my skin in the winter sun. I am renewed.

A thunderous crash echoes through the glen, and Luna growls low at my side. I turn to see an enormous frost giant barreling out of the tree line, its footsteps booming as it charges straight toward us.

My surprise turns swiftly to defiant anger. So this is how it will be? The very day I vow to reclaim my power, the world sends a monster to test my resolve.

"Stay back, Luna!" I shout.

Clenching my fists, I unleash a streaming torrent of flames from my palms. The giant bellows as the fiery onslaught engulfs its torso, blackening its icy armor. It swipes a meaty hand at me, but I leap aside and summon a barrage of glowing violet energy bolts, pummeling the giant's skull relentlessly.

Staggering, the giant rips an entire pine tree from the snowdrifts and hurls it my way. I slice my hand through the air, magically shredding the massive projectile into mere splinters. With a guttural cry, I blast the giant back with a shockwave of pure force. The magical winds drive the creature to its knees.

Still, it rises, blood trickling from its ruined eye. Roaring, the giant slams its fists down. Jagged ice spikes erupt from the earth all around me. I cry out as a spike rakes my shoulder, staining the pure snow crimson. The pain only fuels my anger. How dare this beast harm me when I've already endured so much torment?

I leap into the air on a gust of wind, flying swiftly around the lumbering giant. Gathering my power in clenched fists glowing violet, I unleash my magic mercilessly. Bolts of lightning slice into its body. Shards of razor-sharp ice shred its limbs. My onslaught drives the giant to the very edge of the frozen waterfall as I batter it from all sides.

The frost giant's dying cries echo through the glen as it plunges into the icy depths below. I hover above the waterfall, chest heaving, the last tremors of adrenaline course through my veins. The gash on my shoulder from the giant's icy spike throbs hotly, but I embrace the pain. It is a badge of my hard-won victory, proof that I can and will defend myself against any who wish me harm.

I descend back to the bloodstained snow, where Luna awaits me with worried eyes. Despite my injury, joy and pride well up within me. Not only did I defeat a formidable foe, but also I conquered the paralyzing fear that once gripped me at the vampire king's approach. The frightened girl who cowered helpless in the woods is no more. In her place stands a powerful witch, unafraid and unbroken.

"I'm all right, Luna," I assure my familiar, stroking her soft fur. The warmth of her body soothes my frayed nerves.

Gazing out at the once more now peaceful glen, I sit with Luna nestled close and inspect my wounded shoulder. Pushing back the tattered sleeve, I wince at the ugly gash marring my pale skin. Dark blood oozes from the jagged cut.

I take a deep breath and call on my healing powers, hands glowing violet as I hold them over the injury. Soothing warmth spreads through my shoulder, flesh knitting back together beneath my palms. The bleeding stops, and the raw pain dulls to an ache. It is the best I can do for now.

Once I've regained some strength, I stand and approach the waterfall's icy edge. The frigid water carries traces of the giant's murky blood as it pours relentlessly from the heights.

Kneeling, I wash the stains from my hands and arms, cleansing myself of the battle's residue. The bracing cold helps center my thoughts, the endless water reminding me that life flows ever onward, no matter what storms we weather along the way.

Luna laps at the waterfall basin nearby, her pink tongue darting out to catch the droplets. I smile watching her, this curious creature who has brought such joy and light into my life.

After a time, Luna lifts her head and turns to me. *I must excuse myself for a moment to relieve myself after all that excitement. I will just be in the woods if you need me.*

I nod in understanding. "Go ahead. I will be here."

Luna bounds off into the trees, seeking a private spot to do her business.

Alone now, I settle beneath a towering pine at the edge of the glen. The ache in my shoulder has dulled to a faint throb as my healing magic continues to knit the wound back together. I close my eyes, focusing my energy inward. A deep sense of calm washes over me, the chaos and fear from the battle fading away.

My thoughts turn to Draven, and I remember how it felt being held by him. Our union unlocked something within me, bringing greater balance to my magic. Before, my abilities were unpredictable, emotion-fueled outbursts of elemental energy, but now, I feel this newfound harmony between magic and emotion, power and restraint. I don't want this connection, especially not with him, but I have to admit that if he wasn't part of the family who destroyed everything good for me, I would be open to our mate bond.

A smile touches my lips as I bask in the memory of his tender kiss. Perhaps in time, we could be something more than reluctant allies, something deeper...

My introspection is interrupted by a sudden worrisome thought—Luna has been gone for quite a while.

I open my eyes, scanning the silent snowy woods around me. Unease creeps into my heart, and I rise swiftly to my feet. She should have returned by now.

"Luna?" I call out, my voice echoing unanswered through the glen. "Luna, where are you?" My heart hammers in my chest as I stand and look around. I wander towards the entrance to a nearby cave. "Luna!" I call out again, straining to hear any response over the roaring blood in my ears. Only my own voice echoes back.

Clenching my fists, I summon an orb of violet light to illuminate the darkened cave before me. With no sign of where she has gone, I need to double check she isn't inside.

Holding the glowing orb aloft, I step cautiously into the cave. The soft light reveals a cramped, claustrophobic space with a low ceiling that forces me to stoop as I move deeper inside. The rocky floor slopes downward, slick with moisture. I have to proceed slowly, bracing myself against the walls to keep my footing.

"Luna, please..." My desperate plea goes unanswered. The steady drip of water and the scurrying of unseen creatures break the oppressive silence.

Reaching the back of the narrow cave, I find nothing. No sign of Luna, no clues as to where she might have gone. My magical light reveals no hidden tunnels or passages—just cold, implacable stone on all sides.

Fighting back a rising sense of panic, I stumble back out of the cave into the muted winter daylight. "Luna!" I shriek, spinning around as if she might magically appear, but there is nothing. No tracks, no trail to follow. My beloved companion has simply vanished.

Hot tears spill down my cheeks, quickly turning icy in the cold. She has to be here somewhere. I cannot lose her too.

"Please..." I whisper hoarsely, but only the wind answers, keening through the stark branches.

Panic and dread churn within me at the thought of my familiar lost and afraid. I failed to protect her.

No. I force back the dark thoughts and wipe harshly at my tears. Breaking down will not help Luna now. I must keep a clear head if I am to find her.

Closing my eyes, I focus inward and tap into the well of power within me. I feel its energy thrumming through every fiber of my being, vastly stronger than ever before. With this magic now at my command, I can cover more ground and seek help to locate my missing familiar.

I know where I must go, though the thought fills me with both hope and trepidation. Still, it is my best chance of picking up Luna's trail again quickly. He had been hunting her when he found me.

I activate the teleportation spell as I take in a deep breath, wrapping its power around myself. The winds rise in response, plucking me from the desolate woods. When they die down, I stand at the edge of a sprawling encampment that serves as the center of the vampire king's domain.

It is early evening, the sun's last rays painting the snow crimson as it dips below the horizon. Fires blaze around the perimeter, dotting the camp with circles of flickering light. The smoky smell of roasted meat drifts on the icy air.

In the distance, I spot Draven's unmistakable tall, broad-shouldered frame. He stands with a group of hunters, inspecting the day's kills. Just the sight of him makes my heart constrict with a confusing mix of emotions—anger, longing, fear. I school my features into a mask of calm determination and stride swiftly toward him.

As I approach, Draven glances up. Surprise flashes across his handsome face. "Thorn?" He takes a step toward me but hesitates when I do not slow my pace.

I ignore the others around us and grab Draven's arm as soon as I'm close enough. My fingers dig into his cold flesh. He winces.

"Where is she?" I demand harshly.

Draven's brow furrows in confusion. "She?"

Anger boils up inside me. How dare he play dumb when Luna could be suffering right now?

"My fox. Where did you take her?"

Understanding dawns on his face, followed swiftly by indignation. "That fox is yours? The one I was chasing? You magicked me here against my will entirely naked, and you think I went back out just to hunt your fox?" He yanks his arm from my grip. "I don't know where the creature is."

"But you were hunting her before," I shoot back. "She was there when you found me. Now explain what you've done with her!"

Around us, the other vampires have gone silent, watching our confrontation unfold with interest. I pay them no mind, focused solely on Draven. If he does not give me answers soon, my simmering rage may unleash itself whether I wish it or not.

Draven holds up his hands placatingly. "Thorn, you're not thinking clearly. Yes, I crossed paths with a fox while on the hunt some time ago, but I had no idea it was your companion. I never even got close to the beast before it slipped away. I have not seen it since."

I stare hard into his azure eyes, searching for any hint of deception, but all I find there is earnest confusion and dawning concern. Could it be true? Could he really have nothing to do with Luna's disappearance? Reluctantly, I feel my anger begin to cool.

Draven reaches for me again, more gently this time.

I open my mouth to respond to Draven when a commotion erupts at the edge of the camp. One of the hunting parties has returned, dragging their catches triumphantly.

I catch a glimpse of white fur, and my heart leaps into my throat.

"Luna!" I cry out, shoving past Draven and sprinting toward the hunters. There is my beloved familiar, bound and hanging limply amidst their prizes.

She lifts her head weakly but makes no other movement.

Red-hot rage explodes within me at the sight. With a guttural scream, I unleash a shockwave that knocks the hunters to the ground and propels Luna's body

safely away. I rush to her side, hands sparking dangerously with power.

# 18

## DRAVEN

I watch in stunned disbelief as Thorn materializes in our midst, eyes blazing with fury as she confronts me about her missing fox. Before I can even process her sudden presence, pandemonium erupts.

My brother and his men return triumphant from the hunt, their latest quarry in tow. Amongst the carcasses of deer and elk lies a small white form—the fox. Understanding dawns swiftly followed by horror. This is what has Thorn so distraught.

In the span of a heartbeat, she is upon them, raw power exploding outward in a shockwave that knocks the men off their feet. My brother roars in rage even as he tumbles backward. Thorn snatches up the fox's limp body in her arms before any can react.

I take a step toward her, hands raised in what I hope is a soothing gesture. "Thorn, let us help—"

She whirls on me, violet energy crackling around her. The fury in her emerald eyes gives me pause. "You've done enough!"

My brother regains his feet in a blur of speed, blood trailing from a gash on his forehead. He moves to charge Thorn, murder etched on his face. She tenses, magic flaring in preparation for his attack.

Some protective instinct seizes hold of me, and I intercept my brother in a flash, grabbing his arms.

He strains against me, snarling, "The witch attacked us!"

"She was protecting her familiar," I reply, effortlessly restraining my brother with my newfound strength. I do not struggle at all, though he strains against me with all his might. This power surging through me now exceeds anything I have experienced before. When did I become so strong?

Thorn remains poised for a fight, one hand gently cradling her fox while the other sparks dangerously. My brothers' men fan out, encircling her with weapons drawn.

"Thorn, stop!" I shout. "This will not help your fox."

My brother lunges forward. "The beast is ours by right of the hunt!"

I wrench him back again, my own temper rising. "We did not sanction any hunt for familiars. Stand down, now!"

To my surprise, he hesitates at the command in my voice.

A faint whimper breaks the standoff. Thorn gazes down at the broken body in her arms, her fury visibly receding. She looks back up at me, eyes still hard but no longer murderous.

"Please," I say more gently, "allow me to help make amends."

After a tense moment, she gives a terse nod. With my brother sufficiently subdued for now, I approach Thorn cautiously. Her shoulders relax slightly. Up close, the fox looks badly injured but still draws breath. Hot guilt twists my gut.

"Bring her this way," I murmur.

Thorn acquiesces, following me to my quarters. I can feel my brother's glare boring into my back, but he does not give chase.

Inside the dim privacy of my tent, Thorn lays the fox gently down atop a blanket. I fetch water and bandages, hyperaware of her proximity. The fated mate bond thrums between us, heightening my instincts to provide for and safeguard her. I can only imagine how much harder this is going to be if, no, when the bond is complete.

Kneeling, I inspect Luna's wounds—minor lacerations and a broken hind leg. The bones will have to be set. As I run my hands lightly over the injuries, the urge to soothe away all of Thorn's hurts, physical and emotional, swells within me, but I push that down for now in favor of the fox. Luna's eyes open halfway and regard me warily, but she does not shy from my touch.

I glance up at Thorn. "She's resilient, your friend."
*Like you, beloved.*

Thorn strokes Luna's head, her expression softening for the first time since her arrival. "Her name is Luna." The protective devotion in her voice makes my chest constrict with the need to shelter them both.

I nod solemnly. "You have my deepest apologies. Luna will come to no further harm. I promise."

Thorn searches my face, and I meet her piercing gaze unflinchingly, willing her to see the sincerity of my vow.

After a long moment, she sighs and sinks down beside me. Some of the tension seems to leave her slender frame.

We continue tending Luna's injuries in silence—Thorn with her magic and me assisting in anything requested. The animosity between us has softened. I ache to reach out and trail my fingers down her arm, to gently smooth her worries away, but I restrain myself.

Once Luna is sleeping fitfully under clean dressings, I stand and regard Thorn. Fury no longer pours off of her, but wariness remains in the set of her shoulders. I cannot blame her mistrust, considering my family's role in her pain.

I clear my throat awkwardly, unsure what more I can say to set things right. "Please, make yourself comfortable here for as long as you need to care for Luna. I will... I will keep my brother at bay. You have my oath."

Thorn inclines her head silently. As I take my leave, the connection between us tugs at me like a physical weight, but I must go deal with my brother before he does anything to further endanger my fated mate.

He is waiting outside, scowling and flecked with blood. My protective instincts flare, but I tamp them down. There will be a reckoning eventually, but now, my mate needs me.

"Why do you coddle the witch?" he spits. "Her familiar is rightfully ours."

I fix him with a hard look. "She is not to be touched. Neither of them are."

He opens his mouth to keep arguing.

I cut him off. "The fox is under my protection now. Do nothing more to provoke the witch's ire if you value your life."

His lip curls derisively, but he turns on his heel and stalks off.

I release a breath. There will be further consequences, but the crisis seems averted for now. I return inside to update Thorn.

She sits with one hand resting lightly on Luna's back as it rises and falls with labored breathing. Thorn looks up at my entrance, eyes inscrutable.

I spread my hands placatingly. "You may rest easy. None will disturb you here."

After a pause, she dips her head in acknowledgement.

Her raw display of power left no doubt of her capabilities, yet she refrained from employing that devastating magic against us once Luna was safe. In my tent, her sole focus was tending the injured fox.

Such fierce compassion stirs something in me I have not felt for centuries. I think of her wary eyes regarding me as I treated Luna's wounds. There is a story there, a pain buried deep that fuels her protectiveness.

I find myself wanting to understand this mysterious witch who materialized so suddenly in our world. No, not wanting. Needing. She calls to my very soul in a way I cannot resist, though the bond between us remains rejected.

We are fated mates. That much is clear to me now. My mother was correct. I only felt it grow with our time together. Our paths crossed for a reason. She is the missing piece that will make me whole again after centuries of loneliness. The connection between us is like an invisible tether binding us together. I only hope that her agreeing to stay with me in my tent instead of teleporting away is because she is warming up to me.

I resolve to win back her trust through honorable actions, not probing questions. We have time enough ahead for her unfolding truth. For now, ensuring her safety and recovery here will have to suffice.

I exit the tent, but the irresistible pull toward her remains. I do not yet understand the full extent of our bond, but I know this with sudden clarity—I will protect this witch with my life if need be. Our destinies are intertwined in ways I'm only beginning to grasp. We are meant to walk this path together from now on. Of that, I have no doubt.

Perhaps restoring her faith can also mend the long-broken parts of my own spirit. The bloodshed of my father and brother's endless wars has long since lost meaning for me. This witch—Thorn—has reawakened my noble purpose. I will keep her from harm.

These determined thoughts carry me through the remaining hours of night. At first light, I rise and step outside to stretch by the tent. My brother and some cronies pass by, glaring at me, but they move on without incident. I do not relax my guard.

When Thorn finally emerges near midday, I incline my head in greeting. "I trust Luna is improved after her rest?"

Thorn's expression remains closed-off, but she answers civilly enough. "Her leg will take time to fully mend, but the bleeding has stopped. My magic is working to fully heal her, but the damage was bad enough that I'm having to slow it down." She pauses, as if carefully considering her next words. "You have my thanks for your... hospitality."

I wave a dismissive hand. "It was the least I could do. It's only fair after I intruded on your own hospitality since. Please, stay as long as you need to ensure her recovery."

Thorn's lips press into a thin line. I realize then she likely feels caged here, surrounded by unknown enemies. Does she not see she has at least one ally in me?

I soften my voice. "I know you have no cause to trust me. Give me the chance to prove my good faith."

Something shifts subtly in her eyes. This time, when she inclines her head, it seems less guarded. "We shall see."

I clasp my hands behind my back, hesitant to push any further. "Might I convince you to follow us back to celebrate the winter festival? You and Luna are welcome to stay in my rooms."

Thorn looks uncertain, her emerald eyes searching my face. I keep my expression open and sincere, trying to project that she has nothing to fear from me.

After a long moment, she lets out a soft breath. "Perhaps... it would be best if Luna and I accompanied you back to your capital. She will need several more days of rest before she can travel safely."

I blink in surprise, not having expected her to agree so readily. Cautious optimism swells within me.

"Of course. You are most welcome to join us and stay as long as you need." I hesitate before continuing gently, "I give you my word no harm will come to either of you there."

Thorn presses her lips together but inclines her head. "If we are to travel together, I will hold you to that promise."

Though her words are formal, I sense a subtle shift. She is willing to take a chance on me, however small. Hope blossoms anew.

"You honor me with your trust," I reply sincerely. "We leave at first light two days hence. I will prepare quarters for you near my own and ensure no one disturbs your rest."

I sense my brother and his men watching from across the camp, anger simmering beneath their impassive faces, but they will not challenge me openly. Thorn will be safe.

She follows my glance, and her shoulders tighten slightly. Turning back to me, she asks, "And what of your family? Will they accept my presence?"

"They will accept my decision in this matter," I state firmly. At her dubious look, I soften my tone. "Please do not worry. I know tensions are high, but cooler heads will prevail once we are home."

After a moment, Thorn dips her head. "Let us hope so."

She retreats into the tent, most likely to tend to Luna.

I allow myself a small smile as I turn away. By some miracle, she has placed her trust in me. I do not intend to squander this chance to show her that our fates are intertwined for the better. The journey ahead will not be easy, but with her by my side, I feel hope for the first time in centuries.

# 19

## THORN

The clattering of hooves and wheels on cobblestone heralds our arrival back at the castle. I keep my gaze lowered, clutching Luna close as we pass through the imposing gates. Even after all these years, I still fear discovery in these familiar walls that now tower above, their weathered stones seeming to lean in as if guarding centuries of secrets.

How many years has it been since I last walked here? I've lost count of the decades passed in self-imposed exile. I pause at the edge of the clearing, my boots sinking into the snow. The cold bites my cheeks, but that is nothing compared to the ache in my chest. This place is filled with ghosts.

With slow, hesitant steps, I enter, the crowd dispersing to find their own space. As Prince Draven leads me through the grand halls, I take in the soaring ceilings and intricate carvings adorning the pillars and walls. Priceless tapestries and paintings line the corridors, evidence of immense wealth and history.

I pass ornate sitting rooms and carved wooden furnishings. Crystal chandeliers cast a warm glow over lush carpets underfoot, barely penetrating the cold stone. I keep my eyes lowered though bittersweet memories stir. Once full of promise, these halls are now foreign, my past here locked away.

We come to an elaborately carved door which Draven opens, revealing lavish quarters prepared for my stay. A canopy bed dominates, draped in velvets.

"I hope these rooms are comfortable," he says earnestly, his silver eyes searching my face.

I nod politely. "They're lovely. Thank you."

In truth, I know I will never fully relax here, penned in by the ghosts of my past, but I must try, for Luna's sake. At the very least, the unease I feel helps distract me from the cravings to reach out and touch him. Those lips, his muscular arms, that warm smile, the twinkle in his eyes... they all call to me.

Draven lingers in the doorway. "Is everything all right? You seem... troubled."

His concern undoes me, but I keep my tone even. "Just tired from the journey."

He steps closer, one hand lifting as if to touch my arm, but he seems to think better of it. Our bond flickers between us, an unspoken question.

"I am just across the hall should you need anything," he says softly.

I tense. His nearness will test my resolve to keep him at a distance, yet part of me thrills at his proximity, our connection humming eagerly beneath my skin.

With effort, I take a subtle step back, clasping my hands. "You are most kind. I'm sure I will be quite comfortable."

Draven's eyes darken. He's clearly saddened by my retreat, but he simply bows. "Very well. I shall leave you to rest. Please call if I can be of service."

After Draven leaves, I sink onto the plush bed, the silken sheets pooling around me. I stroke their richness, remembering a time when such finery was a joy to me instead of a reminder of my mistakes.

I settle Luna near the hearth to recover, keeping vigil over her shallow breaths. Her injuries are healing, but she remains weak and vulnerable, just as I once was in this very castle. The thought makes my heart clench. I failed to protect her from harm, just as I failed to save my family all those years ago. Some wounds cannot be healed with magic alone.

Sleep will surely elude me this night.

I cross to the gilded mirror, critically examining my still-youthful features. How easy it would be for someone to pierce my disguise and expose me as an imposter. Panic flutters in my chest at the thought. I cannot be discovered here. The risk is too great.

With trembling fingers, I weave the glamour spell, watching my reflection subtly age. Faint creases frame my eyes, silver strands lace my hair. My true face remains, softened by time's blurred lens. I should have done this sooner, back in the camp, but I had been too distracted. Fortunately, I was been able to avoid most people and traveled with the servants on our way here so I don't think I was recognized. After all, it's been a long time, and I've changed since then. With any luck, our fated mate bond will allow Draven to be none the wiser to these subtle changes. May as well use this blasted curse in my favor if I have to tolerate its existence.

Disguised but heavy of heart, I return to the canopy bed. It dominates the room like a gilded cage, the walls closing in with memories. Just beyond the door, I can sense Draven lingering. Our bond hums eagerly beneath my skin, yearning to reconnect.

I force down the primal urge. I cannot repeat the mistakes of my past, no matter how fiercely fate tempts me. I must cling to reason and self-control.

Yet, being this near to Draven tests my defenses. It takes all my strength to resist the pull of our connection.

I curl atop the silken sheets, restless and alone, as shadows play across the stone walls. Sleep eludes me, just as safety in this place always will.

If so much of my magic wasn't being spent on healing Luna, I would simply magic us back to my cottage, but I can't risk anything going wrong. Somehow, I've become rather attached to that white fur ball.

***

The pale light of dawn filters through the frosted windowpanes, rousing me from a fitful sleep. I rise slowly, shaking off the last wisps of a troubled dream. Luna is curled in a corner, still resting peacefully beneath her blanket of soft white fur. A smile tugs at my lips as I regard my faithful companion. At least one of us managed some real rest last night.

I dress quietly so as not to disturb Luna's slumber. My mind already races ahead to the perplexities this day will surely bring. Ever since realizing the truth of my fated bond with the vampire prince, anxiety has gnawed at my belly like a ravenous wolf.

In my core, I know Draven himself means me no harm. He has shown me nothing but kindness and understanding since we arrived at the castle, yet the echoes of a lifetime's learned distrust are not so easily quieted. I wish fate had chosen any soul but his to bind me to for eternity. Someone untainted by the bloody misdeeds of the vampire royals who wiped out my family and set me on a path of solitary exile. Someone I could give my whole self to without reservation or regret.

But the powers that be in their ineffable wisdom chose differently. Now, this prince of the bloodline I've spent my life fleeing is my destined mate. The bitter irony is not lost on me. Perhaps in time, the walls around my heart will soften and allow affection to grow.

Stepping lightly to the window, I peer out at the castle grounds now bustling in the crisp morning air. How long before the intrigues of court sweep me into their grasp again? I need time to gather my wits and steel my resolve before facing that tempest. This room should feel like a sanctuary, but its walls feel claustrophobic, hemming me in.

I glance back at Luna, still dozing contentedly. Perhaps some time to myself will settle my restless spirit.

I creep silently out the heavy oak door. The guards pay me little mind as I descend the winding stairs. To them, I am just another of the prince's transient guests.

At the base of the stairs lies a seldom used door half-hidden behind a moth-eaten tapestry. I slip through it unseen, finding myself in a familiar dusty corridor. Motes dance in the shafts of light from the occasional high window. The deeper I go, the stronger the scent of parchment, leather, and ancient magic.

Before long, I arrive at my destination—the royal archives. Stepping inside is like entering a lost world frozen in time. I trail my fingers along the rows of leather-bound spines, leaving streaks in the ever-present layer of dust. How many hours did I spend here in another life, when I was still Lady Vivian? Back when my biggest concerns were social standing and revenge, before betrayal and tragedy colored my views forever.

As I walk deeper into the labyrinth of shelves, wisps of mist swirl up to greet me. The spirits that dwell here remember me from my past visits. They whisper excitedly at my return, beckoning me farther into their domain. Like me, these poor souls met their ends at the hands of the vampire royalty and their ruthless factions. Their fates intertwined with mine. We share an eerie kinship. The archives are as much their home as mine.

I pause to touch an icy tendril of mist in greeting. "It gladdens me to see you all again, my friends," I murmur softly.

Their joyful energy lifts my wounded spirit. Here there is no judgment, only understanding.

Perhaps in these archives, I can find some peace of mind with the spirits' company, if only for a little while.

I select a few volumes on magical bonds and vampire lineage then settle into a shadowy corner to read. The ghosts swirl protectively around me as I become absorbed in the ancient pages. At least here, I can momentarily forget the upheaval that threatens the new life I've tried so hard to build. For now, it is only me, the dancing dust motes, the whispering spirits, and the solace of secrets from times long past.

***

The musty pages crinkle under my fingertips as I trace a line of text, murmuring the ancient words aloud. My mind only half focuses on the arcane symbols, still churning with thoughts of fate and fated bonds.

"You must be Thorn!"

I glance up to see a young tween vampire girl bounding down the archive stairs, dark braids swinging. She skids to a stop and dips into a quick, energetic curtsy.

"I'm Princess Kira. It's wonderful to finally meet you!" Her emerald eyes shine with lively curiosity.

I incline my head politely, studying this unfamiliar princess. "A pleasure, Your Highness. Have we met before?"

Kira waves a hand. "Oh no, but you're all my family has talked about since your grand entrance on the hunting trip! I wanted to be the first to meet you, so I volunteered to come fetch you for tea."

She grins, revealing a glint of fangs. I remain guarded, though her guileless enthusiasm is admittedly charming. This princess radiates a simple joy so at odds with my own jaded experiences in this castle long ago.

Kira widens her eyes pleadingly. "Won't you join us? Mother and Audrey are waiting."

Unable to refuse the earnest entreaty, I nod. "It would be an honor then, Your Highness."

"Wonderful!" Kira claps her hands delightedly before looping her arm through mine. "We're going to be the best of friends. I just know it..."

Kira chatters brightly as she leads me through the winding halls. I take in the festive garlands and wreaths adorning every archway, releasing the scents of pine and cinnamon into the air, a small pile of books under my arm to read in my room later. My guide keeps up a steady stream of cheerful chatter, oblivious to my pensive mood.

As we near the solarium, I glimpse frosted windows framing a snowy courtyard outside. Icicles drip from stone eaves, sparkling in the pale winter light. The cold is held at bay inside the sunroom by enchantments, ensuring the tropical plants flourish regardless of the weather.

Steam fogs the glass panes as we enter the humid solarium. Exotic flowers in vivid shades of fuchsia, scarlet, and gold nod from their perches. Orchids cascade down mossy trunks, and tiny birds flit through branches laden with orange fruits I do not recognize. The earthy scents mingle with the vampires' light floral perfumes, soothing my senses.

Queen Vespera rises gracefully from her seat, porcelain skin glowing against her black silken gown. "Thorn, welcome my dear. We are most pleased you could join us."

I dip into a curtsy before the queen, keeping my eyes respectfully lowered. "The honor is mine, Your Majesty."

Despite my calm exterior, nerves jangle within me. The last time I stood in Vespera's presence was when I still wore the guise of Lady Vivian. Eventually, I had to fake my own death to escape after nearly destroying her empire from within. What if she sees through my new glamour and recognizes the deceiver who once infiltrated her family and confidence?

Oblivious to my turmoil, she bids me rise and turns to the elder princess, who steps forward with a smile. "Allow me to formally introduce Crown Princess Audrey, my eldest daughter."

Audrey inclines her head, straight ebony hair slipping over her shoulder like liquid night. As children, we often played together, though she was several years my elder. If anyone might recall Lady Vivian's features beneath this unfamiliar facade, it would be her.

I repeat the curtsy, praying my magical disguise holds true. "The pleasure is mine, Your Highness."

Kira eagerly tugs me to sit between her and Audrey at the table laden with delicate porcelain cups and flaky pastries. A fragrant floral tea steams from the pot as Audrey pours me a cup.

"Tell us, what is it like being a witch?" Kira asks around a mouthful of cream-filled puff pastry. A bit of powdered sugar clings to her lip.

I stir a spoonful of honey into my tea as I consider my response. "In many ways, not so different from anyone else," I say carefully. "Magic runs in my bloodline. It allows me to connect to the elements and channel their energy. I can sense magic in most things and use it to create others. I enjoy the challenge of creating something new from it."

Kira's emerald eyes widen. "That's amazing! What's your favorite spell?"

I can't help a small smile at her girlish enthusiasm. "Well, healing magic has always come most naturally to me. Like when I healed Prince Draven after..." I trail off, unsure if I've said too much.

But Vespera only nods sagely. "Yes, Draven mentioned you tended to him with remarkable skill. He arrived home quite... restored despite his ordeal."

I duck my head, cheeks warming. Of course the queen would notice her son returned satiated. I'm half surprised her eyes haven't glanced at my neck for signs of previous puncture wounds.

Clearly intrigued, Audrey leans forward. "We are most impressed by your arcane abilities, Lady Thorn. It seems the fates smile upon Draven to gift him such a singular mate."

I toy nervously with my teacup under their intent stares. My magic bonding us was involuntary. How to explain that without revealing too much?

"Please, no need to call me lady. The attraction was... instant and profound," I hedge, "but much between us remains unclear."

That, at least, is no falsehood.

Vespera touches my hand gently. "Do not fret, my dear. In time, all shall be revealed between you. Not all of us are blessed with a gods given mate."

"Tell us, how did you come to realize Prince Draven was your fated mate?" Audrey asks.

I sip my tea and choose my words with care. "It was... an unexpected epiphany during our acquaintance."

Vespera nods sagely. "The fated bond is exceptionally rare, even among our kind who mate eternally."

I merely incline my head, unwilling to reveal more.

Perhaps sensing my reticence, Audrey smoothly changes topics, mentioning the upcoming Winter Festival.

"You simply must attend the ball with Draven!" Kira exclaims. "Oh, we'll have such fun together picking out gowns and masks for the occasion."

I glance down self-consciously at my simple garb. "You are too kind, but I fear I have nothing suitable-"

"Nonsense. We will outfit you in style." Audrey gives me an assessing look. "I know just the shops we must visit for a wardrobe fit for a prince's escort."

Their graciousness leaves me touched but conflicted.

I turn inquiries about my past deftly back to them, learning of castle intrigues and romances. Kira, in particular, proves a font of lively court gossip.

# 20

## THORN

I kneel beside the nest of blankets where Luna still slumbers, her breaths slow and even. The gash on her flank has closed thanks to my healing magic, though it will be some time before she regains her strength. I brush my fingertips over her soft fur. Our connection remains intact.

"Rest easy, my friend," I murmur. "I will return soon."

Rising, I make my way to the door at the sound of a cheerful rap. I open it to find Princess Audrey practically bouncing on the balls of her feet with Draven standing behind her, hands in his pockets.

"Hello," Draven says, a small dimple appearing in his cheek. "We've come to escort you to the Winter Festival, if you'll oblige us."

"Oh, please say yes! We talked about it at tea, and we're free this evening." Audrey claps her hands excitedly. "It's simply magical this time of year. We'll show you all the best shops and treats."

I hesitate, glancing back at the sleeping Luna. The pull of exploring the festival finally wins out, and being away from my cottage, I need to find a place to restock on a few things that I've run out of.

"It would be my honor then." I incline my head politely.

"Wonderful! Now we must find you a truly stunning gown for the ball this week. Can't have you on my brother's arm looking anything less than breathtaking."

I duck my head self-consciously. "You flatter me, but I'm afraid my budget is small. With the unexpected stay, I didn't have much on me to begin with. I do need to find an apothecary, though. There are a few items I need to stock up on soon."

"Nonsense. No escort of mine shall be seen in anything but the height of fashion. Draven here will purchase everything you need. Might as well enjoy the perks of being a prince's mate even if you haven't accepted him yet."

I catch Draven's amused glance.

"Best not to argue with her on matters of style," he stage-whispers.

I grab my heavy woolen cloak and wrap it close before following Audrey and Draven out into the torch-lit hallway. Our footsteps echo off the soaring stone walls as we make our way through the maze of corridors. Frosty air kisses my cheeks when we emerge into a courtyard blanketed in fresh powder.

Icicles drip from archways, and stately fir trees dot the grounds strung with lamps that cast a warm glow. The full moon shines brightly overhead, lighting our path across the frozen cobblestones. In the distance, the sounds of music and laughter float on the night breeze.

We pass through an imposing iron gate onto a bustling thoroughfare lined with colorful stalls. Villagers wrapped in furs browse wares by the light of crackling braziers and glowing crystal lanterns—baked goods steaming in the chill, hand-crafted toys, and wreaths of holly berries.

Audrey guides me toward a wider avenue where more elaborate shops stand. Flags snap in the wind above storefronts adorned with garlands of pine boughs and ribbons. I take in the sights and sounds of the unfamiliar festival market with muted awe, reminded of more carefree days from my past. The mouthwatering scents and Audrey's infectious enthusiasm slowly thaw my wariness. For the first time since my reluctant return, I let down my guard and allow myself to enjoy the holiday magic.

My senses come alive, reminded of long-ago visits to my village's humble market with my mother. I lose myself for a moment in memories of hiding in the skirts, clutching her hand as she bartered.

"Ah, here we are!" Audrey tugs me toward an elegant storefront decked in emerald silks and golden filigree. "Madame Claire's shop. She's simply the best."

Bells jingle merrily as we step inside the dressmaker's lavish showroom. Bolts of sumptuous fabrics shimmer under flickering gas lamps—satins in every hue, lush velvets, and finely embroidered taffetas. Audrey cajoles me onto a raised dais in the center of the room as the proprietress sweeps in.

"What treasure have you brought me today, Highness?" Madame Claire circles me appraisingly.

Audrey beams. "Draven's escort for the ball. We simply must make her the envy of every lady at court."

"Hmm, yes, she has fine bones and coloring. I know just the design."

Soon, I am caught up in being draped with silks and taffetas as they discuss styles and colors. Audrey selects a deep emerald green velvet that complements my complexion. The proprietress works swiftly, pinning and marking while her assistants wrap me in the sumptuous fabric.

Watching silently off to the side, Draven catches my uncertain glance. "Just go with it," he whispers behind his hand. "She adores playing dress-up." His crooked smile emboldens me to indulge their enthusiasm.

I stand stiffly on the dais as the proprietress pins and drapes the emerald velvet over me. Despite the sumptuous softness, my skin prickles with unease. This bond between Draven and I feels like a silken cord cinching tighter, slowly suffocating my will.

I chance a glance in his direction. He lounges against the wall watching me, mercury eyes bright with interest. A subtle smile plays about his lips, even before his eyes lock with mine. It's like the air is sucked from the room. Heat spreads up my neck as the mate-bond thrums between us.

The proprietress circles around me, tutting and adjusting the gown's drape, but all I can focus on is Draven's unrelenting stare. The training of decades spent concealing myself is the only thing keeping me upright and outwardly composed.

"You'll be the envy of every lady in the kingdom, my dear," the proprietress declares.

That snaps me out of my trance enough to turn woodenly toward the mirrors. The gown and my reflection are exquisite, but they belong to a stranger, someone whose hand fate has not dealt so unkindly.

When Audrey insists on more dresses, I silently comply.

Draven steps away from the wall, but his eyes remain fixed on mine in the mirror. It's as if he is memorizing every line of my face. It takes all my will not to shudder at the intimacy of his gaze. No one has seen me so bare, without my protective masks, in longer than I can recall. I drop my eyes, praying for strength against the persistent pull of the bond I never asked for.

Before long, I am spun around to view myself in the mirrors. The woman staring back looks like a stranger—regal, graceful...lovely even. Unfamiliar warmth blooms in my chest.

"Utterly perfect!" Audrey declares. "We will take it along with three day gowns in lighter silks."

I start to protest the expense, but Draven walks to me and presses a finger gently to my lips. "Please, allow me this small gift. It is the least I can do for my honored escort."

The sincerity in his dark eyes silences any argument, and his touch ignites my skin. Only centuries of practiced control keep me from betraying the riotous effect he has on my traitorous heart.

I give a mute nod, afraid to trust my voice.

We take our leave once measurements are finished and stroll the market as the stalls begin lighting their lanterns. The sweet scents of roasted nuts and mulled cider hang heavy in the chilled air as we meander down the winding lane of stalls. Vendors pack away their wares, wishing lingering customers good cheer for the season in gravelly voices. Audrey presses piping hot potato cakes and candied violets into my hands as we walk, keeping up a steady stream of delighted chatter.

I nibble the familiar treats dutifully, only half listening as I peer down shadowy side streets in search of a familiar sign. My supply of asrbloom tea is dwindling faster than expected. Already, I feel the subtle scratch of thirst creeping up my throat, a constant companion I've learned to ignore over the centuries. I need to restock my ingredients before the thirst overwhelms me and I'm revealed as being more than just a witch.

Up ahead, a crooked storefront finally catches my eye—weathered timber framed by dark bottles and drying herbs. A tattered awning bears the image of a mortar and pestle. Promising. I slip from Audrey's arm and approach the window, scanning the interior by the light of a flickering brazier.

"Come along, Thorn," Audrey calls out. "We must stop for cider before the vendors close down."

"You go on ahead," I reply distractedly, my focus still trained on the apothecary. "I'll just be a moment."

The shop bell chimes a rusty greeting as I step inside. My nostrils fill with earthy scents—pungent cloves, cinnamon sticks, and the bunches of dried lavender and chamomile hanging from the rafters.

The white-haired shopkeeper glances up from grinding some powdered concoction, blinking owlishly. "Can I help you find something, miss?" His voice creaks like an old door.

I offer a polite smile. "Evening to you. I'm in need of some rare botanicals. Perhaps you might have asrbloom pollen? Or weeping midnight blossoms?"

The old man's bushy eyebrows lift in surprise. "Well now, those are quite exotic ingredients indeed. May I inquire what you aim to brew with such treasures?"

I hesitate, uncertain whether to reveal the truth, but the genuine curiosity in his eyes seems devoid of malice. "An herbal tea to subdue... certain cravings. The family recipe is generations old."

He nods sagely, shuffling over to a shadowed shelf lined with intricate bottles. I hold my breath as he runs a liver-spotted finger along the labels, muttering under his breath. After an agonizing moment, he makes a satisfied grunt and retrieves two small jars.

"You are in luck, miss. My last pinch of asrbloom and a bundle of midnight buds." He sets them gently on the counter. "Odd, though, it's been nigh on fifty years since someone came inquiring after such curiosities. A woman much like yourself, now that I think on it..."

My breath catches sharply. This was an old haunt of mine.

The shopkeeper snaps his fingers. "Aye, that's the one. Knew her way around elixirs and tonics better than most. Traded me a crate of feverfew and witch hazel in exchange for those same ingredients."

I nod nervously, unsure how to answer.

"Your mother?"

Swallowing the lump in my throat, I simply nod. No need to correct his assumption.

He pats my hand gently. "Well then, in honor of your mother's memory, please take these with my compliments."

I open my mouth to protest such generosity, but the look of sincerity on his face stops me. Instead, I clasp his weathered hand in thanks. The precious jars are warm against my skin as I gather my new treasures to make the asrbloom tea once more.

Emerging from the shop, I find Draven lounging casually against the wall while Audrey flits between vendors cooing over trinkets. Though he's seemingly at leisure, his piercing silver eyes find me instantly, sending an involuntary shiver down my spine. The barely leashed power contained in the strong lines of his elegant frame reminds me he is no mere nobleman but a dangerous predator. I would do well to remember that.

"Find what you sought?" His voice remains neutral, but curiosity lurks beneath.

I nod, tucking the jars protectively in my satchel. "Yes, thank you. An apothecary well stocked with rare herbs."

"And secrets, perhaps?"

I bristle under the weight of his scrutiny. He suspects there is more to my midnight tea than I've revealed, but I will not justify my private rituals to this near stranger, prince or no.

Chin lifted, I meet his gaze directly. "The only secrets worth keeping are those that harm no one."

One dark brow lifts, an unspoken challenge.

Audrey's cheerful voice dispels the sudden tension. "Come. The fireworks will be starting soon!" She tugs us eagerly toward the castle gates.

I let out a slow breath, jarred ingredients secure at my side as we are swallowed by the crowd. Their presence chases away the lingering chill inside.

Audrey leads us along the bustling festival thoroughfare, pausing now and then to exclaim over strings of glittering crystals or delicate paper lanterns in the shape of woodland creatures. The sweet scent of baking pies and roasted chestnuts hangs heavy in the chilled air. Up ahead, a cozy restaurant's balcony beckons, framed by twinkling fairy lights.

"Oh, let's stop here!" Audrey clasps her hands eagerly. "They have the most delicious hot cocoa, and we'll have the perfect view for the fireworks."

We follow her up the creaking wooden steps to find the balcony magicked to remain pleasantly warm, though snow-dusted fir trees sparkle just beyond the railing. Draven holds my chair before settling into his own. Audrey immediately launches into reminiscing about her favorite festival memories over the years as we wait for our hot chocolates to arrive. Steam rises fragrantly from the mugs topped with swirls of whipped cream and shavings of chocolate when the server presents them with a flourish.

I cradle the warm drink, letting the rich sweetness melt over my tongue. The subtle scratch of thirst stirs, but I force it back. Later, I will brew a fresh batch of asrbloom tea to calm my ever-present cravings. For now, I want to savor this moment of indulgence.

Beside me, Draven stretches his long legs out casually beneath the table. I'm suddenly very aware of his proximity, our knees occasionally brushing. His presence tugs at our mysterious bond like a persistent undertow.

I chance a glance at his sharp profile silhouetted against the glow of fairy lights and immediately regret it when his quicksilver eyes meet mine.

The air seems to crackle between us. Under the cover of the table, Draven's fingers graze my knee in a feather-light caress that makes my breath catch. His hot gaze bores into me, full of promise and longing. I jerk my leg away, pulse racing in a disconcerting mix of fear and exhilaration. I cannot let him dismantle my defenses so easily. The risk is too great. "So, can I count on you to cover for me tonight?" Audrey asks her brother in a hushed voice.

Draven gives a theatrical sigh, though his eyes glint with amusement. "Yes, yes, I'll provide an alibi should anyone come looking for my reckless older sister."

Their conversation fades into background noise as I study Draven's sharp profile in the fairy light glow. I know I should look away, but I'm helplessly drawn to him like a moth to flame.

I shiver at his heated gaze full of unspoken longing. This dangerous attraction threatens to dismantle all my defenses.

The charged moment is broken by a cheerful
voice calling out, "Ah, here you all are! I've been
searching the festival high and low."

A man bounds up the steps to our balcony, flashing a grin that makes me melt a little.. Audrey sits up
straighter, a pleased flush blooming on her cheeks
though she clearly tries to appear nonchalant.

"Lord Anthony, allow me to introduce Thorn,
our guest of honor this evening," Draven says
smoothly.

Anthony sweeps into an elegant bow and captures my hand, brushing his lips gallantly over my
knuckles. "Thorn, of course! The courageous rescuer of our dear prince. Tales of your daring feat
have spread far and wide, my lady."

I duck my head self-consciously at the dramatic
introduction. "You flatter me, my lord. I'm but a
simple herbalist."

"With an uncommon gift for appearing in the right
place when needed most and a dash of magic I hear,"
Anthony replies earnestly. His handsome face creases

into a roguish wink. "I know I, for one, am grateful for your timely intervention on our prince's behalf."

I study the young lord with interest. His easy charm and familiarity with Draven hint at a longstanding friendship, but there is wisdom in his gray eyes belying his youthful appearance that suggests he has seen much in his life. His eyes have the subtle glow of immortality that all vampires have, but his perfection holds a few flaws showing that he hasn't always been one. I sense a steadfast loyalty in him that goes beyond political alliance or social niceties. Very interesting. As far as I remember, the royal family is strict about the lines between the natural born and turned vampires, yet someone so close to Draven is clearly turned.

Anthony draws up a chair beside Audrey, and they soon fall into lively debate about the upcoming tournament, exchanging playful banter and subtle smiles. I watch the two interact with a bittersweet pang, reminded of what I will never allow myself to have. The glow on Audrey's cheeks warms my heart all the same. Perhaps she has found her match in this steadfast lord. If her family will allow it.

Draven leans in close enough for me to catch his smoky, masculine scent. "Quite an eventful festival, is it not?" His mellifluous voice washes over me. "Does it bring back any fond memories for you?"

I toy with my mug, keeping my tone light. "It's been many years since I attended any such celebrations."

In truth, this city and I share history from another lifetime, but some secrets are best kept close.

Sensing my reticence, Draven changes tack. "For me, this festival always brings back memories of childhood misadventures." His smile turns wistful with nostalgia. "One year, I slipped my minders and ended up causing all sorts of mayhem with some local village boys. Hiding in vendors' stalls, pelting each other with snowballs, pilfering treats..."

I can easily imagine a younger, wilder Draven creating such hijinks. The mental image makes me bite back an amused smile. "Now that I can readily believe, my prince. You seem to have maintained that penchant for mischief."

"Only when there's adequate temptation." His glittering eyes pin me in place.

Before I can craft a retort, the first firework whistles into the sky in a glittering arc of emerald sparks. We turn our attention to the colorful display bursting overhead, bathing upturned faces in vibrant hues. I let the tranquility of the moment wrap around me like a comforting cloak. The nostalgia and cheer of the festival have softened my ever-present wariness, if only for this one night.

As the finale lights the sky with cascading gold, I meet Draven's gaze again. This time, there is only quiet wonder in his expression that surely mirrors my own.

"Thank you," I murmur, "for this small window back to lighter days."

Something solemn moves in his face at my unguarded words. Slowly, Draven's fingers entwine with mine where they rest atop the table, and I find myself allowing it. The tangled connection between us thrums, at once terrifying and exhilarating in its rightness. I know, come morning, I will fortify my defenses once more, but under the fairy lights, cloaked in the magic of this night, I relinquish just an inch of the iron grip on my heart. It feels like coming up for air after an age submerged.

When Draven brushes his lips over my knuckles in a featherlight caress, I close my eyes to memorize the liberating sensation. This gift, I will allow myself to keep.

# 21

## DRAVEN

The last glittering embers of the fireworks display fade into wisps of smoke overhead. All around us, enchanted faces turn earthward once more as the spell breaks. Sounds of laughter and lively chatter fill the chilled night air as crowds begin drifting toward the castle gates.

Anthony catches Audrey's eye with a subtle smile. "Perhaps you might allow me the honor of escorting you back to the castle, my lady?"

Audrey flushes prettily and takes his proffered arm. "I would be delighted, Lord Anthony. After a few drinks perhaps?"

They make their farewells and head off into the dispersing crowd.

Now alone, I rise and offer Thorn my arm. "May I escort you back?"

She hesitates, eyes guarded, but finally, her delicate fingers alight on my sleeve. Even through the layers of my tunic, her touch sends sparks skittering across my skin. I have to restrain the urge to pull her close and breathe in her honeyed scent.

We join the surge of revelers heading back along the winding lane of stalls, now shuttered for the night. Snatches of music and laughter echo around us as families and lovers wander together in the silvery glow of lanterns. The nip in the air reddens Thorn's cheeks.

As we walk, memories surface unbidden of our quiet days together in her cottage, when I was certain I would leave and then never see her again. Against all odds, here she is by my side once more.

"You know, I never did get the secret behind that brick you called bread," I tease lightly as we walk, wanting to keep things light. "Surely even your infamous cooking skills could do better?"

Thorn gasps in mock affront and swats my shoulder, but I catch the reluctant quirk of her lips. "If you must know, that loaf was baked before your untimely arrival interrupted my errands."

"Mmm hmm, likely excuse. I seem to recall you baking a fresh loaf while I was there recuperating. Had the pleasure of watching you punch and knead it within an inch of its life." I mime aggressively punching dough, eliciting a surprised chuckle from her.

"Well, someone had to take out their frustrations when saddled with an unwanted houseguest," Thorn retorts with a pointed look.

"Come now. I was the perfect gentleman. Even offered my expertise on achieving the perfect airy crumb."

Thorn snorts. "Oh, yes, I remember your constant hovering and critiques while I baked. Tell me, do they teach bread chemistry as part of prince schooling?"

"I'll have you know the crown prince receives the most well-rounded education," I reply in mock superiority. "How to manage the cooks is near the top of that list. At least until we have a bride."

Thorn shakes her head, eyes glinting with amusement. "Truly invaluable skills that prepared you so well for being stranded in a blizzard."

"I survived, didn't I? Thanks to a certain witch's anchored bread keeping me nourished." I pat my stomach for emphasis.

Thorn's lips quirk. "Happy to be of baked goods service."

Up ahead, the iron gates of the castle loom.

I slow our steps, wanting to prolong this stolen time together. "Did you enjoy yourself tonight at least?"

Thorn's expression turns thoughtful. "More than I expected to, truthfully. Being here again after so long... it stirred some surprisingly pleasant memories."

Her voice holds a reflective note that piques my curiosity. I didn't realize she had been here before, but I don't press.

I cover her hand resting on my arm with my own. "I'm glad. You deserve a little magic."

Thorn's steps falter briefly before regaining their rhythm. Our bond thrums just beneath the surface, straining to fully reconnect. It's all I can do not to give in to desire and pull her into my arms right there in the middle of the crowd, but I restrain myself, respecting her boundaries. She needs time, and I can be patient. Or at least try to be.

The thought of bidding Thorn goodnight and watching her disappear behind those imposing wooden doors fills me with quiet dread. This magical evening together feels too precious to let end just yet.

I glance down at her hand resting delicately on my arm, wisps of her dark hair trailing over the rich velvet of her cloak. "Tell me, where did you grow up?"

Thorn keeps her gaze fixed ahead, expression unreadable. "Oh, we moved frequently when I was young. My mother sought out remote villages in need of her skills."

She doesn't elaborate further, clearly avoiding specifics.

I try a different tack. "And your interests? Besides medicine and magic, how else do you pass the time?"

A small smile tugs at her lips. "Reading when I can get new material. Used to spend hours as a child hiding away with my nose in a book. And music... I find playing the flute can ease all manner of burdens."

I perk up at this new personal detail. "I would dearly love to hear you play sometime."

"Perhaps..." She toys idly with the sash of her cloak. "If the mood strikes. Now, I believe I'm due a question in return?"

I incline my head graciously. "Ask away, my lady."

Thorn's eyes take on a teasing glint. "Well then... how many hearts have you broken with that roguish charm of yours?"

I press a hand to my chest in mock affront. "You wound me! Here I thought your impression was solely favorable."

Her answering laugh sends warmth cascading through my veins. "Come now. I find it hard to believe you haven't left a trail of lovelorn ladies in your wake over the centuries. You're a prince, and let's be serious. Vampires are known for their more carnal desires."

I hold her gaze meaningfully. "Not as many hearts as you might think. The demands of my station make true romance... challenging."

Lonely, too, though I refrain from saying so aloud.

Something that looks like empathy flickers in Thorn's eyes, but the shutters lower again before I can be certain. I wonder if she, too, knows what it means to feel isolated even amidst a crowd.

We pass beneath the spiked iron portcullis into the castle's outer courtyard, our playful banter continuing as I soak up these glimpses past her prickly exterior. It's like basking in the warmth of spring's first rays after an age of winter's chill.

Too quickly, we traverse the open-air corridors to my wing. Tension coils through me with each step drawing inexorably toward parting.

Thorn pauses outside the heavy oaken door, our joined hands falling back to our sides.

"Thank you for indulging my sister's whims and allowing me to escort you tonight." I infuse the formal words with sincerity, hoping she understands this was no mere obligation to me.

Thorn inclines her head politely, though her eyes shutter again. "I appreciate you both going to such efforts on my behalf."

We hover a moment, the silence heavy between us. I'm struck by the urge to gently tuck back the locks of hair that have escaped her braid, so at odds with her usual severe style. She looks up at me, lips parted as if to speak.

Some magnetic force draws me nearer until I find myself leaning down to press my mouth to hers. For an electric instant, Thorn softens into the kiss, her hands lifting as if to draw me closer...

But then she turns her face away abruptly, eyes lowered. "Forgive me, I cannot... This is unwise." Her words come out barely a whisper.

Regret floods me. Of course she is not ready for such intimacy with our connection still so tenuous. I retreat a step, cursing myself for presuming too much.

"You have nothing to apologize for." I keep my tone gentle. "The fault is mine. Goodnight, Thorn. Sleep well."

I wait until the door closes softly behind her before making my way to my own chambers. The kiss lingers on my lips, sweeter than fae honey-wine and twice as intoxicating. Getting past her thorny exterior will require time and patience, but I find myself more determined than ever to discover the tender heart I know beats beneath the witch's prickly armor.

Half in a daze, I ready myself for bed, my thoughts consumed by Thorn. The mysteries of her past, the secrets flickering in those fathomless dark eyes... they draw me in even as they signal caution. Something wounded her deeply once. I only hope in time she will trust me enough to share those hidden parts of herself and perhaps allow me to help mend them.

Slipping between the cool silken sheets, I close my eyes. Does she lay awake as well reliving those blissful moments in the starlight before fear drove her back behind her walls? I will be patient, I remind myself again, but patience has never been my strong suit.

I fall into a fitful sleep full of tangled dreams where Thorn and I dance together at the Yule Ball, gaze locked as if we are the only two souls in existence. Her lips meet mine again and again beneath the wavering candle flames, but each time I reach for her, she dissolves into mist through my fingers.

I wake well before dawn restless and on edge, but as I rise to greet the new day, determination braces my steps. Last night's thawing, however brief, gives me hope. I need only keep chipping away to uncover the light that draws me like a beacon within Thorn's shadows.

And when at last her armor comes down for good, I will be there waiting.

# 22

## DRAVEN

Sunlight streams in through the arched windows as I make my way toward the dusty depths of the royal archives. Servants and petitioners bustle busily through the sunlit halls, but the archives remain deserted as always. My footsteps echo across the stone floors, past endless shelves stacked high with leather-bound tomes and curiosities from ages past. I'm drawn here seeking insights, nerves still frayed from the spirits' violent warnings during my previous late night research session. The archives stand silent and undisturbed in the bright light of day.

I inhale deeply, letting the comforting scents of ink and parchment soothe my restless mind. Sleep continues to evade me lately, my thoughts consumed by

Thorn. Even here, our fledgling bond tugs at my consciousness, urging me to her side.

I force myself to focus on scanning the shelves, searching for anything related to winter solstice rituals or the amplification of vampiric powers. There must be some clue hidden amidst these millions of pages about the true nature of the fated mate bond and perhaps something about the vampire I'm looking for. There are enough rumors to make me question that her death.

After selecting a stack of promising texts, I settle at my favorite table tucked into a shadowy, isolated corner. One massive volume after another thuds onto the scarred wood as I flip carefully through brittle pages, making notes on spare parchment. Many passages are faded beyond legibility, but I persist. The answers I seek are here somewhere. I can feel it.

As moonlight arcs across the star-strewn sky outside, I chance upon the first obscure reference, a single sentence in an ancient tongue.

"On the winter solstice, the First Blood shall be spilled to renew our power."

I go very still, rereading the ominous line several times. Though cryptic, implications begin taking shape in my mind that chill me to the core. This sounds like some accursed ritual of blood magic, likely enacted upon the turned vampires forced into servitude beneath the first vampire kings, a brutal means of maintaining control.

Jaw clenched, I delve deeper, piecing together fragments from multiple sources. The ritual seems to involve magically tapping into the power of ancient vampire bloodlines on the solstice when magic peaks. The details remain frustratingly vague. What methods did they use to "spill" this First Blood? Some arcane sacrifice? Imprisonment? Or worse... mass extermination?

The lack of clear records makes me wonder if this violent ritual was intentionally obscured over the centuries. But why? What were my ancestors trying to hide about our past? The not knowing eats at me like acid.

I'm attempting to decipher another disintegrating parchment when approaching footsteps break my concentration. I glance up, uneasy, as none usually disturb my nighttime research vigils.

Prince Theron appears in the doorway, immaculate as always in his dark military-style coat. His handsome face is set in hard lines, eyes flashing with annoyance as they settle on me.

"Burning the midnight oil again, brother?" He crosses his arms. "Don't you ever rest?"

I bristle at his condescending tone. "My duties allow little time for leisurely rest." I make a show of rolling up the scroll laid out before me. "Just catching up on some light reading."

Theron snorts. "Yes, I can see your choice of 'light reading' is progressing rapidly." He gestures to the haphazard piles of esoteric texts. "Honestly, Draven, I don't know why you waste time rooting around in the past. Today's challenges should be your only focus."

I clench my jaw, willing myself to hold back the angry retort on my tongue. Theron's lack of interest in our ancestry has always frustrated me. While he seems content to simply inherit the privileges of his princely station without questioning the murky means by which our family secured power long ago, I refuse to be so complacent.

"Have care how you speak," I reply coldly. "The past echoes more loudly than you know."

Theron's eyes flash. "Meaning what exactly? That you've uncovered some great revelation in this dust?"

He sweeps out an arm angrily, sending a pile of books crashing to the floor, and I flinch at the wanton mistreatment of such priceless volumes.

"Watch yourself, brother," I warn softly.

Theron continues his careless destruction, clearly bent on goading me now. Priceless scrolls tumble and crack beneath his boots. When I remain stone-faced, he changes tack.

"Or maybe you're distracted by your new pet witch?" Theron leans over the table, getting in my face. "Do not forget your duties chasing some warm body to rut with."

At that crass assessment of my bond with Thorn, the last frayed thread of my patience snaps. I launch myself up and around the table, slamming into Theron with bruising force. We go down in a tangle of limbs, crashing into shelves and bringing a rain of books down on us.

Theron recovers first, landing a brutal punch to my jaw that snaps my head back painfully. Fury quickly overrides pain. We trade savage blows, all decorum and royal restraint cast aside. Blood drips down my chin as I pin Theron against the stones, fangs bared inches from his throat.

"The rituals we celebrate at the solstice," I hiss, tightening my grip on his collar. "Tell me of their origins."

Confusion wars with rage in Theron's eyes. "Rituals? What nonsense—"

I shake him hard enough to clack his teeth together. "Do not play the fool! The First Blood... the cleansing of impurity. How many had to die to cement our family's power?"

All color leeches from Theron's face. He shoves me back with a roar, reversing our positions to slam me against the wall.

"You tread dangerous ground, little brother." His arm presses hard across my windpipe, and I wheeze for air that I don't need but has become reflex. "Speak of treason again and, title be damned, I will strike you down myself."

Despite the spots dancing across my vision, I cling desperately to consciousness, still seeking answers. "The truth," I gasp out. "Our people... deserve to know..."

With a sound of disgust, Theron hurls me aside. I hit the flagstones hard enough to crack bone, head spinning wildly. Through the haze, I make out his imposing figure looming above me like an executioner.

"You will cease this pointless crusade. Focus your misguided passions on your failed mating, not fanciful history. It wouldn't affect the purebloods anyways." Theron nudges my throbbing side with one polished boot. "Consider yourself lucky the king shall hear nothing of your... doubts."

# 23

## THORN

T he blood thrums hot beneath my skin as I tidy
my chamber. I can feel the thirst rising, that
restless itch that signals the need to feed will soon be
upon me. The copper kettle begins to steam over the
fire, reassuring me that relief is near. The dried petals
I purchased last night at the festival market float atop
the steaming water, infusing their vibrant color and
earthy aroma. No actual blood goes into this brew,
only flowers, herbs, and magic, but it will grant me the
same respite and strength.

A pang of discomfort shoots through me, and I
pause mid-motion, frowning. What was that? I reach
inward with my senses, prodding my own magical
energy gently. There. Another pulse, like a plucked
string, reverberates at my core.

Realization dawns swiftly. Draven. Our bond thrums with his unspoken call, transmitting sensations and emotions whether I wish it or not.

Cursing under my breath, I reinforce my mental shields, trying to block out the unwelcome connection. I want no part of this "destined" entanglement, no matter what sweet words and promises he uses to tempt me.

I've spent decades perfecting the art of solitude, remaining aloof and untethered. The last thing I desire is some mystical vampire bond threatening to tie me down again, forcing unwanted intimacy. Better to sever this thread between us before it strengthens any further. Before either of us gets hurt more deeply.

Another pulse ripples through me, and I clench my jaw, fighting the reflexive urge to listen, to soothe, to go to him. I never asked for this.

With ruthless effort, I force his intrusive presence from my mind, rebuilding my walls stone by silent stone.

Peace. I need peace to think and meditate upon what is wisest now.

I settle onto the wool rug before the fire, slow my unnecessary breaths, and close my eyes. Focus inward. Let the mind be still as a forest pond...

But the very air around me seems to tremble and blur. Draven's call reverberates more insistently. Without warning, the floor drops away beneath me. My stomach lurches as magic wraps me in crushing darkness.

No! I'm being pulled right to him! Panic claws at my throat. I grasp outward blindly with my power, trying to halt the summoning and anchor myself back to my room.

With a gut-wrenching wrench, the darkness splits open. I collapse to my hands and knees, gasping though I need no air. Rough stone meets my palms instead of homespun wool.

Blinking, I peer about cautiously, muscles tensed to spring, but no attacker awaits, only silent bookshelves rising around me like monoliths in neat, familiar rows.

The archives. Somehow, Draven's call hurled me all the way to the castle archives.

Cold fear trickles down my spine. Our bond should not be so strong already that he can summon me thus, no matter how unconsciously. I cannot let this continue. I must go now before—

A thunderous crash echoes through the vast chamber, followed by a pained grunt. I freeze, listening intently. Sounds of a scuffle filter through the shelves then a fury-laced voice I recognize as the elder prince berating someone. Draven's name punctuates the tirade like a curse.

Body coiled tight, I creep between the shelves toward the commotion, peer cautiously around a corner, and inhale a sharp breath at the sight meeting my eyes.

Prince Theron looms over a battered Draven crumpled on the flagstones amidst scattered books and shards of broken wood. Blood, vampire blood, slicks Draven's chin, dripping from his split lip. He's been brutally beaten, one eye rapidly swelling shut, but he glares up at his brother with indomitable defiance.

"The truth... our people deserve..." he rasps out hoarsely.

Blinding rage whites out my vision at seeing him thus. How dare the prince raise a hand to his own? To my mate!

Power surges tumultuously within me, bucking against my restraints like a rabid beast.

In the shadows, my skin ripples as magic flows just beneath the surface. The rows of books begin to tremble, a low ominous rustling rising in crescendo. I taste blood and snarl silently, fangs descending. *Destroy the threat. Protect what is yours.* The primal instincts wells up, demanding release.

With a guttural shout, Prince Theron staggers back as a book launches itself at his head then another and another. He throws up his arms to shield himself from the barrage. Draven struggles to rise, but I pin him safely down with an invisible binding spell, not wanting him hurt further in the chaos.

"Enough! Show yourself, sorcerer!" Theron roars over the cacophony.

Naturally, I don't.

The color drains from his face. He turns and flees the archive, still pursued by a cloud of books hurling themselves at his back.

In the wake of sudden silence, I sag against the shelves, adrenaline rushing out of me. Gods, what have I done? I cannot afford to lose control like that, not even in Draven's defense. I must go quickly before he or anyone else discovers me here.

Steeling myself, I weave the teleportation spell to return home, fighting to ignore Draven's bewildered voice calling distantly for the "invisible spirit" to come forward. His earnest concern for his unseen defender plucks at my heart, but I silence the unwelcome pang. Attachment can only lead to ruin for us both. I must be strong, for his sake as well as mine. If nothing else, this moment has reminded me just how ruthless Draven's family is. I can't become part of it.

With a gut-wrenching twist, I tear myself away, leaving him with nothing but mystery and unanswered questions. The familiar confines of my guest chamber reform around me, and I collapse by the neglected tea kettle, hands shaking. The herbs have over-steeped, but I drink anyhow, the floral brew bitter and astringent on my tongue. It will not fully take care of my bloodlust, but it will hold me over for the night until I can find more or return home.

As my body regains equilibrium, I slump back against the rug, equal parts drained and rattled. This day has only reinforced the danger posed by my bond with Draven. He seems able to summon me without consciously intending to, and the murderous rage that overtook me when I saw him harmed... A shiver wracks my frame. I came perilously close to exposing myself, nearly willing to kill for his sake. That cannot happen again. There is only one way to assure both our safeties now.

Draven's parting words echo through my mind, making my heart ache. "Rest well, unseen spirit..."

I dash the traitorous wetness from my eyes angrily. This is for the best. He is a noble prince, heir to a kingdom, and I... I am the nightmare that his family destroyed hundreds of lives to eliminate. We were never meant to walk the same path.

Tomorrow, I will tell him... it is over. Our stars crossed only for a fleeting moment out of time. No matter what destiny or bonds seek to bind us, we must each follow our own solitary course once more. For his sake and mine.

The decision made, exhausted calm finally settles over my spirit. I curl upon the woolen rug beside Luna, taking comfort in the familiar herbs overhead. Through our connection, I can sense she is nearly healed. Soon, it will be safe to travel with her magically back home. Tomorrow will bring sorrow and parting, but then it shall just be me, Luna, and my woods and quiet days of solitude again.

No matter the ache in my silent heart, that will be enough. It must be enough.

\*\*\*

I stir from my nest of blankets as a familiar prodding nudges at my consciousness. Luna's presence brushes gently against my mind, rousing me from sleep. I blink open bleary eyes to find her silver-furred face peering down at me, green eyes shining brightly despite the early hour.

"Luna?" I rasp in surprise.

She nuzzles against my cheek in response, and I feel a swell of relief to see her recovered enough to wake at last. I run my hands through her soft fur, taking comfort in the strength of our bond after days of worry for her health.

Even as joy lifts my spirit, the persistent throb of thirst stirs as well, never far from waking. I wince as it surges hotly beneath my skin, my body recognizing the creeping onset of need. The tea I brewed last night, meant to curb my rising bloodlust, seems to have lost some potency overnight.

"We must find you more herbs to bring your strength back fully," I murmur.

Even this trivial errand now seems risky with the thirst upon me. What if I cannot restrain my nature amidst the crowds sure to throng the city streets by day?

Luna tilts her head, studying me intently. *Go*, her voice echoes gently in my mind. *I will rest here. While I've slept, I've seen what's transpired. Restock before you reveal yourself. You are not stable enough to take us all of the way back to your home. And bring me back some treats! I prefer the ones with frosting.*

I hesitate, uncertainty and temptation warring within. Part of me yearns to flee the confines of this castle and the entanglements I've found here, to take Luna and disappear into the wilderness once more, leaving only mystery in our wake.

*Coward.*

I flinch from the gentle chastisement, even as I know it's the truth. For decades, I have fled any threat of entanglement, wrapping solitude like armor around my wounded heart. This castle, for all its perils, offers a chance to mend long-neglected parts of my spirit... if I can find the courage to stay.

"Remain in my room. You will be safe here," I concede reluctantly, and Luna's delight ripples through our link. I cannot help a small smile in return. "And try to stay out of trouble."

Her amused huff follows me out the door as I slip into the corridors, wound tight with tension. I keep my steps swift but stealthy, relying on my vampire senses to avoid the few servants beginning to stir in the early light. The last thing I want is conversation, friendly or otherwise, not with the thirst already laying claim to my thoughts.

Rounding a corner, I very nearly crash into a figure stepping suddenly into my path. I pull up short, swallowing back an instinctive hiss, and find myself staring into Princess Audrey's startled face.

Of course. I resist the urge to roll my eyes. So much for avoiding entanglements.

"Thorn!" Audrey exclaims, quickly regaining her composure. "Just the woman I was coming to find."

I fold my hands demurely, keeping my tone light. "How may I be of service, Your Highness?"

Her keen gaze sweeps over me, likely taking in the tense set of my shoulders and darkened eyes, but she simply links her arm through mine. "Come along. We have important business in the city today."

Before I can object, she propels us briskly toward the gates. I force my steps to match hers, senses primed for any threat. I need to head that way anyways. It would only complicate things if I did it alone and ran into her there.

"Business, Highness?" I prompt warily once we pass into the bustling streets beyond the castle walls. The morning sun, though weak in the winter sky, still prickles across my skin, but it is the swirling scents and sounds of the awakening city that truly threaten my restraint. I focus on keeping my breathing steady, my movements natural.

Audrey pats my arm. "Please, it's Audrey, and yes, we have some final dress fittings to attend to before the ball the day after tomorrow. I want to be certain your gown is perfect."

I blink in surprise, some tension easing from my shoulders as her meaning sinks in. Of course, the upcoming solstice celebration. In truth, I nearly forgot about playing my role as Prince Draven's escort for the event. Not that anyone asked my opinion for that role.

I open my mouth to kindly reject the need for more from them, but Audrey's expression—open and earnest, even a touch playful—stops me. When was the last time I shared such carefree moments with another? For all my wariness, part of me yearns to surrender to this silly adventure.

"It would be my honor," I say instead, inclining my head.

Audrey beams and quickens our steps toward the merchant district. I focus on the pleasant bustle around us, letting it drown out the ever-present thrum of blood.

Despite myself, I soon grow caught up in Audrey's infectious enthusiasm as she whisks me from shop to shop. We browse glittering jewels and fabrics, sample exotic perfumes, and share amused commentary on the passing crowds. The thirst still plucks at my veins, but Audrey's bright laughter keeps the shadows at bay.

At the modiste, I stand awkward and self-conscious as the plump seamstress fusses over my ballgown's adjustments. The sumptuous emerald and black velvet creation seems designed for a far loftier lady than I, but Audrey insists it complements my coloring perfectly.

"Simply stunning," she proclaims once the final pins are in place. "Prince Draven will be utterly speechless when he sees you in this."

I duck my head as an involuntary flush warms my pale cheeks. Audrey's knowing look tells me she notices, but she tactfully keeps any teasing at bay. I feel a rush of gratitude for her perceptiveness. There are some matters I do not yet have words for, even to myself.

The seamstress packages up the ballgown with promises to have it delivered to the castle by tomorrow. Audrey then draws me eagerly toward one last stop—another dressmaker she commissioned to outfit me with even more day dresses suitable for court.

My protests over such unnecessary indulgence die on my lips at the sincere delight in Audrey's eyes. Clearly, my acceptance of these gifts means something to her, so I swallow my unease and allow the whirlwind to continue.

A beautiful blonde assistant urges me to try on a gown specially made at Prince Draven's request. Unable to resist peeking at the handiwork, I slip behind the changing screen with the dress in hand.

It proves to be a dream confection of rich burgundy velvet, cinched at the waist with a silver silk sash embroidered with delicate frosted ferns and icicles. The square neckline is trimmed with antique lace and tiny seed pearls like freshly fallen snow. As I smooth my hands over the corseted bodice, I find inner seams lined with discreet flexible boning to support my subtle curves. The full skirts fall in elegant ripples reminiscent of snow drifts, concealing cunning slits to allow freedom of movement. I slip into a pair of heels that both match beautifully and make me want to throw them. I haven't worn heels since I was last in this court. They are something I most definitely haven't missed.

Twirling slowly before the mirror, I can scarcely recognize myself. The gown transforms me into a court lady of refined elegance and taste, utterly unlike the wild, feral creature who roams the mist-veiled, snow-laden forests, concealing herself in winter's shadows.

I wonder what prompted Draven to choose such a creation for me, when my true nature must seem so contrary to this civilized facade. Does he see something in me beyond the wary vagrant exiled to the icy wilderness for so long? Some hidden potential waiting to unfurl like the first flower after the thaw?

Voices sound just outside the curtained alcove, jolting me from my pensive thoughts. I turn at the familiar timbre drawing near, my borrowed finery rustling softly with the motion.

"We have everything well in hand. There's no need to trouble yourself," comes Audrey's lilting voice.

"It's no trouble, I assure you." The smile is audible in Draven's smooth reply. "I wished to check that the dressmaker followed my requests properly for the lady."

My breath stills. Speak of the devil, it seems. The fates conspire at every turn to entangle our paths.

"Thorn is just changing now if you'd like to see how it fits," the blonde chirps eagerly.

Before I can object, the curtain whisks back, revealing me in all my bejeweled splendor.

I freeze beneath Draven's intense silver gaze, pinned in place like a butterfly beneath a collector's needle. Heat blooms across my cheeks, no doubt staining them pink. Curse this fair complexion!

"Exquisite," he murmurs, eyes trailing over me slowly. "You look beautiful, Thorn."

The genuineness in his tone flusters me further. I am no lady, only masquerading as one in this dress, but the way Draven looks at me makes me wish his imaginings were true. It makes me want to become the woman he apparently sees behind my feral facade.

I dip into a wobbly curtsey to disguise my turmoil. "You have a discerning eye, Your Highness. The gown is... beyond compare." I cringe internally at how breathless my voice sounds. Get a hold of yourself!

A hint of a dimple flashes as Draven grins. "The beauty wearing it enhances its splendor."

Audrey makes a small amused noise while I flounder speechlessly. Blast this infernal thirst robbing me of my wits! I settle for dropping my eyes demurely, despite wanting to glare at his smug, handsome face. Insufferable rogue.

"Yes, well, I think that's everything we need here for now," Audrey interjects smoothly, sparing me the need to formulate a clever retort. Bless her tact. "Shall we continue our excursion to the jeweler next? Keep that on, dear. We can have them send back your dress when they deliver the rest of them. It would be a shame to take it off so quickly."

I nod and can't help admiring myself in the mirror, wondering how on earth I'll manage dancing in these fancy heels, when there's a knock. In pops Lord Anthony's sunny face.

"There you are, Lady Audrey! Care to grab lunch with me? I had a few things I wanted to run past you before tomorrow," he asks with a meaningful look that says this is not just any pleasant stroll.

Audrey pinks up prettily. "I would be delighted!" she chirps at him. She turns to me with an apologetic smile. "You don't mind if Prince Draven escorts you to the jewelers instead do you? I'm sure he has an excellent eye to help you choose some accessories."

Before I can reply, the prince speaks, "It would be my absolute pleasure." His silvery gaze settles on me, and my traitorous heart does a little flutter. Honestly, this man!

With a grateful curtsey to the prince, Audrey sweeps out on Anthony's arm, clearly eager to have him alone. She shoots me a significant look over her shoulder as they go.

Hilarious, fate, leaving me alone with my inconvenient crush who I'm desperately trying not to fall for. Just brilliant.

I dip into a courtesy, aiming for poise but nearly toppling on these blasted heels. "Shall we?"

Draven smiles and offers his arm, silver eyes dancing with amusement as I wobble slightly. *Oh, you just love this, don't you?* I internally grumble at him as we head off toward the jewelers. The one place I need to be is the apothecary for more ingredients for my tea, but nope, stuck here playing dress up with Mr. Tall, Dark, and Dangerous. I will get my revenge on Fate the first chance I get.

The jewelers is nestled snugly between two stone buildings, its polished oak door bearing an ornate silver knocker in the shape of an owl. As Draven holds the door open for me with a gallant sweep of his arm, a merry tinkle from the bell announces our arrival.

I blink as my eyes adjust from the bright sunlight outdoors to the cozy interior, lit by a combination of natural light streaming through high arched windows and the warm glow of lanterns lining the display cases. The glass cases shine, meticulously polished to best showcase their glittering contents—gems of every hue and precious metals crafted into rings, necklaces, bracelets, and other finery I can scarcely fathom. My fingers itch to touch and explore, though such frivolous adornments are worlds away from my practical forest life.

An elderly dwarf with a bushy white beard trimmed short comes bustling out from a back room, beaming in delight. His keen eyes gleam beneath busy white brows, taking in every detail.

"Prince Draven, welcome! An honor as always to have you grace my humble shop." He sketches a neat bow then turns the force of his friendly gaze on me. "And who might this lovely blossom be?"

"Fenton, allow me to present Lady Thorn, my personal guest from the northern forests." Draven's hand comes to rest familiarly on my lower back, a subtle possessive touch that makes my pulse skitter. "We are in need of some accessories for the ball tomorrow evening."

"Of course. Of course! My lady, what pleasure it is to make your acquaintance." Fenton makes a gracious bow in my direction, eyes twinkling. "With such beauty before me, I shall take great joy in selecting only the finest pieces to complement you."

I offer him a polite smile in return, though inwardly I'm amused by his obvious attempts at flattery. Still, his warm manner puts me at ease.

Clasping his hands eagerly, Fenton shuffles over to a particular display case near the back. "Now this, I believe, would be just the thing for our fair forest nymph." With practiced care, he unlocks the case and lifts out an elegant silver necklace. "Mined by my cousins in the Blue Mountains from only the finest quality ore." He winks conspiratorially as he lays the piece atop the glass for our inspection. "Silver laced with a touch of dwarven magic, so it will never tarnish or lose its luster. And at the center, an emerald the precise shade of moss in spring, if I may say so, my lady."

I lean in, enthralled by the beauty and craftsmanship of the design. The emerald teardrop glimmers in a setting of delicate silver filigree. Simple yet even my untrained eye can see it is a work of art. I brush a tentative fingertip over the gemstone, half expecting the piece to disappear at my touch.

"It's exquisite," I breathe out.

Beside me, Draven smiles. "Of course it is. I would want nothing less for my mate," he whispers in my ear.

His eyes meet mine, deep wells of quicksilver that see past my surface. "We will take it."

I start to protest such a lavish gift.

Draven silences my objections by taking my hand, his expression unexpectedly earnest. "Please, allow me this small token to welcome you. Seeing such finery grace your lovely neck will bring me great joy." His voice drops lower in a subtle caress. "Though not nearly so much as your smile in this moment."

My cheeks warm at his bold flattery even as my reservations melt away. I cannot deny being touched by his thoughtfulness and wish to make me feel valued.

I swallow my protests and accept gracefully. "You have my deepest thanks. I shall treasure it always."

Fenton beams as he lifts the necklace carefully from its velvet case and hands it to Draven. Moving behind me, Draven gently sweeps my hair aside to clasp the chain in place. I shiver as the cool metal and stones come to rest in the hollow of my throat.

I'm aware of every movement of his body until the clasp clicks shut and he turns me around to face him. His eyes simmer with something I dare not name. His fingers trail feather-light over my nape as he adjusts the pendant, letting it nestle perfectly against my skin. My pulse thrums like a plucked violin string, hyper aware of his nearness, his subtle caress. This feels far too intimate for our precarious arrangement, yet I cannot summon the will to pull away just yet.

Fenton, bless him, seems oblivious to the charged moment passing between us. He clasps his hands in delight once more. "Oh, yes, a perfect match! The lady was made to wear such finery."

Draven's mouth quirks up at one corner. "On that we agree." He takes my hand and presses a courtly kiss to my knuckles, eyes dancing. "My lady shines brighter than any gem."

I reward his audacity with a playful swat against his shoulder. "You are absolutely ridiculous."

Secretly, I admit his attentions leave me flushed and flustered in the most delightful way.

The shop door bursts open, and Lord Anthony enters looking harried. "Your Highness, my apologies, but you're needed urgently."

Draven swears under his breath, clearly irritated by the interruption. "I'm sorry. I need to..."

"Go, if it's that important. I have an errand to run before heading back to the castle anyways."

With a small apologetic smile, Draven pays for the necklace quickly and the two of them leave, and I'm left clutching the emerald necklace, pulse still racing from even that brief contact. Being alone with Draven is exhilarating yet dangerous, like dancing with fire. I must keep my wits about me, though my treacherous heart threatens to overrule my logic when I'm near him.

I turn to the kindly old dwarf and dip into a grateful curtsy. "You have my deepest thanks, sir, for helping select such an exquisite piece." I touch the emerald pendant lying cool against my throat, genuinely moved by Draven's wish to gift me such beautiful finery.

Fenton's eyes crinkle merrily beneath his bushy brows. "The pleasure was all mine, my lady. You and the prince take care now." He waves cheerfully.

Out on the bustling market street once more, I breathe deep of the fresh air and lift my face to the sunshine, letting its warmth soak into my pale skin. An unfamiliar but not unpleasant weight, the pendant glints softly around my neck.

I hesitate, my throat already burning with increasingly urgent thirst. I desperately need to get to the apothecary for more blood elixir before my tenuous control shatters completely. I meander past booths peddling fragrant spices and bolts of sumptuous fabrics, and artisans showcasing their crafts. My fingers itch to explore the wares, but I keep my hands clasped tightly before me, anxious not to draw undue notice.

As I stroll, an uneasy tingle plucks at my senses, the subtle tugging of magical energy. My steps falter as I tense, instantly on high alert. Before I can react, the now-familiar vise grip of involuntary teleportation seizes me. I gasp sharply, the world blurring sickeningly around me.

When my vision clears, I'm no longer amid the sunny market but a dingy, rundown wooden room. Vampires are fighting with each other. Several are dressed in finery that tells me they must be connected to nobles while others are clearly of a much lower class.

My gaze lands on Draven grappling viciously with another vampire, and my heart clutches with fear. Draven is drenched in blood from numerous gashes marring his body. The other vampire has him pinned, greedily feeding from the gaping wound at his throat.

At the horrific sight, the last tattered shreds of my control utterly shatter. Savage, primal bloodlust surges up from deep within, consuming all reason and sanity.

No! I desperately try to cling to some scrap of humanity, but my thoughts dissolve, lost in a rising red haze. The ever-present thirst I constantly keep locked down and controlled is unleashed now with explosive force.

I let loose an inhuman snarl as the monster within takes over. Magic flares wildly around me, lashing the air like the lash of a whip. With blurring speed, I launch myself at the vampire on top of Draven. The vampire has only a split second to look up before I descend on him in a whirlwind of claws and bared fangs, ripping ruthlessly into his vulnerable flesh.

Hot blood splashes my face, and I lunge mindlessly for more. The rich metallic taste only fuels the frenzy growing within me. From far away, I hear chaos exploding as the other vampires react to my sudden berserker fury, but I am deaf now to everything except the screaming bloodlust and hunger driving me.

I carve a path of mangled bodies through the cramped room, consumed by my primal vampiric nature. My vision narrows down to the pulsing veins and frantically beating hearts of my prey. I am the hunter and they my feast. Nothing exists in this moment but the need to rend, to feed.

Only when gentle hands grasp my shoulders, sending a magical warmth through me, do I hesitate in my rampage. Panting, I blink away the haze of violence to find Draven gazing at me with a look of confusion.

"Thorn?" he murmurs.

Shame crashes down on me, horror at what I've done threatening to crush me where I stand. Somehow, Draven's steady gaze anchors me before I can spiral too deep.

Taking in the ruin surrounding us, he says grimly, "We need to talk."

The other vampires—Anthony included—seem shaken but unharmed. They are kept at a wary distance by Draven's upraised hand. With dreadful certainty, I know I have just exposed my monstrous true nature to them all.

Before I can properly panic, Draven turns his compelling gaze on each in turn. "You will forget what transpired here," he commands, voice resonating with power. "We were set upon by enemies and prevailed. No other details remain."

Their eyes all take on a glazed look of obedience. Draven has wiped their memories, saving my secret. All except Anthony, who watches solemnly, clearly still in possession of his wits.

Catching my frightened gaze, he simply bows his head. "Your secrets are safe with me." His sincerity makes me sag with tearful relief and gratitude.

With a reassuring hand on my back, Draven guides me quickly away. My chaotic thoughts swirl like scattered leaves in a storm as we make our harrowing way back to the safety of the castle. I cling to Draven's steady presence at my side like a lifeline, the one fixed point in my unmoored world.

Whatever consequences loom ahead, whether rejection or punishment for my monstrous acts, with Draven, I can weather the coming storm.

# 24

## DRAVEN

Thorn trembles against me, clearly shaken by the violent loss of control. As much as I burn with questions, now is not the time for interrogation. Her needs must come first.

I guide her swiftly from the carnage, one arm wrapped firmly around her slender shoulders. She moves as one hollowed out, numbly putting one foot in front of the other. Once we're back at the castle, I steer her to my private chambers where we can speak away from prying eyes.

Now inside my room, I gently cup her chin and tilt her face up to meet my gaze. Dried blood streaks her skin, marring its usual porcelain perfection. She looks so lost it makes my chest ache.

"Let's get you cleaned up," I murmur.

After leading her to the washroom, I dampen a cloth and tenderly wipe away the gore. She flinches when I uncover the gashes on her hands from her vicious attack. I pour a healing tonic into each cut, erasing all traces.

When no more blood remains, I lift her newly healed palms to my lips in a fervent kiss, ignoring her faint sound of protest. "There. Good as new."

I guide her back to the sitting room and settle us both near the hearth. Now I can focus on her emotional wounds. I rub her cold hands between mine, willing warmth into them.

"Are you hurt anywhere? I saw them feeding on you." Thorn asks softly, brows creased with concern as her eyes search me for injury.

My brave, compassionate fledgling.

I give her a small smile. "I will survive."

She scowls. "That wasn't my question." Her fingers probe my healing throat wound with exquisite gentleness. I wince slightly before I can mask it.

Thorn makes a distressed noise. "How many did I kill?"

"Hush. You saved me, Thorn. Vampires can heal from almost anything. They will all be fine in time.

Technically, you saved quite a few people with that show. They were attacking turned vampires, Thorn, people who have no rights or safety in our kingdom. A place that is supposed to be a refuge for vampires isn't safe for them, and you saved them when I couldn't. Thank you." I cup her cheek in my palm. "Now we have much to discuss, you and I."

Her green eyes, clouded with shame and fear, reluctantly meet my gaze.

*My brave, fractured mate. What burdens have you been bearing alone all this time?*

I wait patiently as she gathers her courage.

Thorn sits silently for a long moment, pale hands clutched tightly in her lap. When she finally begins speaking, her voice is soft and hesitant. "My mother was a gifted healer and witch. She fell in love with a vampire fugitive fleeing the king's persecution. When I was born different, it drew suspicion... Something happened to my village and family as a child. The slaughter." She closes her eyes briefly as if to block out the memories. "Soldiers came under orders from the king to kill me and my family. My mother hid me in the cellar, though it tore her apart to leave me." Her shoulders hunch inward, making her appear small and vulnerable. "I smelled the stench of smoke and death and heard the screams as they tore through our home... and my mother's final agonized cry as they cut her down."

A single tear trails down her cheek. I ache to draw her into my arms but don't dare interrupt as she unburdens herself.

"When the soldiers finally left, I crawled from the ruins numb and in shock. I didn't understand why our peaceful village had been targeted, why innocent lives ripped away. I learned that when I was much older." Her voice takes on a bitter edge. "But I learned quickly why I had to hide my true hybrid nature. The kingdom showed no mercy to those deemed unnatural abominations." Thorn meets my gaze then, eyes burning with remembered grief and anger. "So I survived on the fringes of society, keeping my vampire instincts suppressed with the tea that my mother had taught me to make. Always hiding, always wary of discovery." Her voice breaks on the last word.

My heart clenches at the pain in her words. No child should have endured such trauma and persecution. I long to somehow erase the scars of her past, but these wounds run deeper than any magic can heal.

As Thorn continues, I focus on keeping my expression open and understanding, inviting her to unburden herself fully.

"The tea recipe was my mother's gift, her attempt to give me some normalcy. She created it to help hide and protect my father as well as me." Thorn smooths a hand over her skirts, as if drawing comfort from the memory. "With it, I could blend in and ignore the relentless blood cravings. I could become only a witch." Her jaw tightens, hands fisting in the fabric. "But today, seeing you wounded and in danger, my control shattered." Self-loathing drips from each word.

Unable to stop myself, I cover her clenched hand with my own. "You are no monster, Thorn. You were protecting me, whatever the cost."

She shakes her head bitterly. "I never want to become someone who kills without a reason, a reason for that person specifically. I don't want to become like the people who killed my family."

"You were not yourself," I insist firmly. "The bloodlust took over. I know you would never harm innocents."

Thorn looks unconvinced.

I press on. "What you did today changes nothing between us. Your past, your true nature—those make you no less worthy in my eyes."

Her wary gaze searches mine. I will my sincerity to show through. Slowly, I see her shoulders lose some of their tension. The barest hint of hope dawns in her expression, driving back the clouds of despair.

"You would still have me here, knowing what I am?" she whispers.

I lift her hand and kiss it reverently. "I would never cast you out for being true to yourself. I'm not like my father and brother. You are not a threat. You are my redemption and my hope."

Anthony's face, kind but etched with the lingering sadness he tries to hide, flashes through my mind. His parents also suffered greatly due to the callous power struggles at court. As a young turned vampire, he endured cruelty and mistrust. It was why we bonded so fiercely as outcasts and forged an unbreakable loyalty.

I hope to shield Thorn from the same prejudices that have stained this kingdom and cost Anthony so much. She has faced enough hardship. With understanding and care, perhaps the wounds of the past can finally begin to heal for all.

But if my brother takes the throne, he will only continue the cycle of oppression and fear.

"You are safe with me, Thorn," I murmur. "I swear it."

The lingering fear in her eyes pains me. I vow silently to help heal the scars left by the cruel prejudice she suffered and show her she has a home here now and someone to rely on.

I will do all I can to prevent others from enduring the same tragic fates as those we have lost. I will be the change this kingdom needs. Thorn and Anthony give me hope I can help turn the tides before it is too late. I cannot fail them.

She nods slowly, a tentative, fragile trust taking root between us. We have a long road yet to travel, but this first step of understanding feels significant.

"The village massacre you described... I found records indicating it was your home that was destroyed," I tell her grimly.

I should have realized sooner that the cryptic reports of a slaughtered settlement with suspected vampire hybrids pointed to her hidden identity. I guessed but chalked it off as not possible. After all, she was only a witch.

"Your mother's sacrifice saved you that night."

Thorn meets my gaze at last, her eyes glistening. "Yes, but the scars from what I endured never fully healed."

I reach out to clasp her slender hand between both of mine. "You are so strong to have come through such darkness yet retain your compassion and spirit." I settle back, still clasping her hand warmly between us. "You should rest now. We can speak more tomorrow."

Thorn acquiesces, weariness etching her delicate features. As she curls up on the bed, I remain nearby, keeping silent watch until she succumbs to exhausted slumber. Only then do I allow myself to process the dark truths learned today and what it will take to help Thorn truly heal.

***

I slip from my chambers into the corridors. My mind is churning with all that was revealed today. I need guidance in untangling these knots of past and present. My steps turn almost unthinkingly back toward the tower.

I find the ancient mage awake, poring over some arcane text amidst the clutter of his sanctum. He looks up with no surprise as I enter, merely gesturing for me to take a seat.

"Prince Draven." His gravelly voice echoes off of the small room's stone walls. "What brings you to my tower on this chilly day?"

"Please, I must speak with you urgently." Settling myself on a rickety stool, I meet his questioning gaze directly. "It's about my mate Thorn."

The mage's tufted white brows rise, but he remains silent, waiting for me to continue.

I explain all that came to light with Thorn—her tragic history and hybrid nature kept secret for so long. The heavy weight of guilt and responsibility settles upon me. What path can I take that will not betray her trust yet also brings some reconciliation?

The mage listens intently, bushy brows drawing together. At last, he speaks. "This witchling is more than you think. Her fate and yours intertwined."

"She is my fated mate."

"But she's not allowed that bond to form fully, I see."

"How can you..."

He holds up his hand to stop me. "I have my secrets just as you have yours, although I do wonder…"

I wait for him to continue, but his eyes glazed over while lost in thought. "Yes?" I prompt.

"Bring her to me. I need to confirm something."

If anyone else gave me that request, I would balk, but this is one of the only people I've ever fully trusted. "When she awakes, I will bring her by."

He nods, still lost in thought.

After waiting for a moment to see if he had more to say, I excuse myself. Tomorrow's the ball, and I want a moment alone with her tonight before that. First, though, I need to prepare.

# 25

## THORN

I awake slowly, blinking up at the canopy overhead. For a moment, I'm disoriented, unsure where I am. Then, memory returns in a rush—the slaughter, the loss of control, and Draven accepting me even after witnessing the monster within.

I sit up, cradling my head in my hands. My emotions churn like a stormy sea. Last night changed everything. Was it last night? Draven knows my darkest truth now, yet he still sheltered me with compassion. And I... I let him in, trusted him enough to unburden my past. An act of faith after being alone for so long.

Rising from the bed, I run my fingers through my hair. The residual fog of sleep is slowly lifting, allowing me to take in my surroundings properly. This is not my chamber, I realize with a start. The furnishings are far too fine, masculine in their simplicity. I must be in Draven's private apartments. He brought me there after...

Quickly, I head for the door, cross the hall, and enter my own room.

A whine draws my attention. I look over to see Luna perched expectantly beside the bed, green eyes bright.

"There you are," I murmur, reaching out to stroke her soft fur.

The familiar gesture soothes my lingering anxiety. Luna nuzzles against my hand, her warm presence grounding me.

I move to the window overlooking the western gardens. The sun hovers just above the distant foothills, painting the sky vivid hues of orange and violet. It's nearly sunset. I must have slept the day away. Probably for the best. It was exhausting in body and spirit.

Luna leaps gracefully onto the sill beside me, brushing her tail along my arm. *Ready to talk?* Her voice in my mind is gentle.

I let out a long breath, watching the diminishing rays play across the blanketed gardens. "I suppose I must, though I hardly know where to begin."

I fall silent, struggling to arrange my chaotic thoughts. Slowly, I spill everything that happened since we last saw each other.

I've finished, but Luna waits patiently, radiating compassion. When I remain mute, she ventures, *It was brave, telling him those secrets you've held so long. The first step toward healing.*

I let my forehead rest against the cool glass. "Was it? Or have I foolishly given him power to destroy me?"

Draven seems sincere, yet old fears run deep. If word spreads of what I am...

*You underestimate his honor and his care for you. He will not betray your trust.* Luna sounds utterly certain.

I wish I could share her faith.

"I want to believe that," I whisper, "but it is not so simple to set aside a lifetime of wariness. You were right, though. Confronting the past may be the only way forward, as terrifying as that path seems."

Luna nuzzles my cheek. Her warm breath tickles my skin. *You need not walk it alone anymore. I am with you and now Prince Draven as well, if you allow it. Fate gave him to you for a reason. It would be wise to accept their gift.*

I smile softly at the thought of having allies on this difficult road. Perhaps together we can face the shadows that haunt me... if I can find the courage to fully let Draven in.

"Do you really believe fate could have bonded us?" I ask hesitantly.

Draven seems convinced our stars are aligned, but after shutting off that part of myself for so long, I hardly know how to embrace it.

Luna's eyes shine knowingly. *Really Thorn? You're now second-guessing that the fated mate bond is real?*

A knock at the door cuts short our conversation.

After crossing the room, I open the door to find Draven. He looks refreshed and devastatingly handsome as always in a black doublet embroidered with silver thorns along the collar.

"Good evening." He smiles warmly, clearly relieved to see me recovered. "I hope you are feeling better after some rest."

I dip in a brief curtsy, touched by his thoughtfulness. "I am, thank you, though I fear I slept the day away."

"No matter. It gave me time to prepare a surprise." Draven's eyes dance with anticipation. He offers his arm. "If you would accompany me."

I hesitate only a moment before accepting, letting him draw me close. I give one quick glance back at Luna before I close the door behind me. I swear that fox had a smirk on her face.

Draven's presence is comforting and electrifying all at once. Perhaps I am ready to explore what fate wishes me to find here.

"Let us see what surprise you have in store." I give him a playful smile to mask the sudden flutter of nerves in my belly. His joy is contagious.

Draven leads me through quiet servants' passages until we emerge at the base of a narrow winding stair. I eye the gloomy ascent warily as he gently propels me upward.

"Where are we going?" My whisper echoes eerily off the close stone walls.

"To visit an old friend, one I hope can help provide some... clarity."

Cryptic as ever.

I hold my tongue, sensing Draven will explain no more until we reach our mysterious destination. I recognize the old passages, the very same that I used to visit an old friend, but he couldn't be...

After what feels like endless crumbling steps, we finally halt before an iron-banded door etched with arcane symbols. As Draven knocks sharply, I smooth my skirts and pull back my shoulders, determined to face this unknown trial with poise.

Shuffling sounds precede the door creaking slowly inward. A stooped figure leans heavily on a gnarled staff, blinking rheumy eyes in the gloom. Recognition hits me with the force of a physical blow.

Master Eodan. The ancient castle mage who tutored me decades past when I was nothing but a new vampire in this court deceiving all with my tea and fake name. My knees nearly buckle. He will surely recognize through his mystic sight the truth of what I am.

Draven's hand at my back propels me gently over the threshold before I can bolt

The mage peers at me, bushy brows drawing together thoughtfully beneath his ragged hood. "Welcome, child." His gravelly voice holds no malice, only curiosity.

My nerves settle slightly. Perhaps he does not recall me after all.

Draven clears his throat. "Master Eodan, may I present—"

"The witchling Thorn. Yes, yes." Eodan waves away the introduction impatiently.

My heart sinks. He knows.

The mage's keen gaze bores into me. "You only shared half the story when last we met, child, but I knew."

I clench my trembling hands in my skirts, unsure whether to plead for mercy or flee this exposed perch. Draven's steady presence at my side keeps me rooted in place.

Eodan smiles then, a creaky but kindly expression. "Peace, girl. Your secrets are safe with me." He shuffles closer and pats my hand with one of his gnarled, age-spotted ones. "I am glad to see you well after so long. Last we met, your exit was... dramatic."

Before I can gather my scattered wits to respond, Draven interjects, "You two have met before?" He looks between us, brows drawn together in confusion.

Eodan chuckles, a raspy sound like dry leaves skittering across stone. "Oh, yes, though she went by another name at the time. Came to me near a century ago seeking arcane knowledge, concealing her true hybrid nature." He gives me a knowing look over his hunched shoulder. "You thought yourself clever with that herbal concoction, but you couldn't fool my Sight."

I flush, embarrassment and unease swirling within me. Back then, I was so cautious, so mistrustful of any who might divine the truth. If Eodan chooses to expose me now before the prince...

But the old mage simply pats my hand again. "Fear not, child. Your secrets were safe with me then, as they remain now, but you shouldn't keep all of your secrets to yourself. Tomorrow's the anniversary of renewal winter solstice."

Tomorrow? I nearly forgot.

I glance at Draven and see a myriad of emotions play across his handsome features—surprise, curiosity, and, most unexpectedly, hurt. He must feel stung that I kept even part of my past hidden from him.

Impulsively, I grasp his hand, uncaring of propriety in front of Eodan. "Forgive me," I implore softly. "I only wished to leave that haunted, distrustful version of myself buried firmly in the past. I see now that was foolish."

Some of the tension eases from Draven's posture. He entwines our fingers and squeezes gently. "I understand. All is well." Turning back to the mage, he asks politely, "What prompted your previous acquaintance, if I may?"

I take a steadying breath as I feel both sets of eyes turn to me expectantly. I cannot keep this final secret any longer, not if there is to be true trust between us.

"Draven, there is more I must confess about my time here before," I begin hesitantly. "I was not merely a student of Eodan's. I... I lived at court for a time under a false identity. I went by the name Vivian then." I look down, ashamed. "Everyone believed me harmless, just another court diversion, but I had a secret purpose." I meet Draven's intense gaze. "I discovered ancient records about a ritual used to cement the royals' power—the Winter Solstice reaping. It drained turned vampires to enhance the king's magic. I was investigating how to stop it without getting caught."

Understanding dawns on Eodan's face. "That is why you had to disappear so suddenly back then. You were close to exposing the ritual."

I nod, misery squeezing my heart. "Yes. I intended to find a way to stop it after learning more, but I was found out too soon. There was no choice but to fake my death and flee. I had started to prepare, but I couldn't finish it. I didn't know when to set the trigger. I did discover that it usually happens in the ballroom. It's why the castle was built here specifically. The stones the dungeons are carved out of work as a sort of conductor for this spell to draw the power for this."

To my surprise, Draven enfolds me in a fierce embrace. "We can work on this together. I also found some records of this recently, and Anthony and I have some plans in the works. Plus, it's a bit of a relief to no longer need to look for Vivian. I had heard that she held some knowledge that could constrain my brother after he took the throne. I was following a lead suggesting that she wasn't dead when you found me in the snow. Who could have possibly guessed that I found her when I found you."

I cling to him, tension draining away. The full truth is finally revealed, and I am still accepted. It feels like absolution.

Over Draven's shoulder, I meet Eodan's eyes.

The old mage merely nods, approval shining in his wizened gaze. "Well done, child. The truth shall set you free."

I offer him a tremulous but grateful smile.

After bidding farewell to Master Eodan, Draven leads me up a winding staircase to the castle ramparts. Snow flurries around us, the icy air nipping at my cheeks, but his hand at my back radiates warmth even through his glove.

We walk in pensive silence for a while, both absorbing the truths laid bare in Eodan's tower. I know much still lies unspoken between us, but the revelations shared today feel like a promising start.

Draven halts at an overlook spot, the mountains rising majestically around the castle. He gazes out at the snow-capped peaks, brow furrowed in thought.

"We don't have much time," he says at last. "The solstice ritual happens tomorrow night during the ball. Now that we understand its dark purpose, we may have a chance to stop it." He turns to me, silver eyes blazing with conviction. "With your knowledge and Eodan's guidance, do you think we can find a way to prevent the ritual from absorbing power from my people?"

I consider for a moment, weighing our limited options as the icy wind tugs at my braid. "Perhaps. I learned enough last time to know the foundations of the spellwork, but I will need access to the magic I have set in the ballroom and a way to disrupt the ritual at just the right moment." I chew my lip anxiously. "It will be difficult with so little time."

Draven nods, jaw set with determination. "We will find a way. I cannot allow my family to keep inflicting such atrocities." His expression softens as he brushes a wind-blown lock of hair from my cheek. "You give me hope that change is possible, Thorn."

My heart swells, warmed by his faith despite the daunting task ahead.

I cover his hand with my own. "Then let us prepare. We will face tomorrow together."

Draven's smile steels my resolve.

We climb higher along the parapets until Draven stops before a thick oaken door set into the stone. "Ready for your surprise?"

At my curious nod, he pushes open the door to reveal a cozy chamber nestled at the top of a corner turret, lit by flickering candles and warmed by a merry fire in the hearth. My eyes widen taking in the table set with gleaming dishes and elegant tapered candles. A bottle of wine chills in a silver bucket beside a vase of winter roses.

Draven helps me remove my fur-trimmed cloak. "I thought, after the exhausting day, we deserved a private repast away from prying eyes. Some time to simply... be." His voice drops low on those last words.

My pulse quickens as he guides me to the table, each touch sparking heat beneath my skin. I allow myself to relax into the intimacy of the scene. Tonight is just for us.

We dine on tender pheasant in cranberry sauce, buttery mashed potatoes with chives, crusty bread, and an array of tiny cakes for dessert. Everything is delicious, but it's Draven's company that truly nourishes me. The conversation flows easily, his humor and intellect sparking my own. For the first time in forever, I feel free to simply be myself.

As we finish dessert, soft flecks of snow dance past the arrow slit windows. I gaze out at the whirling flakes, comforted by the cocoon of warmth we've created within these old stone walls.

Behind me, Draven rises and adds another log to the hearth before refilling our wine glasses. "Come.

Let's enjoy the view," he murmurs, drawing me over to the windowsill piled high with plush embroidered cushions.

I sip my wine, leaning into Draven's sturdy frame as his arm encircles my waist. Together, we watch the winter storm unleash its beauty beyond the leaded glass. I've never felt so at peace.

After a time, Draven shifts beside me. "Do you trust me, Thorn?" His words ghost warm against my ear.

I turn to meet his gaze, finding yearning and promise lurking in those quicksilver depths. "Yes," I whisper.

It's true. Despite all that's happened, this vampire has proven himself worthy of my faith.

Joy lights up Draven's handsome face. He brushes back a raven curl that's escaped my braid, his touch trailing sparks across my skin. Ever so slowly, giving me time to pull away, he bends his head and presses his lips to mine in the softest kiss.

My eyes flutter shut as I return the kiss, savoring the tender pressure of his mouth moving with mine. No urgency or heat, just unspoken affection passing through this chaste contact.

When we finally draw apart, Draven grazes his knuckles down my cheek reverently. "You are so very precious to me, Thorn," he murmurs, silver eyes glowing warmly. "In you, I have found something I never dared hope for—a kindred spirit."

Emotion clogs my throat, tears pricking behind my eyes. After lifetimes of hiding, here at last is someone who truly sees me. Who values the real Thorn in all her complexities. I feel sort of silly for having avoided the fated mate connection for so long. So many things that could have simply been worked out if we had just talked. I've never been one to do things the easy way, though, now have I?

I frame Draven's face between my hands, pouring all that words cannot convey into another sweet, lingering kiss. For this one perfect night, the past and future fall away. There is only now, only this, only us.

The peaceful moment shatters at the sound of laughter floating up from the garden below. Curious, I lean over the stone balustrade to peer down at the source. To my astonishment, I recognize the golden head of Lord Anthony beside the chestnut curls of Princess Audrey. They stand pressed close together beneath a tree, heads bent in intimate conversation.

Draven joins me and smothers a laugh at the sight. "Well, well, it seems those two have been keeping secrets from me. They're a good match, though."

I glance at him in surprise as understanding dawns. "They appear quite... smitten with one another."

"Indeed, though it's hardly surprising. Audrey has been enamored with Anthony for years. I'm glad to see he finally returned her affections." Mischief glints in Draven's eyes. "Shall we have a little fun?"

Before I can ask what he means, Draven grins. With a flick of his arm so quick I hardly see the movement, he creates a gust of icy wind to swirl down from the ramparts into the garden below.

The brisk air disturbs a nearby bush, dislodging the blanket of fresh snow clinging to its branches. A sparkling cascade rains down over Anthony and Audrey, who laugh in delight as they twirl together amidst the shimmering flurry. Joy fills me seeing how clearly besotted they are.

Above, I shake my head at Draven, unable to hide my smile. "You are incorrigible."

Draven's expression grows serious again. "Yes, but their love cannot last. Not when Audrey is expected to make a political match. My father would never approve a turned vampire for his daughter." Regret tinges his voice.

My heart clenches, reminded anew of the petty prejudices that still persist, even here.

I slip my hand into Draven's, giving it a consoling squeeze. "Let them have this happiness however fleeting," I say softly. "We cannot know what changes tomorrow may bring."

Draven nods, eyes distant in thought. I sense him contemplating all the ways tradition shackles us needlessly but also how, with care, those chains might be broken, one link at a time.

Below, the lovers begin drifting back inside, bundled close beneath Anthony's cloak.

Draven draws me into the turret room and kicks the door shut against the cold. We settle together on the cushioned seat, my head tucked against his shoulder.

This time, it is I who initiate the kiss, seeking to rekindle the tenderness from before. Draven responds ardently, hands tangling in my hair as he claims my mouth. We take our time rediscovering one another, the rest of the world forgotten beyond these walls.

The king may be against us, but tonight, we are invincible. Tonight, we are us, and that is all that matters.

# 26

## THORN

I stir slowly, nestled in silken sheets that still hold traces of Draven's spicy masculine scent. Blinking awake, I find myself curled against his side, his arms wrapped securely around me. Memories from last night wash over me—the romantic dinner we shared, slowly opening our hearts to one another, eventually finding our way here, to his chambers, to share this bed.

Heat blooms in my cheeks even as a smile tugs at my lips. My lonely existence already feels a lifetime away. Being here, held in Draven's tender embrace, feels profoundly right in a way I've never known before.

I trail light fingertips across Draven's bare chest, tracing the contours of muscle and pale skin. He doesn't stir, dead to the world in slumber, dark hair

charmingly mussed. Contentment glows softly
within me. Fate may have drawn us together, but
this intimacy exists through choice alone.

After a few more stolen moments admiring my
new mate, I slip carefully from beneath the covers.
Draven mumbles in protest, reaching for me even
in dreams, but I gently disentangle myself. I should
dress and ready myself before the day's demands
intrude on this treasured interlude.

I press a feather-soft kiss to Draven's brow, retrieve a robe, and silently make my way back to my
own chamber across the hall. Inside, I find Luna
already awake, tail swishing in greeting.

*You're glowing this morning,* she remarks knowingly.

I quickly turn away to splash water on my flushed
face, hiding my smile. Trust Luna to notice everything, no matter how subtle. A gentle knock on the
door has me pulling the robe tighter around me. I
open it a crack to find Draven on the other side.

"My bed got cold without you in it."

My cheeks warmed. Am I blushing? Do I blush?
Apparently I now do.

"Get dressed. I have a surprise," he says with a twinkle in his eye.

"A surprise like last night?"

"Maybe not that good of a surprise. More like a family tradition. You are family now after all."

"All right," I acquiesce with a yawn, opening the door wider. "Give me a few minutes to dress, and I'll meet you downstairs."

Draven beams, darting forward to plant a swift kiss on my cheek. "Perfect! Don't keep me waiting too long."

With that, he practically bounces off down the corridor, leaving me staring after him in bewilderment. What has gotten into that vampire this morning?

Shaking my head, I shut the door and begin preparing for this early adventure.

As I wash my face and neatly braid my hair, I feel a smile creeping over my lips. Truthfully, Draven's excitement is endearing. This surprise of Draven's will provide a nice change of pace. It's been so long since I've had a family. This could be good, a chance to enjoy lighter moments together beyond the weight of the past or our tangled destinies. Something fun before whatever happens tonight. The prospect warms me as I dress in a simple forest green gown.

I turn to Luna with a smile, taking in her sleek coat and bright eyes. "Well, you're looking much better today."

She stretches leisurely, tail swishing. *I feel as good as new thanks to your healing powers,* Luna replies, hopping gracefully down from the cushions.

My heart is glad to see her fully recovered.

As I finish braiding my hair, Luna comes over to nuzzle my hand affectionately. *I'm happy to see you so at peace for once. This prince seems to have been good for you.*

I give a slow nod, thinking it over. "Yeah, Draven's got me rethinking how wary I've been about accepting anything from fate lately, but I'd be lying if I said I wasn't still worried about whatever this winter solstice ritual is going to bring tonight." I let out a heavy sigh, feeling the weight of all the unknowns pressing down. "We've got no idea what we're walking into with these solstice celebrations. Whatever it is, it can't be good."

Luna tilts her head thoughtfully. *I can keep watch around the castle as events unfold. My senses are keen, and I can blend into the shadows easily.* Her golden

eyes gleam knowingly. *And a familiar has more abilities than most realize when needs arise.*

I chew my lip, still worried but also relieved to have
Luna healed and able to assist. "Please be careful. It
would break me if something happened to you."

Luna snorts delicately. *Please, I'm no helpless kit. I've
more than a few tricks hidden beneath this fur.* She
gives me a vulpine grin. *Besides, now that you have
accepted our bond, my own powers have grown. I'll be
keeping a close eye on things. Don't you worry.*

I have to chuckle a little at Luna acting all smug.
Having a sly fox on watch does make me feel better
about facing the unknown tonight. For now, though,
I'm just gonna try and go with the flow and see where
this wild ride with Draven takes us next. Things are
always more interesting with him around, that's for
sure.

With a final scratch behind Luna's ears, I head
downstairs to find Draven. He waits for me at the
base of the grand staircase, silver eyes lighting up as I
approach.

"Ah, there you are," he greets me warmly, drawing
me close to place a swift kiss on my lips. "Ready for
our adventure?"

"As ready as I'll ever be for one of your escapades," I reply with a wry smile.

After taking my hand, Draven leads me through the bustling main halls then down a deserted servants' passage. Our footsteps echo off the cold stones.

"Where exactly are we going?" I ask, glancing around the unfamiliar gloomy corridor. This isn't an area I've ever explored, even in my past life here.

"Somewhere I spent much time as a boy, back when I sought to escape my rigid lessons," Draven says over his shoulder.

I raise my brows curiously. "Should I be concerned you're leading me to some secret dungeon?"

Draven chuckles, the rich sound bouncing around us. "Would you like that? Are you hoping for a dungeon? No, nothing so nefarious. Just a quiet place for us to gather today."

As we meander through the dim corridors, we eventually reach a small wooden door hidden away in the shadows. Draven's hand pushes it open, revealing a cozy kitchen that has been untouched and left to gather dust. The buckets of dirty water tell me that it has been cleaned only today for this particular purpose. The large stone hearth and neatly arranged shelves of cookware give the room a sense of warmth and comfort.

Draven gestures me inside. "Welcome to the old servant's kitchens. As children, my siblings and I would sneak down here to pilfer treats."

As he speaks, I notice figures already waiting for us by the long prep table. Queen Vespera looks up from rolling out dough, her face lighting in a smile. Princess Audrey and Lord Anthony are bickering playfully over a bowl of sugar as they measure ingredients. Kira's bouncing on the balls of her feet sneaking sugar.

"You're just in time. We're about to mix up some cookie dough," Audrey declares cheerily.

I glance between them, touched they've welcomed me into this private family tradition. "Cookie baking was your mysterious surprise activity?"

"Well, you are one of us now, are you not?" Vespera replies gently. "We thought you should help prepare the solstice treats, as is custom."

Warmth blooms in my chest at her words. After lifetimes alone, to be so readily accepted means everything.

Draven grins and presses a quick kiss to my hair before putting on an apron.

Soon, we're all busy creaming butter, whisking eggs, and mixing batter the color of sunsets. Laughter and banter fills the cozy kitchen as we work side by side.

Draven keeps sneaking nibbles of cookie dough when he thinks I'm not looking. I retaliate by flicking flour across his nose, making him sputter in surprise. Even Vespera hides her smile behind one elegant hand at our antics.

Princess Kira giggles as she watches us, her doe eyes lighting up with delight. Though the youngest, she joins in preparing the dough with enthusiasm, scattering flour across the tabletop.

As we bake, the looming solstice rituals fade from thought. Here there are no divisions between natural born vampires and those turned. No expectations weigh upon me as Prince Draven's fated mate. We are simply family, finding joy in shared laughter and sweets.

While we wait for the first batch to bake, I study those gathered around me. Vespera moves with refined grace even while scooping dough onto trays, every motion elegant. Audrey's eyes keep straying to Anthony, who steals glances of his own when her

head is turned. An unspoken affection glows between them, binding two souls despite their differ-
ences.

My own gaze finds Draven. He's leaning casually
near the ovens. Our eyes meet across the room, and
an invisible thread seems to connect us. Though
I'm unsure where fate will lead us, I'm deeply grateful for the joy this bond has brought me.

The warm scents of baking cookies fill the
kitchen. We sample the results eagerly, mouths full
of molten chocolate and bursts of cinnamon. Kira
laughs in delight with each new treat, leaving a
smudge of icing on her nose that makes Draven
chuckle and wipe it away fondly.

As we finish our baking, talk turns to reminiscing about past Winter Festivals. I listen with joy as
Draven recounts lively tales of him and his siblings
sneaking down here for midnight feasts or stealing
whole trays of tarts upstairs. His eyes dance with
nostalgia and mischief.

"One year, young Draven somehow rigged a trap
above the kitchen door to shower me in flour when
I walked through," Vespera adds wryly. "I was finding the stuff in my hair for days."

We all laugh at the image while Draven ducks his head with an impish grin. "You must admit I was quite inventive," he says cheekily.

The queen just shakes her head in amusement.

I find myself blending into the reminiscing, sharing my own stories of Winter Fests long ago, back when my world was whole. The bittersweet memories bring smiles tinged with sorrow but also hope that I may find similar joy again now.

Too soon, the grandfather clock signals mid-morning. We begin tidying up, the lightness of our shared moments drifting away like flour dusted across the worn wood floors. The memories glow within me, kindling hope. For a few precious hours, I felt part of something beyond myself, beyond my solitude. Whatever comes tonight, I will hold onto that.

Vespera sighs as she unties her apron. "I'm afraid duty calls, but thank you all for this lovely interlude." She touches my shoulder lightly. "I hope you know you are welcome here, Thorn."

"Thank you," I reply thickly. I curtsy respectfully as she takes her leave, queen once more despite her casual garb.

Audrey glances at the clock and gasps. "Oh, my, is it really almost noon already? I must start preparing for the ball!" She gathers an armload of freshly baked cookies and sweets. "The handmaidens will need at least four hours just to style my hair, and don't get me started on picking the perfect gown!"

I smile in amusement at her dramatic flair as she sweeps toward the door in a flutter of skirts.

Anthony sketches us an elaborate bow. "Well, I suppose I should go make myself presentable as well. Can't have the princess showing me up in front of all the nobility." He winks.

Audrey tosses her head imperiously, though her eyes sparkle with laughter. "As if you could ever match my sense of style, Anthony."

"You wound me, my lady!" Anthony presses a hand to his heart in mock affront.

Audrey's laughter echoes down the passage as she departs, Anthony following with a grin and a wave.

Draven draws me close, his arms encircling my waist. "Did you enjoy yourself?"

"Very much so. I almost wish this day would never end." I nestle into his embrace, wanting to cling to these beautiful moments a little longer before the coming night.

Draven's expression grows serious. "Whatever this ritual holds, remember you are not alone to face it." He tips my chin up, gazing intently into my eyes until I nod.

Together, we gather up the rest of the cookie trays. As we make our way back upstairs, I feel hopeful. With Draven beside me and a newfound family at my back, I am ready for what is to come.

***

The grand doors of the ballroom feel like a portal to another world, a world where I'm not just Thorn with dirt under my fingernails and a knack for talking to plants. Here, in this sea of twirling silk and whispered secrets, I'm a lady—or, at least, pretending to be one.

"Deep breaths," I mutter to myself, stepping over the threshold.

The green and black velvet of my dress hugs every curve, making me acutely aware of how out of place I am. Draven's necklace presses cool and reassuringly against my collarbone, its emerald heart pulsing with a warmth that must be magic. Or maybe it's just my pounding heart reflecting back at me.

I can do this. I'm just in a room full of vampires who, the last time I saw them, wanted to kill me. What's the worst that could happen?

*Don't answer that, brain.*

The ballroom is a stunning display of opulence and wealth, decorated in deep crimson and gold for the winter solstice festival. Candles flicker on every surface, casting a warm glow over the room. The vampire nobles are dressed in extravagant gowns and suits, their pale skin contrasting with the rich colors of the room. The king and queen sit on their thrones, regal and imposing, while Kira sits with her friends at a table adorned with silver and crystal. Audrey is already on the dance floor with a noble I don't recognize while Anthony watches with a scowl from the side of the ballroom. How those two haven't been discovered as a couple by the rest of the court, I will never know.

I breathe deep in an attempt to calm my nerves. The air is heavy with the scent of burning candles, fragrant pine from the decorations, and the subtle hint of blood that lingers on the vampires. The rich aroma of spices and roasted meats wafts from the buffet table, making mouths water in anticipation.

As I scan the crowd, little flickers of memory dance at the edges of my consciousness. Me, standing in front of an angry mob, their accusations stinging like hornet bites. Traitor, they hissed, and the word clung to my skin, a label I couldn't shake off.

My feet freeze on the polished floor, and I can almost feel the bite of cold iron manacles on my wrists again.

"Get a grip, Thorn," I tell myself through gritted teeth, forcing my legs to move.

The past is a ghost that loves to haunt at the most inconvenient times, but I won't let it ruin tonight. Tonight, I'm with Draven, and we're going to dance until these memories are nothing but dust. Well, at least until the ritual is started. I wish I had more time to figure out what exactly that ritual looks like. I feel so unprepared.

"Remember who you are," I whisper, my own reflection in the mirror-like sheen of the ballroom floor giving me a determined nod.

*That's right, Thorn. You're a survivor, a fighter, and you clean up pretty nice in velvet too.*

"Easy for you to say," I mutter under my breath, casting a glare at the chandelier above as if it's personally responsible for my racing pulse.

The crystal lights flicker and dance mockingly, refracting light as if they're in on a secret joke.

"Focus," I command myself, clenching my hands into fists then releasing them, trying to let go of the tension knotted within. Draven gave me this necklace, this dress, a symbol of his trust and belief in me. I can't dishonor that with my own doubts.

I take a step forward, another, feeling the swish of velvet against my legs. I'm doing this. I'm moving through a ballroom full of potential enemies with my head held high because that's what Thorn does. She doesn't cower. She struts, even if it's just a well-rehearsed act.

Tonight is about new memories. My resolve hardens like the crust of a well-baked loaf. Memories of betrayal and fear might bubble up like an overzealous potion, but I'll keep them at bay with a spoonful of defiance and a dash of sheer stubbornness.

"Plus, I've got killer dance moves," I add with a smirk, even though no one's close enough to hear.

"Let's see you try to frown when I'm twirling across the dance floor."

The past can lurk in the shadows all it wants, but I won't let it take the lead tonight. Not when I have a chance to waltz with destiny—and with Draven.

"Thorn, love, are you all right?" Draven's voice cuts through the whirl of the ballroom like a knife, smooth but impossible to ignore.

Turning on my heels, I flash him my best "everything is peachy" grin. "Me? Pfft, I'm fine. Just taking in the... splendor of it all." My hands do a little twirl to encompass the grandeur of the room, hoping it distracts from the panic I can feel nipping at my insides like an annoying fairy with a point to prove.

He steps closer, his gaze searching mine. It's unsettling how he can read me so well. The whole fated mate thing really cranks up the dial on the intuition radio.

"You don't have to pretend, not with me," he says softly, his hand reaching out to trace the line of the necklace, the one that seems to pulse with reassurance against my skin.

"Draven, honestly, I'm—" I start, but the words fade as his fingers brush mine. He's trying to be my rock, my anchor in this sea of high society sharks, and damned if I don't want to cling to him like the last life vest on a sinking ship.

"Come on," he says, offering his arm with that lopsided smile that spells trouble and thrills in equal measure. "Let's dance."

The music swells around us—a cue straight out of a play—as we step onto the dance floor. His hand finds my waist, and I rest mine on his shoulder, our other hands clasping together. As we begin to move, something just clicks. Our bodies seem to sync up effortlessly, like two parts of the same spell coming together to create magic.

"Look at us," I whisper, a laugh bubbling up. "Who knew becoming official would suddenly make us fantastic dancers?"

"To be fair, it's always been one of my skills, but it's never been like this. It's much more natural dancing with you."

The world narrows down to just him and me, spinning through space as if the ground beneath us has transformed into clouds, but even with the intoxicating rush of dancing with Draven, I can't fully let go.

My eyes dart past the twirling gowns and sharp suits, over to where the king and crowned prince hold court. They're the picture of royal poise, but something about the set of the king's jaw and the way his eyes track the room sends a shiver down my spine.

"Notice anything off with Tall, Dark, and Regal over there?" I murmur, tilting my head ever so slightly toward the throne.

Draven's gaze follows mine as we continue our dance, moving with a grace that belies our vigilance. "They're on edge. More than usual," he says, his voice a low growl only I can hear. "Something's brewing."

"Fantastic," I mutter. "Just tells me that we are right. It's happening tonight."

We share a look, one that says we're in this together, come hell or high water. As much as I would rather face a mountain troll bare-handed than deal with royal vampire intrigue, I know there's no one else I would rather have by my side than Draven.

Because when push comes to shove, if there's a battle to be fought or a mystery to unravel, there's no denying it. We make one hell of a team.

The rhythm of the music still pulses through me, a siren's call to lose myself in the endless sea of twirls and dips, but as Draven's strong hands steady me from yet another spin, a whisper in my mind halts any thought of further revelry.

*Thorn.* Luna's voice echoes within the confines of my skull, her mental touch as light as a moth's wing against a lantern. *The crowned prince is making a rather sneaky exit stage left.*

I blink, subtly craning my neck to see past a flock of feathered headpieces crowning the heads of nobility. Sure enough, there is a ripple in the crowd, vampires parting ways for royalty on the move.

*Interesting,* I muse silently back to Luna, feeling the corners of my mouth twitch with curiosity. *Time to play shadow.*

*Be careful,* she warns, a mother hen even in telepathic form. I chuckle at calling my fox familiar a hen.

*Always am,* I shoot back, though we both know that is a stretch of the truth.

"Where are you going?" Draven's voice pulls me back, a thread of concern lacing his words.

"Need some air," I lie smoothly, detaching myself from his embrace with practiced ease.

While I know we are in this together, I don't want to require him to face down his own family. It would break me for him to have to fight or possibly kill his own father and brother, but they have to be stopped.

With a phantom kiss pressed to his cheek, I slip away, melting into the throng of bodies. My feet carry me with silent purpose, skirting the edge of the ballroom.

But as fate would have it—or just my rotten luck—a hand clamps down on my shoulder, spinning me with an unexpected force. The world comes to a screeching halt as I find myself staring into a pair of eyes that recognize me not as Thorn but as someone I once was.

"Vivian?" the voice drips with incredulous surprise, the name hitting me like a bucket of ice water.

"Ah," I stammer, my heart pulling a drum solo against my ribs. "You must be mistaken."

"Your resemblance is uncanny," they insist, peering at me with an intensity that feels like tweezers trying to pluck out my secrets.

"Coincidence, I assure you," I reply, the words tumbling out in a tumbleweed of nerves.

But inside, panic claws at my chest. Vivian is a ghost meant to stay buried, and if this specter of the past doesn't take the hint, things will go sour fast.

"Sorry, but I really must catch my breath," I say, offering a smile that I hope looks more genuine than it feels. "Excuse me."

"Could it be that you're related? You just look so much like her," the inquisitor presses, leaning in too close for comfort. Their eyes are eager, almost hungry, and a shiver runs down my spine that had nothing to do with the ballroom's chill.

I laugh, but it sounds like a crow cawing—an omen of bad luck. "In another life, perhaps," I quip, side-stepping their probing gaze.

My mind is already sprinting through lies as slippery as eels. If they dig deeper, I'll have to spin a tapestry of half-truths tight enough to snare them in confusion.

"Your features, though..." they murmur, relentless as a hound on a scent.

"Common stock. You'll find them in any village," I reply with a shrug that I hope conveys nonchalance rather than the screaming alarm bells inside me.

"Perhaps," they concede, but their suspicion hangs between us, a noose waiting to tighten.

It is then that chaos erupts like a potion gone wrong. The king's voice booms across the grandeur of the ballroom, each syllable a thunderclap of doom. "Bring her here!"

I look around the room to see who the king could be demanding and find to my horror that his finger is pointing directly at me.

I don't even have time to curse before vampires encircle me, their eyes glinting with malice—and is that excitement? In another life, I might have found it flattering to command such attention. Now, it is about as welcome as a swarm of bees at a picnic.

"Great," I mutter under my breath, taking a discreet step back as my fingers twitch toward the hidden dagger strapped to my thigh. "Party's over, Thorn."

The vampires close in, their gazes cold and calculating. I tense, ready to fight, but a firm hand grips my elbow.

"No need for trouble, my dear," the vampire from earlier says. "His Majesty simply requests an audience."

I doubt that highly but allow him to steer me through the parted crowd toward the throne. All around, whisperings break out like hissing fires.

"Vivian," the king purrs as we approach, his tone deceptively warm. "What a delightful surprise."

His calculating eyes say otherwise. They rake over me, searching for cracks in my disguise.

"The pleasure is mine, Your Majesty," I reply, dipping into a curtsy, "although I'm afraid you have me confused with someone else. My name is—"

"Do not play coy with me, witch," he snap, cold fury blazing through the glamour. "I know precisely who you are. I was suspicious when my son brought you back. How you dug your claws into him, I will never know, but it's so good to see you alive."

Before I can react, he makes a sharp motion with his fingers. My illusion peels away in wisps of glowing magic, leaving me exposed. Gasps echo around us. The king's smile holds all the warmth of a dagger's edge.

"Vivian," he purrs again, savoring my true name. "Did you really think I wouldn't recognize a traitor in my own court?"

My heart stutter. I glance desperately for Draven but find only enemies. Their hungry eyes tell me my fate has already been decided.

I take a deep breath to steady my nerves. "Your Majesty is mistaken. My name is Thorn, not Vivian."

The king's eyes narrows. "Do not play games with me, witch. I know exactly who you are and why you have returned." His voice drips with contempt.

"I speak the truth," I insist. "Vivian was a name I once went by, before I was forced to flee this court under false accusations."

Murmurs ripple through the crowd.

The king raises a hand to silence them. "False accusations, you say? You were caught red-handed stealing forbidden texts from the royal library, texts containing powerful blood magic, which you intended to use against me."

"That's not true!" I cry. "I discovered a plot—your plot—to slaughter innocents in a bid to expand your power. I had to run for my life when you marked me as a traitor for uncovering your deceit."

Gasps echo around the hall.

The king's face contorts in rage. "Lies! I would never harm my people. Do not listen to this witch's poisonous words. She is clearly mad and deludes herself with fantasies."

I shake my head sadly. "I speak only the truth. The people deserve to know how you've betrayed them."

The king rises from his throne, magic crackling around him. "Enough! I will hear no more of these outrageous fabrications. Guards, seize her!"

As vampires close in, I prepare to make my stand, praying Draven will fight by my side. The battle for the truth has only just begun.

"Touch her and you die!" comes Draven's sharp command from somewhere behind me.

His presence is a torch in the dark, the silent promise that I'm not alone in this twisted dance, but I can't focus on that. Not now.

"Sorry, boys," I say with a grin that feels more like a snarl, "but I don't do well with cages."

The first vampire lunges, more shadow than substance, but I'm ready. Instinct and adrenaline are a potent brew, fueling my defiance. I pivot, ducking low as the room becomes a blur of motion.

"Guess it's time to fight fire with fire," I whisper to myself, summoning the magic that simmers in my veins, feeling it coil like a spring—or a serpent—waiting to strike.

I feel their hesitation, the vampires recoiling as if Draven's words are tangible things, strikes against their undead flesh, but I know it wouldn't be enough, not with the king's command ringing in their ears like a twisted benediction.

*Psst, Luna, you there?* I call out silently, casting my thoughts toward my familiar, hidden somewhere among the shadows. *Kinda could use an escape plan right about now.*

Her reply is instant, a cool thread weaving through the hot tangle of my thoughts. *East balcony. Hidden passage behind the tapestry. Move quickly, Thorn. The crowned prince is up to something and is on his way back. You can have a better vantage point from there.*

*East balcony,* I repeat mentally, plotting my next move as I feign a stumble, using the momentary distraction to slip through the ring of encircling vampires.

*Right. Because nothing says "cozy" like darting through cobwebbed secret corridors during a royal smackdown.*

"Stay back!" Draven warns again, his tone dripping with the kind of menace that would make lesser creatures flee. There is a reason he is feared, respected—a predator cloaked in prince's finery. And he is all mine. Talk about relationship goals.

*Thorn, now!* Luna's urgent whisper echoes in my mind.

Not one to ignore sound advice—or the chance to avoid being vampire chow—I make a break for it, skirts whipping around my legs as I dart toward the balcony. The ballroom blurs past in a swirl of color and sound, my pulse pounding a staccato beat in my ears.

"Sorry, gotta dash. Wouldn't want to ruin your fun," I toss over my shoulder with a smirk, though it is mostly for show.

My skin prickles with awareness, the sensation of being hunted prickling along my spine. I've been playing this game long before tonight, and I'm not about to get caught now.

"Over my dead body," Draven growls from behind me, a vow wrapped in shadow and steel.

*Let's not add that to the evening's entertainment, okay?* I try to think at him, hoping he catches the edge of desperation in my silent plea.

*Focus, Thorn,* I chide myself. *You have a date with a dusty old tapestry to regroup and fight back.*

With that, I leap onto the balcony, my fingers finding the edges of woven history and pushing them aside to reveal salvation—a narrow passage just waiting for a damsel in distress to make her less-than-graceful exit.

A group of vampires rushes me, attempting to climb up onto the balcony after me.

"Big mistake," I mutter under my breath, feeling the energy pulse and swell within me.

With a defiant cry, I unleash it, sending a wave of force that knocks the vampires back. They stumble, surprise etched on their pale faces, and I don't waste a second. I dart forward, slipping through their loosened grasp like water through fingers.

"Nice try, boys," I taunt, my sarcasm a thin veil over the fear that claws at my insides.

"Thorn!" Draven call out, his gaze tracking my every move with fierce intensity.

"Keep your crown on. I'm not leaving you," I shoot back even as my heart hammers against my ribs.

Just then, the grand doors swings open with a resounding thud, and in strides the crowned prince, his presence commanding the room's attention. His hands are adorned with a pair of crowns that glint ominously under the chandelier's light. He joins the king at the dais, and together, they begin to chant words that make my blood run cold.

"Son of a vamp," I whisper, the realization hitting me like a thunderbolt.

The ritual. They are going to do it now while everyone is focused on me. This is part of the plan. No one will see what they are doing before it is too late. The king always knew who I was. Or did he?

As the chanting fills the air, an echo of ancient magic, memories surge within me, pieces of arcane knowledge slotting into place.

"Looks like story time is over," I say to myself, steeling my nerve. This is bigger than any secret or fear I harbored. I must stop whatever madness is about to unfold.

"Thorn, what are you—" Draven starts, but I wave him off.

"Trust me. I've got a history with dusty old books, and they're about to pay off," I reply, my focus narrowing on the prince and king.

The chants grow louder, the vibrations of power threading through the air, wrapping around us in an unseen snare, but I'm not about to let the past repeat itself—not here, not now. With everything at stake, I square my shoulders and prepare to rewrite our fates.

"I'm done letting someone else write my story," I declare, my voice cutting through the cacophony of chants and murmurs that fill the opulent throne room.

The truth is a burning starburst within me, demanding release. It is time for Thorn, the unassuming half witch, half vampire with more secrets than a grave keeper, to step into the light. Time to take revenge for everyone and everything I've lost to this corrupted royal line.

"Who are you?" someone hisses from the crowd, their suspicion a tangible thing wrapping around my throat.

I recite the prophecy that was the entire reason my family was killed:

"Born of two worlds, blood and magic entwined,

This child of darkness shall see the throne declined.

For when day bleeds into endless night,

Her power shall end the tyrant's might."

My words echo, defiant and bold, reverberating against stone walls adorned with ancient tapestries. Power surges through my veins as though it is liquid fire. I pull at the magic within me, feeling it respond like a loyal beast awakening from slumber.

Shock ripple through the assembly like a wave.

The words tumble from my lips, ancient and commanding, as I continue the chant that will activate the spell I secretly embedded throughout this cursed hall. Snow bursts through the arched windows in swirling gusts, carried on an unnatural wind that howls like a wolf baying at the moon. Symbols etched into the floor and walls begin to glow an eerie emerald, casting the room in an otherworldly light.

My words begin to drown out the king and crown prince's own chanting as my power overwhelms theirs.

The magic ignites within me, coursing through my veins, and I raise several feet in the air as power radiates from my body in shimmering waves. My hair whips about me as if alive, tendrils of inky black with strands of silver sparking like lightning. Below, vampires stalk toward me, their eyes feral. One leaps upward, claws extended, only to be blasted back by a bolt of energy from my fingertips.

Luna is below me in an instant, her fangs bared, swiping at any who dare approach. A fierce snarl rips from her throat. *Touch my Thorn, and you shall not live to regret it!*

On the floor below, Draven roars, felling vampires left and right in a desperate bid to protect me. Our bond hums between us, his determination fueling my own. I've never been stronger. None of us have.

The chant pours from my lips, guttural words in a language not heard for a millennium. The markings flare brighter, the windows rattling in their frames. This is the moment I prepared for. The king thought he defeated me, but he only unleashed my true power. Now, we will see how prophecy spoke truth.

As the final syllable leaves my lips, the very stones of the throne room shudder. The prince and king stare at me, their smirks fading into terror as they sense the shifting tides of power.

# 27

## DRAVEN

The air in the grand ballroom is electric, buzzing with an energy that prickles at my skin and sets my senses on edge beyond anything I have ever experienced before. I can hear the softest whisper of fabric against the marble floor, the quietest intake of breath from the assembled crowd, and above all, the rhythmic cadence of Thorn's chant as she floats ethereally on the balcony. In the chaos around me, I shouldn't be able to pinpoint each sound, but somehow, I can. My eyes remain locked on Thorn, her silhouette backlit by the moonlight that spills through the grand arched windows.

The marks, those intricate symbols glowing from the stone walls, begin to pulse with an otherworldly glow. It is like watching the heartbeat of the castle itself, each throb of light sending a wave of power that reverberates through the room. The colors shift, dancing between shades of silver and a luminescent blue that mirror the night sky just beyond our reach.

"Show off," I whisper under my breath, reluctantly admiring Thorn's display of raw magic.

The marks grow brighter still, their luminance painting the faces of the onlookers with awe and not a small amount of fear. The symbols seem to twist and turn, alive with the force of Thorn's incantations.

As the chanting reaches a crescendo, the entire room is bathed in the radiant glow of the marks, casting long, wavering shadows behind the columns of nobles and courtiers clutching their finery. You can almost taste the magic in the air, thick and heady like the scent of a storm on the wind.

Thorn commands the mystical energies swirling around us. The light from the marks etch every line of concentration on her face, every determined crease, illuminating her as the true focal point of this supernatural maelstrom we find ourselves caught in.

A vampire lunges with fangs bared, a blur of dark fabric and pale skin. I pivot on my heel, my nails elongating into claws. They meet flesh in a whispering sigh as the vampire staggers back, its hiss fading into a gurgle. I grunt, eyes flicking back up to where Thorn is suspended in midair, her silhouette framed against the luminous glyphs that dance like fireflies on a summer's eve.

"Stay close," I murmur, more to myself than to Luna, who has already materialized at my side, her fur glowing ethereal in the ballroom's enchanted light. She doesn't need the reminder. She is as intent on protecting Thorn as I am. Her sharp teeth gleam, a silent promise to any who dare threaten her charge.

*Right behind you,* comes Luna's telepathic response, cutting through the chaos like a knife through butter.

I am shocked. The occasional awkward silence while they watched each other made me assume Luna and Thorn communicate telepathically, but never before has Luna spoken to me. Can I now because of the fated mate connection, or did Luna just never deem me worthy? Either way, clever girl. Never one to miss a beat.

My gaze never wavers from Thorn, even as I parry another attack. The connection between us is a pulsating chord of energy, taut with the strain of battle yet unbreakable in its resolve. She is the reason my heart beat, the drum to which I march, and if anything happens to her...

"Over my dead body," I growl, spinning to catch another bloodsucker off guard.

Luna is a white streak of fury, darting between legs and snapping at any who ventures too close to our corner of the room.

I taunt another assailant, knocking him off balance with a well-placed kick. My father's loyal vampires are relentless, but so are we. Every time one gets too close, Luna will harry it, giving me the opening I need to strike. We are poetry in motion, a symphony of snarls and slashes set against the backdrop of Thorn's incantations.

"Keep it up, Luna," I say, breathless with exertion but buoyed by the adrenaline surging through my veins. "We're the wall between them and her."

*Always,* she shoots back mentally, her voice as fierce as the fires of magic that Thorn wields above us.

With every enemy that falls, with every protective circle we draw around our witch, I can feel the weight of destiny pressing down upon us. This is our moment, the crucible that will forge our future, and nothing, no power-hungry vampire or twisted crown, will tear that away from us.

"Thorn," I whisper, a silent prayer that she'll stay safe, that she'll remain untouched by the darkness clawing at our heels. Because if fate bound us together, then I'll be damned before I let anything sever that bond.

"Audrey, stay close!" Anthony's voice cuts through the cacophony of battle.

For a moment, my gaze turns to find him as he positions himself between my sister and a snarling vampire with ambitions far above its station. The two fight off swarms of vampires as they make their way toward Luna and myself.

"Like I have a choice," Audrey quips even as her eyes darts around the room, seeking escape. The space has shrunk to a cage of fangs and fury, walls closing in as the vampires circle like sharks scenting blood.

"Charming time for humor," Anthony shoots back, his sword flashing silver arcs in the dim light as he parries a blow meant for Audrey's heart. He is grace under pressure, a dancer whose stage is the battlefield, each step a calculated risk to keep them both breathing.

"Can't help it," she retorts, fingers twitching at her side where her own weapon rests unused—for now. "Humor is my shield, remember?"

"Then let's hope it's as strong as mine," he mutters, another swipe of his blade sending an opponent staggering backward.

His movements are precise, efficient, but even I can see the fatigue setting in. They're outnumbered, and each passing second sees their odds dwindling.

My gaze flickers upward as a sudden, intense glow catches my attention. The king's crown, perched atop that regal head, pulses with an ominous red light that seems to drink in the chaos below it. The air grows thick with magic and malice, the atmosphere charged with foreboding.

"Uh oh," I breath out, a knot forming in my stomach. "That can't be good."

*Understatement of the century,* Luna's telepathic voice buzzes in my head, laced with concern. Even without looking, I know her fur is bristling, her senses on high alert.

"We need to end this. Now!" Audrey shouts over the crowd as they step beside us.

"Working on it." Anthony grunts as he takes down another vampire, yet for all his skill, for every vampire that falls, another rises to take its place, as if the very shadows conspire against them.

"Any bright ideas?" Audrey calls, ducking under a clawed hand that seeks to claim her.

"Survive," I answer grimly, locking eyes with my sister. "We survive, and we protect Thorn. That's the only plan that matters."

"Right there with you," Audrey confirms, her gaze flitting to the crown above and back to Anthony. A silent understanding passes between them, one of warriors linked by something deeper than blood or battle. It is the acknowledgment of a threat beyond their comprehension, one that will test the bonds of fate itself.

The crimson glow from my father's and brother's crowns casts a sickly hue across the ballroom, and an eerie stillness descends like death's own cloak. I watch, my heart hammering against my ribs, as vampires around us freeze mid-stride, their eyes glazing over with that same sinister red.

"Draven," Anthony rasps beside me, his voice brittle with sudden age. "What sorcery is this?"

I turn to him, and my blood runs cold. Wrinkles etch deep into his once-youthful face, his hair graying at the temples. The life seems to be draining out of him, aging him before my very eyes. A red thread, thin as spider silk but vivid against the chaos, links him—and all the others—straight to the king and the crowned prince. Compulsion. A puppeteer's strings pulling taut.

"Damn it," I spit, feeling an icy dread settle in my stomach. This is serious, a darker turn than any of us anticipated.

Thorn floats above the balcony like some avenging angel, her eyes blazing with an inner light. Her lips part, and though she whispers, the word cascades through the chaos with the force of a storm's calm eye.

"No."

It is soft, barely a breath, but it slams into the room with the weight of mountains. The white magic, which has been relentlessly striking the king and crowned prince, falters at her command, the glowing arrows freezing mid-air before dissipating like mist at dawn. The marks on the walls cease their furious glow, settling into a gentle pulse that matches the rhythm of my still-racing heart.

"By the stars," I murmur, my gaze never leaving Thorn as she takes control of the room without uttering another sound.

The air stills, and then, as if conjured by her will alone, the white magic coalesces above us, swirling into two formidable spheres that hum with power. Thorn's arms rise, and with a fierce grace, she directs the orbs toward my brother and father. They hurtle across the room, streaking like comet tails, and strike true.

The balls of magic collide with their targets.

With a sound like cracking ice, the crowns atop the heads of the king and crowned prince are knocked askew, fissures racing along their once-immaculate surfaces. The metal twists, the jewels dulled, and as they clatter to the stone floor, the oppressive aura that blanketed the room lifts just enough for a collective, shuddering breath.

Thorn floats down beside me, her descent as graceful as a feather caught in a gentle breeze. She looks every bit the savior they didn't know they needed, and my chest swells with an odd mix of pride and protectiveness.

"Draven," she says, her hand finding mine, grounding me, "we need to decide what to do with them." Her chin tilts toward the king and crowned prince, who are slowly regaining their bearings, looking more vulnerable than I've ever seen.

"Right." The word comes out sharper than I intend. I take a deep breath, tasting the new freedom in the air. "I've got a proposition for you."

"Propose away," she says, the corner of her mouth twitching.

"Let's not kill them. My youngest sister and mother, it would break them," I plead. "Imprison them below. Strip them of their titles and power. It'll be a living lesson for anyone else who gets big ideas about controlling the masses."

"Mercy from a vampire," she muses, her gaze searching mine. "That's not the usual narrative."

"Hey, I'm all about breaking stereotypes," I quip, but my heart hammers against my ribs, waiting for her verdict.

She studies the fallen royals, their faces etched with uncertainty. "For you," she begins, "and for the sake of your mother and sisters, I'll agree to leniency, but, Draven, they can't go unpunished."

"Understood." I nod, feeling a rush of gratitude. "Thank you, Thorn."

"Let's hope this is the right call." Her fingers tighten around mine, a silent promise linking us together.

"Either way," I say with a lopsided grin, "we'll face the consequences together."

Somehow, standing there with Thorn, the half witch who stormed into my life and turned it inside out, I know we'll handle whatever comes our way.

Thorn's fingers weave through the air, spinning invisible threads that bind the fallen royals' hands behind their backs. The glyphs on her arms shimmer with a gentle luminescence, reflecting her newfound resolve.

"All right, your highnesses," she says with a commanding yet calm tone, "let's take a walk to your new quarters."

As we escort the once-mighty king and his heir, my father and brother, toward the castle's depths, I can't help but admire her—Thorn, the witch who defied every odd and now chooses mercy over vengeance.

# 28

## DRAVEN

The incessant babble of the war room buzzes like a hive of disgruntled bees, each council member more agitated than the last. I lean against the cool stone wall, the tension in the air prickling against my skin as if it knows something I don't.

"Execution," Councilor Vargas spits, his hawk-like gaze flitting over the assembly. "Let the traitors feel the kiss of silver. It's the only language these dogs understand." His words are met with solemn nods from some corners, while others exchange uneasy glances.

"Exile," Lady Marcelline counters, her smooth-as-silk voice laced with an edge that can slice through bone. "Banish them beyond the kingdom's borders. Let their immortal lives be a slow torment in solitude." Her proposal hangs in the air, a thinly veiled compromise between mercy and cruelty.

"Rehabilitation," Elder Jasper ventures, stroking his white beard thoughtfully. "We must seek to heal, not just punish. Let us guide them back to the light. Let Draven take the throne in their absence while they are given a chance to change." His optimistic tone seems almost naive amidst the sea of hardened faces.

"Draven." Thorn's voice floats toward me, a whisper meant for my ears alone.

I nod subtly, feeling her hand squeeze mine beneath the table. Her touch is a reminder of our shared dream, a life far from the suffocating walls of the castle.

"Enough!" I finally burst out, my voice slicing through the barrage of arguments.

A hush falls over the room, all eyes on me. Even my mother, the queen, arches an eyebrow in surprise.

"Look, I get it," I say, trying to sound more confident than I felt, "everyone's got their knickers in a twist over this mess, but let's not forget that we're talking about people here, not just pawns on a chessboard."

I shoot a brief glance at Thorn, her steady gaze bolstering my resolve.

"Remember that they are still a loved father, husband and brother," I continue, threading my fingers through hers while casting a quick glance at my mother. "They are safe in the dungeons below. All of you should be well aware of the things we have in place to stop any escape attempts. Many of them devices of your own creation. And frankly..." I smirked, despite the gravity of the situation. "I'd rather spend my days enjoying her company than sitting on some dusty throne, playing judge and jury to every squabble that breaks out."

Murmurs ripple through the council members as they digest my words. Some look shocked, others contemplative, but all seem to recognize the sincerity in my voice.

"Life's too short for endless power plays," I quip, hoping my humor will ease the tension, "especially when there's magic to explore, love to cherish, and, let's be honest, better food to eat outside these walls. My father and brother will stay where they are."

Thorn squeezes my hand, her silent laughter shining in her eyes. We are both ready to forge a path of our own, away from the lure of the throne and closer to the simple enchantment of our cozy life.

Gathering the last shreds of my courage, I square my shoulders and clear my throat. The room falls silent, all eyes on me—Draven, the reluctant heir with a penchant for dramatic pauses.

"Listen up," I say, the words tumbling out in a rush, "we've been going about this all wrong—two sides at each other's throats when we should be holding hands or whatever." A snicker escapes me, but I am quick to smother it with a cough. "What I mean is, we need unity, not another round of 'who hates whom' more."

A few nods, some skeptical looks. Typical.

I plow on, "I propose Anthony and Audrey as our next king and queen."

I let that hang in the air, watching as brows furrowed and whispers take flight like startled bats in the night.

"Think about it," I urge, feeling Thorn's presence like a warm ember at my back. "A pureblood vampire and a turned vampire ruling side by side, it's like... like a fairytale ending without the cheesy ballads."

Laughter ripples through the chamber, softening the edges of the tense atmosphere. I grin, pleased with the effect.

"Audrey's got the lineage and training, and Anthony's got the grit. Together, they're the perfect blend of old blood and new beginnings." I spread my palms wide, as if offering them a neatly wrapped gift. "They'll usher in a new era, one of peace and understanding. The whole 'fear and loathing' vibe is done. The prejudices we held were only a wall put up so we felt no guilt when something would happen to a turned vampire. Did no one else notice that the spell my father and brother produced only targeted turned vampires? The crowns are gone, destroyed thanks to my mate. We no longer need to hold that opinion."

There are nods now, thoughtful expressions painting the faces of even the most hardened council members. I can sense the shift, the sway of opinion like the tide turning beneath the moon's gentle coaxing.

"Besides," I ad with a wink in Audrey and Anthony's direction, "they're both easy on the eyes. Can't hurt the royal image, right?"

That draws outright laughter, and I feel Thorn's amusement pouring into me, her silent chuckle mingling with mine. It is a good sound, a sound full of hope and promise for a future where love isn't just an afterthought.

"Who's with me?" I ask, throwing down the gauntlet, challenging fate itself with a devil-may-care smile.

And just like that, the future seems a little less daunting, a bit more enchanting, as the room warms to the idea of two hearts ruling as one.

# 29

## THORN

The first glimmer of dawn hasn't even kissed the sky yet, and here I am, wide awake as if sleep was last season's fashion. A tingle of excitement zips through me like a lightning bug in a jar. Today isn't just any day. It is The Day—the grand opening of our tea shop, a dream Draven and I have been steeping for what feels like forever.

I hop out of bed back in my cottage, my feet barely touching the cool wooden floor as I flit to the wardrobe. I slide into an outfit that is basically "me" stitched into clothing—a moss-green tunic, soft as a whisper, and skirt with strategic slits in the layers that let me leap into action if needed. Little swirls of leaves, vines, and flowers are sewn along the hem of the skirt and cuffs of the tunic. And let's not forget the boots—sturdy, comfortable, and the softest things I've ever worn.

"Looking sharp," I mutter to my reflection, giving myself a cheeky wink before I bolt downstairs where the heart of our home beats—the kitchen.

"Morning, love," Draven calls, his voice smooth as melted chocolate. There he is, my rock in human form, standing at the stove wearing an apron over his usual attire—a shirt that hugs his muscles just right and trousers that tell tales of adventure.

"Morning," I chirp back, plopping down at the table as he pours me a cup of tea. The steam dances up to greet me, wrapping me in a warm embrace. "Smells like victory."

"Or chamomile," Draven corrects with a chuckle, sliding into the seat opposite me.

"Which is the scent of victory for anyone with sense," I shoot back, the corners of my mouth betraying my attempt at sternness. We clink cups in a quiet toast to the future.

"All right, boss lady," Draven says, eyebrow raised in that way that always makes me want to spill my secrets. "Walk me through today's battle plan one more time."

"Simple," I start, ticking off on my fingers. "We charm their socks off, fill their bellies with the best tea this side of the kingdom, and make them feel at home enough to never want to leave."

"Charm I can do," he says with a grin that will undoubtedly have the same effect on our patrons. "But remember the part where they actually have to leave at closing time."

"Details." I wave him off, taking another sip of the liquid calm.

We go over the checklist—tea leaves, check; clean cups, check; mystical ambiance, double check.

"Think we're ready?" I ask, though it is less of a question and more of a nudge for affirmation.

"Thorn," Draven says, reaching across the table to give my hand a squeeze, "with you, I'm ready for anything."

His confidence in us is the secret ingredient that makes everything sweeter. I squeeze back, our connection as tangible as the magic that hums in the air around us.

"Then let's show this city what true magic tastes like," I declare, standing up with a flourish that almost—but not quite—knocks over my chair.

"Let's," he agrees, and together, we stand on the threshold of our shared dream, ready to leap into the unknown with nothing but our wits, our wills, and each other.

As I stack the last of the cups on the shelf, a gentle nudge against my leg draws my attention downward. Luna, with her pristine white fur catching the first light of dawn like a personal sunrise, winds between my ankles in a figure-eight of affection. Her sapphire eyes hold a wisdom that belies her feline form, and I can't help but smile.

"Morning, Luna," I greet her, scratching behind her ears in our customary fashion. Luna purrs, a sound as comforting as the tea still warm in our bellies. "I don't know what we'd do without you."

"Probably forget half the things on that checklist," Draven chimes in from across the kitchen, his voice warm with humor.

"You're not wrong," I admit. "She's got a better head on her shoulders than both of us combined."

"Thankfully, one of us does," Draven agrees, bending down to scoop Luna into his arms. She settles there as though she molds to fit against his chest, a familiar sight that never fails to tug at my heartstrings.

"Looks like someone's ready for the big day," I say, reaching out to let Luna bat playfully at my fingers.

"Ready and more than capable," Draven affirms, planting a soft kiss on Luna's head. "Isn't that right?"

"Absolutely," I say, interpreting Luna's contented blink as agreement. "Look at her, the epitome of grace under pressure."

"Unlike some of us," Draven teases with a pointed look.

"Hey now," I retort with mock indignation. "I'll have you know my middle name is 'Grace.'"

"Only when you're not knocking over chairs," he quips, eyes sparkling with mirth.

"Details," I sniff, rolling my eyes but unable to suppress my own grin. "Shall we?" I gesture toward the door, excitement spiraling within me like a summoned wind.

"Let's not keep our customers waiting," Draven replies, setting Luna down so she can lead the way.

We follow in her wake, stepping out into the brisk morning air that promises new beginnings. The streets are just starting to stir as we teleport from my small cottage where it all started to the heart of the capital, the early risers casting curious glances at the shop windows, anticipating the day's treasures. Our steps echo in unison, a rhythmic dance of anticipation that carries us to the front of our very own tea shop.

"Here we are," I breathe, a mix of awe and nerves knotting in my chest.

"Home away from home," Draven concurs, fishing out the keys from his pocket. With a flourish that is all for show, he unlocks the doors and pushes them open.

The scent of tea leaves, rich and varied, waft out to greet us, a welcome as tangible as any embrace. Inside, the tables wait patiently, their surfaces gleaming with care, while the chairs stand at attention, ready for the stories they'll soon cradle.

"Would you look at that," I murmur, stepping inside and letting the reality of it all wash over me. The shop is like a dream given form, every detail a testament to our journey.

"Perfect," Draven says simply, his hand finding mine.

We survey the fruits of our labor. Together, we crafted a haven not just for ourselves, but for a whole community yet to come.

"Couldn't have done it without Luna's supervision, though," I add, glancing back at our furry sentinel who has taken up a regal position by the windowsill, her watchful gaze surveying her kingdom.

"Or each other," Draven reminds me, his grip tightening ever so slightly.

"Especially each other," I agree, leaning into him. "Let's brew some magic, shall we?"

"Let's," he echoes.

Side by side, we begin the enchanting symphony of our grand opening. The chime above the door tinkles its merry tune, and like a spell being broken, customers start to trickle in. They come in pairs, in groups, alone with books or with laughter spilling from their lips—each one seeking the sanctuary of our tea shop.

"Welcome," I greet them, my voice carrying the bright note of opening day enthusiasm. "Find a cozy corner or a window seat. Today, the world is yours."

Draven, ever the charming host beside me, offers up a menu that has clearly been practiced. "Might I recommend the morningtide blend? It's a vibrant start to any adventurer's day."

"Or for those more nocturnally inclined," I chime in, winking at a patron who looks like he just stumbled out of a fairytale or a tavern brawl, "our Midnight Melody is a lullaby in a cup."

Our movements are a dance we rehearsed in dreams, his steps a beat behind mine, creating an effortless cadence. We weave between tables, pour steaming liquid, and exchange smiles as if they are a currency minted by joy itself.

"Your laughter is the best tip," Draven tells an elderly woman whose giggle reminds me of wind chimes.

"Though coin doesn't hurt either," I add, and we share a conspiratorial grin.

When there's a lull, I lean against the polished counter, taking a moment to really look at our tea shop. The shelves are a library of color holding jars of tea blends meticulously organized, each label penned in Draven's elegant script. Aromatic promises are sealed behind glass, waiting to be fulfilled. The walls are a gallery of memories—a painting of the very first herb garden I grew, a candid one of Draven caught mid-laugh, and a sketch on a day I swore I would never forget and haven't. Every piece is a fragment of us, arranged with purpose. Every sip served is a sharing of our story.

"Thorn," Draven calls, drawing me back to the present. "Table three is ready for that story you promised."

"Of course," I say, pushing off from the counter. "Can't let them go thirsty for tea or tales."

With a flourish of the silver teaspoon, I sprinkle a dash of crimson safflower into the delicate mix. The asrbloom tea is an alchemy of its own, a blend that takes more than just skill. It requires a whisper of magic and a heart full of intent. Each ingredient has been chosen with care—star anise for its licorice kiss, rose hips for a blush of vitality, and a secret hint of enchantment that makes it kindred to vampire taste buds.

"Watch it," I mutter under my breath. "Too much elderflower, and you'll have them dancing on tables instead of sating their thirst."

"Wouldn't be the worst opening day spectacle," I imagine Draven's voice teasing back if he stood beside me, but my partner in tea and love is out there, weaving his charm among our patrons, leaving me to the sacred art of brewing.

"Infuse with love, they say," I say to the steam curling from the pot, "as if love is the sort of thing you can bottle and sell."

Yet, as I seal the lid, I close my eyes for just a moment, letting the warmth of all I feel for Draven seep into the concoction. If love can be shared through tea, then let this batch be a testament.

"Brace yourselves, folks," I announce to the room as I carry out a tray with several teapots and cups, grinning at the expectant faces. "The potion master has done it again. Drink deep, and feel the magic."

As I set down the tray and Draven's and my eyes met over the rising steam, something unspoken passes between us—a silent vow, a shared dream, and the quiet certainty that together, we are home.

\*\*\*

I nudge the door open with a hip-check, stepping out onto the cobblestone path that leads up to our tea shop. The capital is alive with its usual hustle, merchants peddling their trinkets and bards crooning for coin. A whiff of roasting chestnuts drifts past, mingling with the petrichor left behind by an early morning drizzle. I fill my lungs with the crisp air, the kind that nips at your nose and makes you grateful for warm scarves and warmer company.

"Taking a breather?" Draven's voice comes from the doorway, his eyebrow perched in that half-amused arch I know so well.

"More like soaking it all in," I reply, my breath misting before me. "This city... It's got a pulse, doesn't it? And now we're part of it, our little sanctuary in the midst of chaos."

"Sanctuary" was the right word. We've crafted not just a business, but a refuge, a place where magic meets mundane over cups of liquid enchantment.

I glance back through the window at the cozy interior, heart swelling like dough left to proof.

Draven steps up beside me, his shoulder brushing against mine, a solid presence that sends a familiar thrill down my spine. "We've done good, Thorn. Really good."

"Understatement of the century." I flash him a grin then turn back inside, feeling that tug in my chest that calls me back to our shared dream.

\*\*\*

"All right, last sweep?" Draven asks as the sun dips below the horizon, painting the sky in strokes of fiery orange and dusky purple.

"Last sweep," I confirm, tying up the final bag of trash with a flourish.

The clatter of dishes has been replaced by the soothing scrape of brushes on china, and the scent of lemon soap rises in soft tendrils. Luna pads silently between us, her white fur catching the fading light, a ghostly sentinel even in the quiet after-hours.

"Hey, careful with that cup," I tease as Draven carefully places a delicate teacup on the drying rack. "It's survived a hundred years and two dragon attacks. It'd be a shame if you were its demise."

"Haha, very funny," he retorts without looking up, but the twitch of his lips betrays his amusement. "You know I handle everything you treasure with utmost care."

"Everything I treasure, huh?" I lean back against the counter, crossing my arms and watching him work—a dance of precision and purpose.

"Every last thing," he says, straightening up and turning to face me, his hand finding mine amidst the bubbles and suds.

"Even the grumpy cat?"

"We have a grumpy cat?" he replies, and I can't help but laugh.

Cleaning up isn't just about tidying. It is reaffirming the life we've built together, brick by brick, dream by dream. Our fingers intertwine, soap slipping between them, and I feel it again—that profound sense of gratitude for this man, this moment, this magic we've spun from nothing but hope and hard work.

"Come on," I say, giving his hand a gentle tug. "Let's finish up here. There's a pot of asrbloom tea with our names on it, and I intend to enjoy every last drop before we call it a night."

"Lead the way," he says with that half-smile that always seems to say more than words ever could.

We work until the tea shop gleams, a silent vessel waiting to be filled with tomorrow's laughter and stories. When we hang the closed sign on the door, I know, deep in my bones, that we are exactly where we are meant to be.

I pour the last of the asrbloom tea into two chipped mugs that survived the day's frenzy. The shop hums with a satisfied silence, the kind that only comes after a space has buzzed with life and laughter. I settle beside Draven on the cushioned bench by the window, tucking my feet beneath me.

"Today was..." I start but trail off, lost in thought.

"An absolute whirlwind of delight?" Draven offers. He takes a sip of his tea.

"Delight's one word for it," I agree, chuckling. "Never thought I'd see the Baroness of Blythe trying to haggle over a scone."

Draven laughs, a warm sound that fills the room. "And her face when you threw in an extra for good measure. Priceless!"

"Ah, but your face when little Timmy decided your lap was the perfect throne for his cookie kingdom." I nudge him playfully.

"Ah yes, King Timmy," he says, rubbing at a phantom crumb. "May his reign be sweet and full of mischief."

We lean against each other, our sides brushing in the quiet comfort of shared memories. It feels like weaving threads of gold into the tapestry of our lives—a tapestry that shimmers with spells and soft whispers, holding the promise of more days like this.

"None of this would've been possible without you, Thorn," Draven says earnestly, his hand finding mine. "You're the heart of this place."

"Us," I correct softly, squeezing his hand. "We're the heart of it. That's what makes it special."

He nods, and we sit there, two halves of a whole, until the last drop of tea vanishes from our cups.

"Ready to lock up?" he asks, standing and offering me his hand.

"Let's do it," I reply, feeling the familiar rush of anticipation as I think about what tomorrow might bring.

The metallic click of the lock echoes through the empty street as we step outside. Draven's hand is warm in mine, anchoring me to the moment. Luna trails behind us, her tail wagging gracefully with joy. We walk in sync, our shadows stretching long and playful behind us under the light of the half-moon.

"Look at us, huh?" I say, a wistful note coloring my words. "From a half vampire, half witch and a vampire to tea shop connoisseurs."

"Only the beginning, my fierce enchantress," he murmurs, lifting our entwined hands to kiss the back of mine.

"Speaking of beginnings, think the world's ready for what we'll brew up next?" I tease, bumping my shoulder against his.

"Let them come," he says, his voice laced with the thrill of future challenges. "We'll be ready for them, side by side."

"Side by side," I echo, knowing it for the truth it is. Our dreams are spun from starlight and shadows, bound tight by love and the certainty that, together, we can face anything the fates toss our way.

# Witchy Rustic Bread

3 cups flour, bread or plain/all purpose
2 tsp instant or rapid rise yeast
2 tsp cooking / kosher salt, NOT table salt
1 1/2 cups very warm tap water

In a bowl, combine the flour, yeast, and salt. Summon the water and
stir with a wand of wood until a sticky dough forms. This will be
and sticky (not kneadable)

Cover your dough with a blessed cloth. Let it rest in a warm corner
your cottage until it doubles in size, wobbles, and bubbles. (2-3 hour
Set in a fridge for up to a day if you aren't ready to cook it yet. C
longer it takes the better it tastes

Awaken your fire beast (oven to 450°F) and place your iron pot w
its flames to heat for 30 empty. If you do not have a dutch oven yo
can do a pan in the oven below your bread pan with water in it.

Dust your workbench with flour-dust. Shape your dough into a r
pile and flip it so it's smooth side up on parchment paper. Messy
good! Place it into your dutch oven.

When your pot glows with heat, carefully place the dough inside
using the parchment as a charm of protection from sticking.

Seal the pot with its lid and return it to the flames for the count c
breaths. Then remove the lid and bake until golden as dragon's go
(about 12 more breaths).

Allow your magical loaf to cool before slicing, lest you release its s
too soon.

May your bread rise true and your kitchen be blessed!

# Author Note

How to Dump a Vampire was actually a book that I never had on my radar. To be completely honest, How to Be a Good Villain was going to be a complete standalone with no other books written in the world. But when some author bad behavior hit social media my brain thought it would be so much fun to join the many many authors who decided to write a snowed in story and publish it. The trick though, is that most people I knew were writing contemporary romances and at this point you know that's not quite where I fit in.

So I took a bit of time to process how I could write a good chunk of a book with two people snowed in together in a fantasy setting. The closer I got to finishing How to Be a Good Villain the more I was seeing what this world looked like as a whole and what it could be as a series of standalone books. All based around women who are villains in their own societies. So if a villain was snowed in with a love interest, what could I add to it that would make this interesting and fun. Of course magic needed to be involved. But what if one of them was a starving vampire? What if they were fated mates and one of them didn't want that?

As I started to write this book the first half of it flowed so incredibly smoothly. The characters spoke to each other and me (yes, I'm a pantser for most of my books) and the sass and banter just flowed. Once it hit time for her to panic and send him back I had to think about what the rest of the stakes were for this world. I had already figured out that she was hiding from his family and I knew from the moment I added in the tea that she was part vampire, but I wasn't sure how to let that all play out yet. I had to go back and add in little moments as I explored the world and stakes further to layer the world and still let it feel simple and easy. Afterall, I want this series to stay fantasy romcoms.

Then, I was approached by a company wanting a short story. A company that I can't name yet (I will add the name to the ebook and print books after the book is complete but it's huge! Something I couldn't ask to get into myself) wanted me to join in an anthology. One that some major authors I admired had been part of last year and I had always wanted to be a part of. As I thought about what to do for it, I realized that I had two side characters from this world get a happily ever after but the readers never see how they met. Yes, Audrey and Anthony are getting their own short story so you get to see how they meet!

Also, fun fact, but Audrey's name originally was Amaya. Then a very kind backer of the early kickstarter for How to Be a Good Villain chose to back a tier that allowed them to choose the name of a character of one of the royal siblings. Audrey Rona was created because Audrey means strong and noble and Rona is a family name of the grandmother who is mentioned in passing in the book. Huge thank you to F.Farlander for being a part of this with me!

Made in United States
Troutdale, OR
09/26/2024

23165379R00239